ROLL OF THE

DICE

SHERRYL D. HANCOCK

Published by Vulpine Press in the United Kingdom in 2019

ISBN 978-1-83919-301-9

Cover by Claire Wood

www.vulpine-press.com

Also in the *MidKnight Blue* series:

CHAPTER 1

Joe and his children walked through the halls of the hotel, both kids carrying bags from their shopping excursion. It had been a few days since Joe had spoken to Randy, and things were very strained at this point in their relationship. When he got to the room, there was a man standing there, holding an envelope. He handed Joe the envelope and walked away without a word. Joe looked at the kids, who stood staring up at him. He shook his head, shrugged, and walked inside. He tossed the envelope on the dresser, not sure what it was but assuming it was some kind of summons for a court case; he'd gotten them often enough over the course of his career.

He spent the next two hours with the kids, watching TV, getting them baths, then settling them in the bed in the second room in the hotel suite. Once they were asleep he took a shower himself, and afterward sat down in his robe with the envelope. He took out a sheaf of papers and glanced down at the plaintiff's name. He was stunned to see *Randy Sinclair*. He read back over the words. *The plaintiff, Randy Sinclair, petitions for dissolution of the thirteen-year marriage to Joseph Michael Sinclair.* Joe was sure he'd just been struck with a blunt object. He stared at the words for ten full minutes, unable to believe that Randy had actually filed for divorce.

Her reason given was "irreconcilable differences." He read on to find that she had asked for literally nothing except half-time custody of Kat and JT. She hadn't asked for alimony or child support. She hadn't asked for anything. He couldn't believe what he was reading. How did she expect to support herself? She made nothing off the center; it was purely non-profit. She hadn't even asked to keep the property Sinclair House sat on. Was she giving up the center too? Where would she live? She hadn't asked for either of the houses they owned in California, nor had she asked for any part of the vast estate they owned in England. Was she crazy?

Glancing at the clock, Joe knew it was too late to call Robert in England to find out what his rights were in all this. Although, what did he have to complain about? The fact that she wanted a divorce? The fact that she wanted shared custody of the children? Did she actually think he'd fight her to keep the kids with him full time? His wife had suddenly become a stranger to him, and it made him ache more than he ever had in his lifetime. As he lay on his bed that night, thinking about everything, he felt a sense of calm come over him. He started thinking that maybe it was just time. That they'd run the course of their marriage, doing for each other all they could do, and now they were ready for a change. The thought terrified him, and sent him walking over to the small wet bar in the room for a drink. Once he felt a little numb, he looked at the thought again. It was a scary thing to contemplate after all these years. Suddenly being single again. But Randy had made her wishes known now, and Joe didn't have the energy to fight it at this point.

What he wanted to do, however, was get away. With that thought in mind, he got on the phone. By the time he was able to call Robert, he had himself and both kids booked on a flight to England, that morning. He told Robert what time he'd be arriving and asked to meet with him. He called Susan, asking her to go over to the house and pack enough for the children to be gone for at least two weeks. He called Randy, calmly informing her that he was taking the kids to

England, that he might be gone longer than he'd originally planned to keep them for. He could hear uncertainty in her voice, but she agreed to it. Not that he had any intention of heeding any kind of forbiddance anyway. They were his children too, and he wanted them with him. His last call was to Midnight. It was 7:30 a.m. by that time, and he caught her in her car on the way to the office.

"Night, it's me," he said, his tone edgy.

Midnight picked up on it instantly. "What's wrong?"

"I need to take some time off," he said, watching the kids play on his bed. The one he hadn't slept in that night.

"Okay…"

"Look, I need to get some things straightened out in my life, okay? It could be a while," he added, trying to avoid having to explain too much.

"Joe…" Midnight began, not sure what to say.

She knew he was sickened by the fact that his cousin had nearly killed himself over Joe and Stevie's affair. She just wasn't sure what to say to try and ease his mind and heart.

"Night, don't, please?" Joe said, forestalling anything she was about to say. "I just need to go. Can you do without me for a while?"

"Yeah, Joe, we'll get by," she said hesitantly. "I just don't like you running off to do this. You might need us."

"If I do, I'll call, okay?" he said briskly.

"No, you won't," Midnight replied wisely, sighing. "I don't want to lose you," she said, telling him what was in her heart at that point.

"I don't want to lose me either, Night," he said gently. "That's why I need to get away for a bit. I'm taking the kids and I'm going home to England."

3

Midnight nodded, remembering well the last time he'd run home to England. It had been after Randy's car accident, when she'd literally died for a minute. A dirty cop was responsible for the accident, the same dirty cop who'd put a hit out on Donovan and eventually on Midnight herself. Joe had been determined to protect his family, quitting the department and going home. It had been Midnight's "death" that had brought him back, and he'd stayed after that to put the men that had tried to have her killed either behind bars or in the ground.

"Are you coming back?" she asked, knowing that it was possible he was easing out this way.

"Yes," he said. "I'll be back."

Midnight breathed a sigh of relief. "Okay, well, I'll just put you on a leave of absence. Please call me and let me know how you are, okay?"

"I will," he said, feeling his throat constrict, knowing he was running again but unable to think of another solution.

They hung up a few minutes later. Joe got the kids' things together and met Susan at her and Dave's house an hour later.

"Do you know when you'll be back?" Susan asked worriedly.

"No," Joe said, shaking his head. "But I will be."

Susan nodded sadly. She knew things were very strained for Joe. Not only was he estranged from Randy, but the incident with Christian had sent him reeling. She honestly wished that she had the right words to ask him if he was really okay. But she'd never known how to talk to Joe. He was so far beyond her realm of understanding in a man. He was a mass of complications, with his background and ways of handling things. He was very much like Christian, and she knew when not to push things with either of the Sinclair men. Impulsively, she reached out and hugged him.

"Please be safe," she whispered.

Joe hugged her tight, knowing he was leaving a lot of things up in the air but not able to assure anyone of anything, other than the fact that he'd be back.

An hour later he and the children were on a plane to England.

***

Christian and Stevie spent hours lying together that very first day back together, with Christian dozing off and on, then waking to kiss Stevie softly on the head or the cheek. When he woke the third time she was leaning up on her elbow, watching him. His eyes connected with hers, and he could tell she was thinking about what was going to happen now.

"We need to talk, don't we?" he said quietly, resigned.

"Yes, we do," she said, nodding.

They both knew that they couldn't get past the hurts that had been caused if they didn't talk about them.

"What happened, Steve?" Christian asked, looking up into her eyes.

She looked back at him for a long moment, then sighed, shaking her head. She lay back down next to him, resting her head in the crook of his arm, her face turned up to look at him.

"Joe and I had started talking when we were going to court," she began. "He told me about the stuff with Randy, and asked me about the house and stuff. So I told him about what was going on with that, and how you hadn't really mentioned anything about moving with me." She looked up at him. "Why was that, Christian?" Her tone wasn't in any way accusing, simply questioning what she hadn't understood.

His lips tightened in contrition. He knew that had been a major turning point in their relationship. It was his turn to sigh.

"Fact was, Steve, I wasn't ready for that with you," he said, looking pained.

"Why?" she said. "We were already living together."

"I know that. But you were buying a house, and it was safe to figure that I should pay for half... and buying something together... that's a lot." His eyes begged her to understand.

"So you felt like you should be helping me buy it, or you shouldn't be living there, right?"

"Yeah," he said, blowing his breath out.

She nodded, remembering how freaked out he got about major commitments. She'd been surprised when he'd actually suggested they move in together. She also fully understood his fear of commitment; she was exactly the same. Being in love with someone didn't always allay that fear, either.

"I guess I was just afraid that we'd get so..." He trailed off as he shook his head again. "I don't know... I guess that things would change for us. That we'd become..."

"Boring?" she asked, raising an eyebrow.

"Yeah," he said, grimacing.

"Christian, I don't think we could be boring if we tried. We've both got too much fire in us for that."

"Yeah, well, I guess I wasn't thinkin' like that," he said, grinning.

Stevie nodded again. "Well, I didn't know all this at that point, and I just figured you were trying to tell me you didn't want to live with me anymore. And then all that shit with Seattle…"

It was Christian's turn to nod, looking embarrassed.

"You were sleeping with her, weren't you?" Stevie asked, her tone indicating that she already knew that.

He looked at her for a long minute, then shook his head, realizing he'd misunderstood the term "shit with Seattle"—he'd thought she'd meant him going to Seattle the week she closed.

"No, Steve, I wasn't."

Stevie looked stunned. "Then what were you just nodding about?"

"I thought you meant the week that you closed on the house, my going back then."

"That was on purpose, though, wasn't it?" she asked, determined to have been right about something.

"Yes, that was on purpose," he said. "And no, I wasn't sleeping with the woman there, but if you'd been pushing me about the house, I probably would have."

"Why?"

"To put distance between us," he answered honestly.

Stevie nodded, understanding how he thought. "I'm sorry," she said sincerely. "I really did think you were already screwing around on me. That combined with the house thing, I just thought you were trying to tell me it was over."

"Mixed messages," he said. "But why didn't you ask? I mean, if you'd asked I would have told you. I just didn't want to bring it up and get into a nasty fight about it."

It was her turn to grimace. "You know me," she said, sounding disgusted with herself. "I never ask."

"No, you don't," he said, remembering well the last time they'd been torn apart, simply because she'd misread his feelings about Susan.

When Susan and Dave had announced their plans to marry, Christian had disappeared and gotten horrendously drunk. It had been Stevie who tracked him down and got him back to his room at Joe's safely. In trying to get him to lie down before he passed out, she'd caught the look of devastation in his eyes. She'd assumed it was because he was still in love with Susan, when in fact it was because Susan had finally found true love, and he was afraid he'd never find that with anyone. At the time he and Stevie had been so busy playing it casual that neither of them had been willing to admit they were in love with each other. He'd chastised her about not asking him about it then, and apparently she hadn't learned anything from that time. Then again, neither had he.

"You could have said something too, Christian," she said gently.

"Yeah, I know," he said wearily.

"But the thing with Joe, that just happened. We never meant to hurt anyone. I guess we were both feeling really unwanted, and… and it just happened," she said, her eyes searching his.

Christian nodded slowly. "It hurt like hell."

"I'm sorry," she said, wincing at the words as well as his tone.

They were both silent for a while, and Stevie leaned her head against his chest, feeling drained suddenly. There had just been so much happening lately.

"I don't want to lose you again," he said after a long while.

She raised her head. "I'm not going anywhere again."

He looked back at her, staring directly into her eyes. "I want more than that."

"More?" she asked, mystified.

"Yeah," he said, moving to lever himself up on his elbow. "Marry me."

"What?" she breathed, her eyes widening.

"I need you with me, Stevie, for good. I can't live without you, and I bloody well don't want to. Marry me," he said, his eyes never leaving hers.

"You don't have to do this," she said, reaching up to touch his cheek. "I'm not going anywhere. I'm yours."

"I know," he said. "And I want everyone else to know." He turned his head, kissing her hand that rested on his cheek, then looked back down at her. "And I want a house with you, and kids, and a white picket fence, and even a fucking Volvo if you want one." He wrinkled his nose on that part, making her laugh.

"I don't think we need to go *that far*," she said, grinning. They were both sports car people, not family vehicle people at all.

He said nothing, simply waiting, holding his breath, for her answer.

She stared up at him for a long moment. "Ask me again," she said softly.

He narrowed his eyes at her, trying to figure out what was going on in her mind, but he was willing to do anything for her at this point.

He lowered his head to hers, his lips brushing her lips. "Stevie O'Neil, will you marry me?"

"Yes," she said, kissing his lips.

The kiss started out soft, deepening to hunger, then heating to passion. He moved to his back, pulling her over with him, his lips never leaving hers. They kissed hungrily for a long time, just enjoying the feel of being together again. Then his hands moved to pull her shirt from her jeans, sliding reverently over the exposed skin. Stevie gasped against his lips. It always felt like this with him, and she reveled in it.

Piece by piece he removed her clothes, then reached up to pull his shirt off. He wanted to feel her against him again.

"God, I've missed you so much," he groaned when their skin touched. He kissed her again. "I need you so much," he said against her lips.

"I love you. I need you. I want you."

She kissed his chest, then his neck, moving to his ear.

"I want to hear you," she said.

"What?" he asked, still touching her, caressing her back.

"I want to hear you," she repeated, moving to look down at him. "I want you to drop that control of yours and give me everything."

He nodded then, understanding what she meant. He tended to be very controlled even during lovemaking, not making too many sounds. It wasn't intentional, just habit. But he understood that she wanted him to let her hear his reactions to her now. And he was willing to do anything for her.

When they made love, it was with more heat than they'd ever experienced in their two-year relationship. Stevie was spurred on by his moans, gasps, and words, which heated her to the point of near explosion before his body ever slid inside hers. Her fervor served to excite him further as well, making their union more explosive than ever.

Afterward they both lay, trying to catch their breath.

"Oh my God," she breathed against his neck, where her face was pressed.

"And a few other deities I can think of," he said, grinning.

She laughed. "God, I love you."

"Good thing, considering you just said you'd marry me and all."

"Uh-huh," she said, nodding.

"Haven't changed your mind, have you?" he asked, not sounding too concerned.

"After that?" she asked, raising her head and looking at him like he was nuts. "If anything, I would say that would have made my decision even more solid."

"Good." He looked very satisfied. "I love you," he said, staring into her eyes.

"Good thing," she said, grinning as she leaned down to kiss him.

They spent the rest of the night lying together and talking about whatever came to mind. They made love a few more times, not really getting too much sleep, and not caring either.

They slept in the following day. Stevie called and talked to Spider, asking him for the day off. He approved it. They spent their free time relaxing. While Christian was asleep at one point, Stevie cleaned up the apartment. In the end she counted fourteen full-sized tequila bottles and God only knew how many bottles of Tequiza beer. At the hospital they'd been told that Christian's blood alcohol had been literally off the charts, and that for all intents and purposes that alone should have killed him. It made her sick to see the amount of bottles he had lying around. And she had no idea how many he might have disposed of before.

When he woke later, he commented on the apartment being clean. She told him she was getting used to her wife role. He laughed, shaking his head, knowing she was far from the June Cleaver type woman. She ordered them lunch, since he had no food in the apartment.

While they ate, sitting in the living room, he glanced over at her.

"So when do you want to do the deed?"

She grinned. "I thought we already did."

"Not that one," he said, laughing.

"Oh, you mean the really scary one?"

"Yeah, that one."

She shrugged. "Today, tomorrow, next week," she said, her eyes twinkling with humor.

"Seriously?"

He wanted to know if she meant she wanted to get married soon, or if she wanted a so-called "long engagement," which to Christian had always meant one of the two didn't really want to get married and was only humoring the other person.

"Christian," she said, reaching out to touch his lips. "I don't care when, where, or how, just so long as you're mine."

He nodded. "My sentiments exactly." Then he gave her a pointed look. "What do you think about Vegas?"

Again, he wasn't sure if she'd want a big wedding or not.

"Vegas sounds like us," she said, grinning.

"No," he said. "Monte Carlo sounds like us, but Vegas will have to do."

"Never been to Monte Carlo," she said, shrugging. "So I

wouldn't have a clue."

"Well, I'll have to take you there sometime."

"Maybe."

"So Vegas then?"

"Yes, Vegas. Don't they have a Monte Carlo hotel there?"

He grinned. "Yes, as a matter of fact they do."

"Then that's where we should get married."

"You got it, babe."

"Good."

She was surprised at how easy it was to talk about getting married now. For years she'd abhorred the idea. She'd never seen the point—why buy the cow when she could get the milk from many different cows for free? She had never found anyone she was willing to put up with on a full-time basis. That was until she met Christian Collins.

Stevie realized now that she'd wanted a commitment from him all along. Her own independence and the knowledge of his staunch attitude about commitment had kept her from even thinking about the long term. Now it just seemed so natural that they would get married. Look at Rick and Midnight; they had all the fire of about ten people, and yet they made their marriage work. It was practically legendary in the department. She and Christian could make it work too, and they would. She was sure of that.

***

Things on Donovan and Jeanie's case were stalled. Now that they knew who the supplier was, they needed to make a case. However,

Rosa's attitude had cooled significantly toward Donovan, and since he couldn't in good conscience sleep with her again, it was difficult. They started working the angle of trying to figure out which young men were selling for her; Jeanie handled that part, since they didn't want to tip Rosa off. Donovan had a short conversation with Rosa, telling her that he still wasn't sure about that "assignment" she'd offered him for "extra credit." She'd nodded, giving him a condescending look that said she thought he was a coward.

When they were out of class and away from the college, he and Jeanie spent hours talking and enjoying getting to be with each other again. Suddenly the past was gone, and they were starting again. It was like they were even now; she'd been there for him when he'd needed her, as he had done for her. They were on even ground again. But they both knew they needed to make this case. They just weren't sure how. Donovan couldn't let go of the fact that he'd botched it.

***

Susan was tense, more so after Joe left town. She felt totally adrift. Dave was back on his usual undercover work the day Joe called to ask her to pack the children's clothes. It was the first time Susan used the code Dave had given her to tell him she needed him.

While he was undercover he was almost impossible to contact, so he had given Susan a way to do so without risking his cover being blown. Susan texted him, putting in the numbers the way he'd written down for her: "25 10 19 00 1199." On paper it was just a series of numbers; in a text it would just look like child's play. Dave had explained the code to her in case she ever lost the paper he'd written it on.

"The 25 is my radio call number, 10–19 means return to base, the 00 stands for you, since there are no 00 radio call numbers, and 1199 means an officer needs assistance." He'd leaned down to kiss her lips then, staring directly into her eyes as he pulled back. "It'll tell me you need me home now. I want you to use it when you need me."

Susan had never used it, never wanting to cry wolf. On this particular day she felt so bereft, she just wanted him to be there to hold her. Right after she sent the message she had second thoughts, but she had no clue what to text to keep him from responding, and didn't want to take any chances. She worried for the next half hour about the ramifications of her silly, emotional decision.

Thirty-two minutes after she'd sent her message, Dave strode in the door looking worried. Susan stood up from the kitchen table.

"What's wrong?" he asked, seeing that she had been crying.

Even as she started to shake her head, he walked over to her, taking her in his arms.

"David, I'm sorry, I just…" she began, feeling like a silly girl. "I was feeling so awful, I just, I didn't think about it before I messaged you. I'm sorry."

"What happened?" he asked, tilting her face up to his.

She sighed, feeling foolish. "Joe called this morning. He had me pack the children's clothes for a trip. He's taking them to England, David…" Her voice trailed off as she shook her head miserably. "I'm sorry, this wasn't important. I was just being an emotional little girl. I'm sorry, David."

His lips on hers stopped her apologies. He pulled back, looking down at her.

"Don't apologize," he said softly. "When you need me, I want to be here, okay? Why do you think he left? Because of Blue?"

Susan shook her head. "I don't know. He looked so unhappy, and I guess I just felt that... I just wish everything would be right again," she said, sighing.

Dave hugged her to him. He knew she was extremely worried about Christian, and now with Joe leaving, that added to her worry. Susan was very close to the family she worked for. She'd known Joe since she was born, and she'd been thrilled to take care of his children. It upset her no end that he and Randy seemed to be drifting farther and farther apart. Not to mention that if Joe left and went back to England, her job may be in jeopardy as well. It wasn't the main concern, but Dave knew she wouldn't be as happy working for any other family.

"It'll be okay, hon," Dave said softly. "Everyone just needs to settle down again."

Susan nodded, leaning her head against his chest, taking comfort in his confidence that things would settle back down eventually.

"I'm sorry I bothered you about this," she said.

"It's okay," he said, grinning at her. "I was just lounging on the beach."

"Really now?" she asked, raising an eyebrow.

"Dealers don't do much during the day," he said, his tone indicating what he thought of the people he was stuck dealing with on a daily basis.

"So I didn't take you away from anything important?"

"Nope."

He didn't tell her that he'd been in the middle of negotiations to buy three kilos of cocaine while lying on that beach. That he'd had to make some quick excuse about a source wanting to meet with him.

He knew if he told her that, she'd be less likely to text him next time. It was bad enough that he had to be away from his wife for days on end; he was bound and determined to be there for her when she needed him enough to send that message.

They spent the rest of the afternoon talking about all that was happening. Dave did his best to allay all Susan's fears, but he could see that although she was doing her best to appear totally comforted, she wasn't. He excused himself to discreetly make two quick phone calls to get out of his next two meetings, so he could stay home with her for a few days. It was the first time he'd canceled a meeting in his career, but to him, being a good husband was more important now than his job.

He took her to dinner at The Marine Room that night. It was the restaurant he'd taken her to on their very first date, and it had come to mean a lot for the two of them. He purposely steered the conversation to happier topics. Susan was more grateful than she could express. They talked about her birthday, coming up on the first of the month. Dave asked her again what she wanted, and as always she said she wanted him home safe. He had much bigger plans than that; he'd been working on them for months. It was his intention to show her just how important she was to him with this present. He knew for a fact she'd probably give him all kinds of hell for what he was buying her, but he also knew that it was what he wanted for her.

That night he took his time making love to her. He fell asleep holding her close. There was no doubt in her mind that she was loved, and that no matter what, he would be there to take care of her. The next morning they went out to the beach and she watched him surf. It was a ritual for them now. After he climbed out of the water, he lay down next to her on the sand and they talked as the sun rose in the sky. By the time they left the beach at eleven she was feeling much better about everything. When he left the house early that afternoon, she kissed him deeply.

"Thank you, David," she said, her sapphire blue eyes staring up at him. "You take such good care of me."

"That's what you married me to do, isn't it?" he asked, grinning.

"No," she said. "I married you to take care of you."

He hugged her close. "And you take perfect care of me, honey," he said, kissing her cheek. "I love you."

"I love you too, David," she whispered back.

When he walked to his car, Susan watched him, feeling very happy. For the millionth time in their two-year marriage she thanked God for this man. He winked at her as he pulled out of the driveway. She waved, smiling brightly. Everything wasn't fixed in their world, with their friends, but Susan was once again buoyed by the spirit of the man she was married to, and that helped endlessly.

***

Erin Shandley walked into the office at 7:30 a.m. and was surprised to hear someone tapping away on the computer. She was even more surprised when she looked into Christian's cubicle and found that it was Christian himself sitting there.

"You're here," she said, sounding stunned.

Christian glanced up at her and grinned. "Brilliant deduction, Rin."

Erin narrowed her eyes. "You scared the shit out of me, Christian Collins."

18

Christian looked immediately contrite. He stood from his chair and pulled her into his arms.

"I'm sorry, Erin."

Her tiny fist struck his chest lightly. "Don't you ever try to hurt yourself again, do you hear me?" She looked up at him, and the glaze of tears in her eyes made him feel worse.

"I hear you," he said softly, his light blue eyes looking down into hers.

She nodded, looking satisfied with his answer. Then she glanced up again, her eyes searching his face.

"Are you okay?" she asked.

"I'm here, aren't I?" he said as he moved to sit back down.

She sat across from him, nodding. "Yeah, you're here, but that doesn't mean everything is okay with you, Blue."

"Well, everything is okay," he assured her. He reached over and took her hand. "I'm getting married."

"You're what?"

He grinned. "You heard me."

"To Stevie?" she asked hopefully.

"Duh, Shandley," he said, having picked up Stevie's habit of referring to everyone by their last name.

She grinned, biting her lower lip. "What happened? I mean, I thought… well, I mean… What happened?" she stammered, trying not to bring up anything that would hurt him.

Christian nodded, understanding what she was trying to ask.

"She came to see me when I got out of the hospital," he said. "We talked, and I told her I can't live without her." His voice softened on the last, and he shrugged. "She wanted me back too, and I wanted to

19

make it permanent this time."

Erin nodded, her eyes shining. "I'm so happy for you, Blue. You two belong together."

"Thanks," he said, grinning. "You're the first one to know."

"Cool," she said, grinning too. "When does everyone else get to know?"

"Know what?" asked a voice from the other side of the partition.

Christian stood and looked around it. He was happy to see Rhiannon standing at her desk, looking healthy and happy.

"So you're back, huh, Rhi?" he said, walking over to her and hugging her.

"Yeah, you too, I see," she said, reaching up to hug him back.

"Can't have the entire property unit go to shit."

"Hey!" Erin said, laughing.

"Oh, sorry."

"So, know what?" Rhiannon asked, raising an eyebrow at the two of them.

"Oh, that I'm getting married," Christian said casually as he leaned on her desk.

"You're what?" Rhiannon exclaimed, her face reflecting the shock he'd just given her.

"Getting married," he repeated, more slowly this time.

Rhiannon was quiet for a moment, and Christian could see she was trying to figure out what could have happened and who he could be marrying.

"Before you blow a gasket, Rhi, I'm marrying your sister."

Rhiannon started to smile. "What kind of bat did you hit her over the head with to make her regain her senses?"

Christian looked repentant as he said, "I think it was the Vicodin-tequila-check-out-time bat."

Rhiannon nodded sadly. "I'm sorry you went through that."

Christian shook his head. "It wasn't her fault, Rhi. I made the choice—it was just the wrong one."

"Yes, it was," Rhiannon agreed, knowing that it would be so easy for Christian to blame Joe and Stevie for his suicide attempt. She found that she respected him more for taking responsibility for it. "So when are you two going to get married?"

"I don't know yet. We're thinking along the lines of Christmas Night."

"Cool," Erin put in, always the romantic. "A winter wedding, how sweet."

Rhiannon grinned. "Easier to remember your anniversary date too," she said slyly.

Christian laughed.

"So why didn't my rat of a sister call me and tell me?" Rhiannon asked, putting her hands on her hips.

Christian shrugged. "Maybe she doesn't want you there."

He promptly got poked in the ribs for that. The three of them laughed.

News spread quickly throughout the department that not only was Christian Collins back from his near-death experience but he was getting married. Midnight was down in his office three hours later.

"What is this I hear?" she said, reaching out to hug Christian as he stood up.

"You mean the getting married thing?"

21

"Yeah, that," she said, grinning.

He smiled. "Yeah, that."

Midnight nodded, looking pleased. "I'm glad you two got it together."

"Me too," Christian replied seriously. "Have you seen Joe? I need to talk to him."

Midnight grimaced. "He, uh…" She hesitated. "He left for England this morning."

"He did?"

"Yeah. He said he needed to get things together."

Christian nodded, blowing his breath out. He knew he was indirectly the cause of it.

"I'm sure in a day or two you can reach him at the estate," Midnight said. "I can give you the number if you want it."

Christian shook his head. "I have it. I'll call him. Thanks."

Midnight pinned him with a look. "Christian, we all have to handle things our own way, okay? For Joe, going home is easier for him sometimes."

Christian nodded, appreciating her desire to make him feel better. He knew he needed to talk to Joe in order to put things right.

That night, he was on the phone to Joe's parents' house. He was surprised when he got through on the second ring.

"'Lo" Joe said, watching as the kids ran up the stairs for the millionth time since they'd arrived.

"Joe, it's Christian."

"Oh," Joe said, surprised. "Hey," he added, not sure what to say at this point.

"Hey," Christian replied, glancing up as Stevie sat down on the bed next to him, watching him closely.

There was a long silence.

"Look," Joe said, sighing, "I just want you to know that I'm sorry…" He trailed off as he shook his head, knowing that "sorry" was never going to cut it.

"Nah, man, it's okay. Everything is cool," Christian said. "In fact," he went on, having just had a thought, "I need you to do me a huge favor."

"What would that be?" Joe asked, not believing for a second that everything was okay between them.

"I need you to be my best man."

"Your what?" Joe asked, his brow furrowing.

"Best man," Christian repeated, grinning as Stevie's mouth dropped open. "You know, at my wedding."

"Your wedding," Joe said, his tone humoring. "Right, okay, yeah."

Christian chuckled. "Seriously, man. Stevie and I are getting married."

"Wow…" Joe said, stunned and nearly speechless.

"Yeah," Christian said. "That's about what I thought too."

"So you two figured it out."

"Yeah…"

"You belong together," Joe said sincerely.

"Yeah," Christian said again, his eyes trailing over to Stevie. "I guess I needed to know I could lose her to someone else to realize that."

"Christian…" Joe began, his tone once again apologetic.

"No, man, it's cool—it really is," Christian said. "I've never felt this way about anyone, and I guess I needed things to go hideously wrong to know that I did have it right the first time."

Joe nodded. "Well, I'm sorry that it had to happen. I'm sorry for my part in it."

"She explained it to me," Christian said. "You don't need to be sorry."

"Well, I am anyway."

"Just tell me you'll be my best man."

"You tell me when and where, and I'll be there," Joe said, feeling the beginnings of his soul being restored.

"We're looking at Christmas Night in Vegas."

"That sounds fitting," Joe replied with a grin.

"Doesn't it though?" Christian said, laughing.

They talked for a few more minutes, and both hung up feeling worlds better.

***

That same evening, Donovan and Jeanie were lying in bed talking. They'd made love when they'd gotten back from "school," and he'd made them dinner. They'd eaten, then talked over wine sitting on the couch, and ended up kissing and subsequently making love again. Being back together had them feeling insatiable with each other. Donovan found it quite amusing; Jeanie did too, saying that she had forgotten what good sex was. Although he said nothing, Donovan was secretly pleased that she hadn't found anyone she enjoyed more in their time apart.

"So, what do you think we should do here?" Donovan asked, his hand pressed against hers, which lay on his chest.

They were discussing the case again. Both were starting to feel like they were getting nowhere fast. Jeanie glanced up at him, biting her lip. She had an idea, but she wasn't sure how he'd feel about it.

"I kinda had an idea…"

Donovan chuckled. "Let's hear it, Franco," he said, knowing she was trying to let him play the lead still.

"Oops," she said, looking contrite as she grinned. "Guess I'm going back to that deferring to you thing, huh?"

"Yeah, so knock it off," he said, smiling at her.

"Okay, so I have this idea," she said directly, making him laugh. She grinned. "I think we should bring in a ringer."

"A ringer?"

"Yeah." Jeanie nodded. "Someone we know Rosa will go for."

Donovan looked thoughtful for a moment, then nodded slowly. "And you're thinking Blue, aren't you?"

"Yeah…" Jeanie hadn't been sure how Donovan was going to take it.

Christian was such a spectacularly handsome man, with striking looks that would catch any woman with even a drop of sense's attention. His combination of jet black hair, darker skin, and light blue eyes, along with a tall, strong build, made him impossible to miss. And more than likely impossible for Rosa to resist.

Again Donovan nodded. "Yeah, I think you might be right."

Jeanie smiled warmly, glad that he wasn't the type of man to be jealous of another guy's looks. Donovan was nothing if not confident in his own appearance and unique appeal.

"Think we could get him?" Jeanie asked, not sure if it was even possible.

"Well, he does have peace officer powers, even if he doesn't use them."

"And we already know he can do undercover work and pull it off."

Jeanie was thinking of the work Christian had done against the dirty cops who had tried to have Donovan, his sister Randy, and even the chief killed. Christian had been the one to get inside their little ring, gaining their confidence by distancing himself from the Gang, even going so far as to let Rick think he was involved in Midnight's "murder." Rick had attacked Christian at Midnight's funeral, because he'd walked up with the man everyone had been sure was running things, Frank Devereaux. Christian had allowed himself to be ostracized by everyone so he could find out who had been responsible for the hits.

In the end, he'd been the one to rescue Susan when the dirty cops kidnapped her to use her against him. Christian had ended up shooting Devereaux, taking a bullet in the stomach in the process of blocking Susan from being shot. He had proven himself that day, and he hadn't even been through the police academy at that point. Now he had.

"We'll need to talk to Spider about it," Donovan said, unhappy at the prospect of having to confess his mistake but understanding that he would have had to eventually anyway. It would definitely come up during the prosecution of the case.

The following morning, Donovan called into the office and requested a meeting with Spider, telling him they had a bit of a problem. Spider agreed, telling Donovan to be there at 10:00 a.m. When Jeanie and Donovan walked into Spider's office, they were surprised to find Midnight there as well.

"We were meeting on budget issues," Spider explained. "Midnight wanted to stay to hear what was going on."

Donovan glanced at Jeanie. She shrugged slightly, shaking her head. Midnight would have heard eventually anyway. Donovan nodded, as if having gotten her message telepathically. Midnight noticed the exchange, as did Spider; they glanced at each other, both wondering what was up. Donovan and Jeanie at least seemed to be getting along again. Things had been strained between the two for months, and everyone knew it.

Donovan gestured to the only other chair in Spider's office, and Jeanie took a seat, glancing up at Donovan as he closed the door and went to lean on Spider's low credenza to the side of the desk, looking distinctly uncomfortable.

"So what's going on?" Spider asked, looking between the two.

"Well," Donovan started, "basically, I fucked up."

Spider looked surprised. Jeanie stepped quickly into the silence.

"He didn't fuck up," she said, giving Donovan a narrow look. "He was human. He got into a relationship with one of the professors at the college."

Midnight raised an eyebrow, glancing at Donovan, then looked back at Jeanie.

"It just so happens," Donovan said, his tone still self-effacing, "that this particular professor is our suspect."

"She's our suspect *now*," Jeanie said.

"You think it's a professor pushing this stuff?" Spider asked.

"I know it is," Donovan said.

"How?" Midnight asked.

"Because she wants me to sell it for her," Donovan replied.

"She initiated the offer to sell?" Midnight asked, sounding like a lawyer.

Donovan nodded, looking unhappy.

"Then what's the problem?" Midnight spread her hands in confusion.

"The problem is, I was screwing her at the time," Donovan said, his face indicating the disgust he felt in himself. "And she'd managed to get me hooked on X while I was doing so."

"What?" Midnight breathed, sitting up straighter.

Her eyes took on a worried look as they searched his face, as if looking for signs of the addiction even as she questioned what he'd said.

"She was giving me Ecstasy every night, when I went over there. She was slipping it in my drink," Donovan said, his voice even but his eyes belying his true feelings. "And I'm such a great narc that I didn't even notice the side effects I was experiencing till she had me hooked then started backing it off to cause withdrawals."

"But you guys were after Rohypnol," Spider said. "The side effects aren't the same."

"Spider, I knew I was tired all the time, I knew I was a time bomb with my temper. I should have figured it out."

"She wasn't even a major suspect," Jeanie put in, hating that Donovan was still blaming himself. "And I saw what was happening with you, and I never suspected either."

"Jay, I wasn't letting you be around me long enough to notice anything, besides the fact that I'd become an asshole," Donovan said. "And you're new at this."

"No, Donovan," Midnight said, her tone brooking no argument. "Spider and Jeanie are right. There's no way you could have known. This woman obviously does this a lot and catches young men unawares."

"I'm a narc, Midnight. I'm not unaware."

"Nonetheless, Pony," Midnight said, using his long-time nickname to soften her words. "How would you have ever guessed that a dealer would hand out product to get her prospective sellers hooked? I mean, that's a huge risk on any level, but to actually become intimate with these guys too? She has no idea how they might react to that stuff—what if one of them became enraged and injured her?"

"She's lucky I didn't kill her myself when I found out what she did," Donovan said.

"Exactly," Midnight said. "And that could happen with any of these guys she does this to."

"But I don't have proof that she's done this to the others."

"Chances are she has, and that's why they wouldn't give her up," Spider said.

"But we need proof," Midnight said, narrowing her eyes slightly. "And I'm betting you two have come up with an idea."

Donovan nodded toward Jeanie. "Jay did."

"What is it?"

"I thought if we brought in a guy that this woman couldn't resist going for, we could get everything on a wire."

Midnight nodded. "Are you thinking Blue?"

It was well established among the women in the department that

Christian Collins was the most incredible-looking man in the place. Spider and Donovan exchanged a look, both grinning and shaking their heads. It was hard, living up to a guy that looked like Collins did.

Jeanie noted the exchange and grinned, as did Midnight.

Jeanie nodded. "Yeah, we figure since he has peace officer powers, and we all know he can lie with the best of them, literally and figuratively…" She winked over at Donovan, even as he shook his head. "We figure he'd be a ringer for this."

Midnight nodded, glancing over at Spider. "You okay with this?"

Spider shrugged. "Whatever we have to do to make this case. We need to take this woman down. She's dangerous." His tone was ominous on the last. One of his men's life had been endangered by this woman's game, and that did not sit well with him.

Midnight looked at Donovan. "Have you gotten yourself checked out?" she asked, sincere concern for him coloring her voice. "Are you okay?"

Donovan nodded. "The first few days were brutal," he said honestly, looking over at Jeanie. "But Jay took care of me." His voice softened on her name. He turned back to Midnight. "I still get the headache every so often, but it's getting lighter every day. I'm fine."

Midnight nodded, looking satisfied with his answer. "Good."

"Midnight," Donovan began. "I'm sorry. I know this is going to be a bitch to prosecute and it's going to make the department look bad. I'm sorry I wasn't thinking with the right body part."

Midnight stood up, walking over to him. Since he was sitting on the low credenza, she was at eye level with him.

"I'm just glad you're okay, Donovan. And don't worry, we'll get the bitch and make her sorry she messed with one of my favorite people," she said with a wink.

She leaned forward and hugged him. Donovan hugged her back gratefully. There seemed to be no end to Midnight's ability to be loyal to her friends and loved ones. She'd defend any of them to the very end. It felt good to be someone she was that dedicated to.

CHAPTER 2

Christian was sitting at his computer when Jeanie and Donovan walked in. He glanced up, his expression already wary. He could see by the look on Jeanie's face that they were about to ask him for something. He glanced back at Erin, who smiled warmly at both of them.

"Blue, can we talk to you a minute?" Donovan asked, gesturing with his head toward the parking lot.

Christian nodded, moving to stand up. He followed them outside. Erin watched them go.

"So what's up?" Christian asked as he moved to lean against a car in the motor pool, reaching for a cigarette and lighting up.

"How are you?" Jeanie asked.

"I'm good. Fine, in fact. Did you two hear?"

"Hear?" Donovan queried. "About…" He trailed off, not sure if Christian meant about his suicide attempt. Since Christian had refused to see anyone, he didn't know who all had made it to the hospital.

"Nah, I know the whole friggin' department knows about my attempt to check out," Christian said, grimacing at the fact that it had quickly become departmental knowledge. "I meant about me and Stevie."

"You and Stevie?" Jeanie repeated hopefully. She'd always thought they made a good couple.

Christian grinned. "Yeah, we're getting married." He was starting to get used to the word.

"Oh my God!" Jeanie said, laughing and moving to hug him.

Christian hugged her back carefully, holding his cigarette away from her.

"Congrats, man," Donovan said, extending his hand. "Can't believe you're actually gonna do it."

"Yeah, well…" Christian said, his face growing serious. "I don't want to lose her again."

Donovan nodded, knowing that feeling all too well.

"We need your help," Jeanie said.

"With?" Christian asked, thinking they'd want him to write a program or something.

"It's with our case," Donovan said.

Christian nodded, still thinking it would be computer related.

"We need you to go UC for us," Jeanie said, biting her lip in uncertainty. She wasn't totally sure Christian would go for it.

"What?" Christian asked, looking stunned. "You mean you want me to go play narc?" he asked, shaking his head. "That's not my thing, guys. I'm more of a behind-the-scenes player…" He held up his hands, as if in defense.

"We need you on this, Blue," Jeanie said, reaching out to touch his arm. "There's this professor at the college that's getting young, good-looking guys hooked so she can get them to sell drugs for her. We need to stop her."

Christian's black brows furrowed, and he looked at Donovan. "You're the good-looking narc—why can't you handle this?"

Donovan grimaced, curling his lips in disgust. "I did. I fucked up. I had no idea what I was dealing with until it was too late and she had me hooked."

Christian was stunned. Donovan wasn't one to mess up when it came to police work. Donovan waited for the sarcastic rejoinder he was sure to get for making such a huge mistake. Christian Collins was well known for his ability to make a person feel extremely inferior when he thought you'd screwed up, or if he wanted to screw with you to piss you off.

After a long pause, Christian nodded. "What do you need to me to do?"

Jeanie glanced back at Donovan, having known he fully expected to take a lot of shit from Christian. She read surprise in his reaction to Christian's question. He wasn't going to say anything? In reality, the snide comment about how Donovan's fucking around had fucked him up had been on the tip of Christian's tongue. But he'd realized from the look on Donovan's face that the other man was beating himself up enough; he didn't need Christian's knives to carve himself up any further. Christian had recently gained a deep understanding of moments of weakness, and realized that even the slightest could cause you irreparable damage. It had made him quickly rethink drilling Donovan.

When Donovan was apparently too stunned to answer, Jeanie started talking.

"We need this woman to approach you. So we want to get you in as a transferring student. But we're going to need to get right to the point, so we want you to play up the angle that you already do some dealing and that you have bigger distribution sources. We're hoping her greed will get the better of her."

Christian nodded. "How does she get you hooked?" he asked,

looking at Donovan.

"She puts it in a drink, which she makes sure to hand you every time you show up."

Christian nodded again. "X, right?"

"Yeah…" Donovan said, looking mystified. "But how—?"

"I've had it," Christian said simply. "I know how it's easily administered, what it's used for, and how it works on people."

"You've had it?" Jeanie asked, surprised. She knew Christian had a colorful past, but she hadn't realized how colorful.

Christian nodded, looking unrepentant. "It's pretty wicked stuff," he said, looking Donovan over. "You okay, man?"

"Yeah," Donovan said, realizing that Christian was excusing his slip by indicating that the drug he'd been slipped was quite strong.

"Okay," Christian said. "So when are you gonna send me in?"

"Is tomorrow too soon?" Jeanie asked.

Christian looked thoughtful, then shrugged. "Nah, I can do it tomorrow."

"Great, thanks, Blue," Jeanie said sincerely.

"No problem." Christian looked at the two of them then, noting how close they stood, and the fact that Donovan's expression had been a bit proprietary whenever any man had walked by looking at Jeanie. He nodded back toward the office. "She know you two are back together?"

Jeanie was clearly surprised. Donovan shook his head, realizing that he should have known that nothing got past Blue. He also knew that Erin tended to make people feel protective of her, wanting to shelter her from getting hurt. It had become evident when everyone had leapt to defend her against her abusive ex-husband a few years before. The Gang had turned out as a whole for the meeting between Donovan and Tyler Shandley. All Donovan had done was tell Joe what was happening. Joe had spread the word, and the Gang had been there to stand against the man that had hurt Erin.

Christian had been working with Erin over the last six months, and Donovan was sure she would have confided in Christian with her concerns about Donovan. Regardless of his rough exterior, Christian Collins was every bit as gallant as his cousin, so it served to figure that he would want to make sure Erin wasn't hurt here.

"No," Jeanie said, looking penitent.

Christian canted his head to the side. "She wants you both happy, Jeanie," he assured her. "But she has a right to know, don't you think?" He glanced back at Donovan.

Donovan nodded in agreement.

A little while later, in the office, Erin looked over at Christian.

"So what was that about?" she asked.

Christian glanced up, narrowing his eyes slightly, as if trying to discern what she thought it was about.

He shrugged. "They just want me to do some UC stuff."

"Just?" Erin repeated, giving him an astonished look.

"Yeah."

"Isn't that considered somewhat dangerous?"

"Maybe a little," he said. "So?"

"You're a computer geek," Erin said, the beginnings of a grin on her lips.

"Shut the hell up, Erin," he replied, laughing.

"Hey, I'm just looking out for your well-being," she pointed out.

"I'll show you well-being…"

Erin grinned, glad that he was happy again.

"They're back together, aren't they?" she said after a few minutes, her tone not holding any real question.

Christian stared back at her for a long moment, then nodded, looking a bit pained. Erin nodded too. She'd felt it when they'd walked in. Taking a deep breath, she turned back to her desk. She tried not to let it hurt her. She'd known all along that Donovan would never love her like he loved Jeanie. That she had stumbled into the middle of a tragedy and she'd merely been one of the actors in the play, not the star. She had always known that things would work out the way they were meant to. It just hurt to realize that now there was no one in her life again.

She felt Christian behind her before he actually touched her shoulder. She nodded, trying to be brave, but when his hands closed over her shoulders, she gave in to the urge to cry. Turning around blindly, she found herself pulled against his chest. She sobbed and sniffled against his shirt, while he told her it would be okay, that she'd find the right guy for her soon. She nodded, knowing he was right and hoping soon would be very soon.

Stevie walked in a couple minutes later and stood watching them. She heard what Christian told Erin and wondered at it, but figured it had to do with Donovan, because Donovan was the guy Erin had her heart set on. Stevie smiled softly, realizing again what a big softy Christian really was. He was a lot like Joe, he just liked to pretend he wasn't—whereas Joe was straightforward in his chivalry, Christian tended to downplay his.

Christian sensed Stevie there, and turned his head to look at her. He caught the smile she wore and quirked his lips in a sardonic grin, as if reading her thoughts. Erin looked up at him, and then over his shoulder, standing on her tiptoes to be able to see.

"Hi, Stevie," she said, stepping away from Christian.

"Hi, Erin," Stevie said, smiling at the younger girl.

"Congratulations," Erin said, moving to sit on her desk as she wiped at her cheeks.

Stevie nodded. Christian went to sit in his chair, reaching out to take her hand and pull her down onto his lap. She grinned at his affectionate gesture, and wondered if he was worried that she was mad that he'd been comforting Erin when she walked in. Looking down into his eyes, she could see that yes, he was worried about that. She kissed his lips softly, then his cheek, in her own way telling him that she wasn't the least bit upset.

Stevie had gained a greater respect for his feelings for her. Knowing that his devastation at losing her had caused his attempt to end his life made her sick to her stomach, but also told her a lot about how much he loved her. It meant more than she could express to him.

"You about ready for lunch?" she asked, knowing he really shouldn't be at work. He had been exhausted the night before, having overdone it by going into the office so soon.

Christian nodded. "Yeah, I could eat."

"Erin?" Stevie asked as she stood. "You want to come?"

"No, but thanks," Erin said, smiling shyly. She was grateful for Stevie's invitation, but didn't want to impose on the two of them.

Stevie nodded, looking unhappy that Erin hadn't accepted. Christian stood up, looking over at Erin.

"You sure?" he asked.

"I'm sure."

"Rin, come with us," he said beseechingly.

"No, I'm okay."

Christian gave her an "Oh really?" look. Erin laughed, shaking her head. "Okay, so I'm not okay, but I don't want to impose on you two."

"You're not imposing, Shandley, come on," Stevie said, walking over and grabbing her hand, pulling her up off the desk.

Erin was constantly amazed by the people she worked with. They were always there for each other, and it felt really good to be included in that. She walked out with Stevie and Christian.

In the hallway, Stevie saw Bill Harris coming out of an office. He looked down the hall at the three of them, sneering. Stevie stared back, refusing to break eye contact. The look on her face was challenging, daring him to say something. Harris said nothing, only giving Stevie a dirty look and shaking his head.

Once in the stairwell, Christian glanced over at her. "What was that about?"

"Oh, the usual," she replied, shrugging.

Christian's expression was considering as he glanced over at Erin; she'd seen Harris' look too.

"He hassled you again?" Christian asked Stevie.

Stevie sighed. "He always hassles me, babe. He has nothing better to do with his time."

"Was it about me? Or about Joe?"

Stevie continued walking down the stairs, glancing back over her shoulder at him to see if it bothered him to talk about her and Joe. It didn't seem to.

"It was about Joe," she said. "He wanted to know if it hurt when

I fell from grace."

Christian's lips tightened. He didn't like that the same guy who had physically assaulted Stevie once, in this very stairwell, was hassling her again.

"And you said?" he asked mildly, knowing her well enough to know she didn't just take anyone's shit.

Stevie was silent for a minute as they got to the floor her car was on. As she went through the door, Christian caught her sly grin.

"Oh, God, what did you say?" he asked, knowing it must have been a zinger.

Stevie shrugged casually as they got to her car, looking at him and Erin over the top of it.

"I just asked what bugged him more, the fact that I could make it with a captain in this department, or the fact that he couldn't even make sergeant in this department." Her tone was sweet, her smile ingénue, and Christian almost choked.

He started laughing then, and Stevie laughed too. Erin's eyes had widened to saucers when Stevie said the part about "making it with a captain," but when she saw that Christian was obviously okay with it, she saw the humor in what Stevie had said. She laughed too.

"Donovan and Jeanie want me to help them out with their case," Christian said casually as they drove out of the parking lot a few minutes later.

"What? A new program or something?" Stevie asked.

"Ah…" Christian said, rubbing the bridge of his nose with his index finger.

It was a sure sign he was hedging, and Stevie caught the movement. "Spill it, Collins."

40

"They want me to help them make their case at the college."

"Uh-huh…" she said, knowing there was more.

"Well, the case kind of took a strange twist, so they said they need me."

"What kind of strange twist?" she asked, raising an eyebrow. It wasn't like Christian to be so evasive.

"The dealer is a professor who snags good-looking guys, drops some X on them, then lays them. She gets them hooked then backs off the drug, so they will beg her to sell it to get their fix," he said, his tone informative, even as his light blue eyes sparkled.

"Whoa, whoa, whoa," Stevie said. "Back up here. Lays them?"

Christian grinned, nodding.

"And they want you to do what exactly?"

"They want to send me in to catch this professor's eye."

Stevie narrowed her eyes. "Why doesn't Donovan do it—he's good-looking. Or won't Jeanie let him?"

"Uh…" Christian said, grimacing.

"Oh shit," Stevie said, realizing what that meant. "You mean she already nailed him?"

"Yeah," Christian said, glancing back at Erin apologetically. Erin bit her lip, looking worried.

"Wait, did she give him X?" Stevie had suddenly realized the connotations.

"Apparently."

"Fuck…" Stevie breathed. "Is he okay?"

"He seemed fine," Christian said. "But they're doubly deter-mined to make this case now."

"Understandably." Stevie gave him a narrowed look. "I don't

41

like them using you for it though."

"Why not?" he asked evenly.

Stevie detected the note of irritation in his voice. "You're just… You're not a trained narc, Christian," she said, trying to make sure it didn't sound like she was putting him down.

"I wasn't a trained narc when I dropped the dime on Devereaux either," he said, narrowing his eyes.

"I know that, but—"

"But nothing. You weren't a trained narc when you made the case on Tiempo—would you appreciate being treated like an amateur after all you went through?" he asked, raising a jet black eyebrow. "I went to the same academy you did, Steve."

"I know you did, I know," she said, shaking her head. "I'm just…"

"Just what?"

She looked over at him, her eyes backing up what she said. "I'm just worried, Christian, okay?"

"Okay," he said gently. "Steve, I'll be fine. It doesn't sound like this woman is dangerous, just crazy."

"Crazy means dangerous."

He was silent for a minute, then looked over at her. "Would you feel better if you could be on the other end of the wire?"

Stevie looked thoughtful. "Yeah, that would make me feel better."

"You can be my backup," he said, grinning at her.

"I'll always be your backup," she said, smiling.

He winked. "But this time, bring your gun."

She laughed.

Joe met with Robert the day after getting back to England.

"What can I do here?" he asked, indicating the divorce papers he'd handed Robert upon arriving at the Debenshire home.

Robert had had time to read them, since Annabelle had insisted on feeding Joe, citing that he was far too thin. Robert had retired to his office, telling Joe to meet him there once Belle was done fattening him up.

"Well, Joe, there isn't much you can do," Robert said gently. "Randy has not asked for anything, so her petition for divorce should be fairly quickly granted. There is nothing to contest, unless you want to fight her for full custody of the children…"

Robert trailed off. He didn't think that would be a good idea. He also didn't think it was Joseph Michael Sinclair's style to hide behind children. Joe was already shaking his head.

"No, you don't understand." Joe took a deep breath, blowing it out slowly. "I don't want the divorce, but I know that neither of us is happy anymore. By the same token, I want Randy taken care of. I mean, Jesus, Robert, she didn't even ask for Sinclair House. Is she just going to walk away?"

Robert stared back at Joe for a long moment. He'd known him his entire life, having been Joseph Sinclair Senior's lawyer as well. He could see the turmoil in the younger man's eyes.

"What do you want me to counter with, Joe?" Robert asked carefully.

Joe sat back on the leather couch. He wasn't sure how he'd got here. How did he end up losing his wife at the age of forty? This wasn't how it was supposed to go. He was supposed to retire in a few years and live out his life with her... Why wasn't it going that way?

Joe lifted his head, looking at Robert, his face serious and sad.

"Look, I want her taken care of. I want her to have $5,000 a month alimony, $2,500 child support. She can have the house we live in now. And Sinclair House was a gift to her, so she keeps it. I also want her to have a lump sum settlement of a million. Okay?"

Robert nodded, ever astounded at the Sinclair generosity. Joe could have literally walked out of his thirteen-year marriage without giving Randy a cent, and the fact that she hadn't asked for anything would have made that even easier. But that was not Joe's way, and Robert couldn't help but feel pride for the man he considered his other son.

Joe stood up, eager to get this over with. "And if you think of anything else, throw it in. I'll sign whatever you write up, okay?"

Robert nodded. "I'll have it messengered over to you by the end of the day."

At the front door, he hugged Joe as a father would. "I am sorry this is happening, Joe," he said sincerely.

Joe nodded. "Thanks."

Robert nodded.

Over the next week, Joe spent the days with the kids and the nights out on the town. He drank at first by himself, but then little by little people he'd known from his youth started hearing that he was around. Then they started finding him at the bar he was hanging out in. Slowly but surely he built up a crowd. He still felt very out of place, but it did feel better to have people around him.

Eventually, he ended up accidentally inviting them all over to the estate for a party. He'd been talking to one of the guys he'd run with in the gang he'd led, and said something about the estate, and the man had taken that to mean party. The word had spread, and the next thing Joe knew, he had a major house party going on. Some of the people he'd known in his old days had actually grown up to be respectable human beings; some even had kids. They brought their spouses, girlfriends, kids, and then they brought friends. Their friends brought their friends, and the next thing Joe knew, the house was full of people and he was looking for an escape.

In the end, he found himself a nice, quiet terrace at the back of the home he'd lived in from the time he was a baby. It was an oddly nice day out, not the freezing weather he was used to in England but not exactly warm either. The sun was out, so the children were taking full advantage of the company that they had. They were currently attacking each other with silly string and Nerf balls; it had become a contest.

Joe sat with his drink in hand. He'd switched to margaritas with extra tequila to keep from getting too drunk too quickly. He wore comfortable faded jeans, a long-sleeved polo shirt, black with a light blue stripe, and black hiking boots. He also wore his sunglasses, and his hair, just past his shoulders now, was tucked back behind his ears. He looked like the consummate relaxed rock star.

Jordan Tate couldn't help but notice him. She'd been attempting to escape from an overbearing producer type trying to monopolize her time, so she'd gone outside to walk around the perimeter of the house, admiring the architecture. She'd heard about the host of the party. Of course, she couldn't credit half of what she'd heard.

Some people said the owner of the home was a young man

who'd inherited it by way of shady means. Some said he'd killed his parents to get their money. Others said his parents had been murdered. Still others said they had died in a car accident. The man himself was also a mystery to many. Some said he was a tax exile, staying out of England for so many months so as not to pay the government so much. Others said he was a cop in the States; still others said he was a drug dealer. The terms hoodlum and black sheep came out a lot too when people described the owner of the beautiful home. Many had been there literally for days. And the party just seemed to be growing.

Jordan was a guest of someone who had been invited by someone else. She had no idea why she was here, other than that she was taking a break before her next big tour in Europe. The name Jordan Tate was famous in the pop/rock music industry. At thirty-five, she'd been a household name for three years, and her second album had just gone triple platinum. She was thrilled. She'd grown up all over Europe. Her father had been a high-level federal employee, and as such had moved his family to Europe when Jordan was five. She'd grown up learning many languages and cultures, but she'd found that she liked England the best, because of the music that came out of the country. All the bands she'd loved as a teen had been English, from Duran Duran to Def Leppard, to The Stones and even Ozzy Osbourne.

She decided when she was fifteen that she wanted to be Lita Ford when she grew up. She was very pretty, with dark brown hair shot through with lighter reddish highlights and amber eyes that looked like molten gold. She had a body that most women would kill for, with slim hips and a small waist, but ample breasts to keep her from looking too thin without giving the impression of being fake. She worked out constantly, toning her body to the point of perfection.

Her heritage was Albanian American, and she had her mother's golden complexion.

Her father had seen to it that she got heard by the right agent when she wanted to get discovered, but it had taken six years after that to get anything good going. Now she had it going, and she was just enjoying the ride. She'd come back to London to spend a couple of months relaxing and to prepare for her European tour before she hit America again. It was going to be exhausting, but she was going to love every minute of it.

Walking around a set of bushes, Jordan saw the man sitting on the small terrace at the back of the house. His long legs were extended in front of him, his ankles crossed. His arms were resting on the arms of the chair, and he slouched comfortably. He had a drink in one hand, and was grinning at something the children were doing on the lawn. His profile was very handsome; he had a strong jawline, with nicely tanned skin and a dark blond goatee. His eyes were hidden by sunglasses. His hair was dirty blond, falling to just past his shoulders; it gave him a very rakish, wild but modern look. Jordan couldn't help the natural reaction to what was, from what she could tell, a nicely formed body. His legs were long, but she could detect the hint of muscle from the snug faded jeans. There was no paunch at his mid-section where he was slouched, and his shoulders appeared broad. It was enough to perk her attention. She watched him from the side, glancing over at the group of children playing in the garden.

Jordan was determined to at least talk to this man. She wasn't sure that her guess was right, but she thought he was likely to be the host of the party. Jordan had heard just enough conflicting information to be extremely curious, and if this was indeed the man himself, she was doubly curious.

As she stepped closer, she heard a phone ring. She watched as he sat up, leaning down to pick up the phone lying next to his chair. Jordan knew it was highly impolite to eavesdrop on his conversation, but she found she couldn't help it.

"'Lo," he said into the phone, still watching the children.

Jordan's breath caught in her throat as she saw him smile. Obviously, whoever was on the other end of the line had said something to make him happy. Or maybe it was the person.

"Yeah, yeah," he said, grinning still. "What's goin' on?" he asked, his English accent clear. He listened for a few moments, nodding. "When does he want to run it?"

Jordan listened intently, trying to see if she could pick up some clues about him from the conversation.

"Well, Night," he said, putting a foot up on the stone railing that ran around the terrace, "he can run it, but I don't think he's qualified." He made a face that Jordan couldn't help grinning at, then shook his head. "Yeah, he is, but he's not really going to hinge on accuracy." His voice trailed off as the other person talked again. He nodded a few times. It was obvious he was listening to their point of view. "Right," he said. "But the way I see it, if they are going to clear leather, I want them prepared to hit what they aim for." Again he listened, nodding, and finally he sighed. "Night, it's your choice…"

Jordan stepped around the bushes and walked over to the terrace, not wanting to continue eavesdropping. Joe glanced up at her. She couldn't see his eyes appraising her because of his sunglasses. She only saw a slight smile that curled his lips as he inclined his head. He was still listening to the person on the phone. He gestured to the gate at the side of the terrace. Jordan smiled and opened it before walking over to him. She leaned against the stone rail.

"Night, look," he said, "if you want to send them through, go for it. But if you want to wait, I'll come run the range when I get back." He listened again. "Yeah, he can just run the first ten KDs and then I'll be there." He nodded a few times. "Yeah, I heard. I'll be there too," he said, grinning. Then he laughed softly. "Yeah, ought to be entertaining. Okay, babe, I'll talk to you soon."

He hung up, looking up at Jordan as he set the phone back by his feet.

"Hi," she said, smiling.

"Hello," he replied, his tone more reserved.

"Sorry if I interrupted."

"You didn't."

Jordan nodded, glancing at the children as they got particularly loud. She turned back and saw him smile over at the kids.

"Yours?" she asked.

"Oh God, no, only two of them," he said, laughing.

"Which two?"

"The boy in the black and the girl in the yellow," he said, pointing them out.

Jordan nodded. "Twins?" she asked, noting that the children were about the same size.

"Close enough," Joe said, grinning. "They're only a year apart."

"Wow," she said, widening her eyes. "That must be difficult."

"You have kids?"

"No, I have a hard enough time taking care of myself," she replied wryly.

He laughed.

"I'm Jordan Tate," she said, extending her hand.

"Joe Sinclair," he replied, taking it.

"Ah, so you are our elusive host."

He inclined his head to indicate she was right. "I guess that would be me."

"And I note that you're hiding out here."

"And I note you're doing the same," he replied, grinning.

Jordan laughed, nodding.

"I'm basically not a big party person," he said, then raised an eyebrow at her. "What's your excuse?"

"I'm escaping an overbearing producer who wants to do my next album."

"Album?" he queried, grimacing. "Should I have known your name? I mean, if I wasn't out of the loop, would I have?"

Jordan laughed, waving off his concern. "It's nice, actually, for a change—but yes, I'm kinda famous."

"Kinda?"

She grinned. "Uh-huh…"

"Kinda like local, no commercial value, eclectic type, never be on MTV kinda? Or 'Oh my God it's Jordan Tate, and can I touch her and never wash my hand again' kinda?"

Jordan laughed. "I think I'm somewhere in between those two."

"Ah, so I can probably safely converse with you without fear of being overrun by hysterical groupies?"

"Yes, I think you're safe."

"Thank God."

"I'll do that and get back to you."

"I'll wait here."

"Not speaking to God these days, Mr. Sinclair?"

"Haven't spoken to him in years," he replied dryly.

"So I'm guessing a stimulating dialogue on theology is out, huh?"

"Au contraire. Not being on communication levels with an entity doesn't forbid a very definite opinion on said deity."

"Wow…" Jordan breathed, enjoying his obvious quick wit. "You wouldn't by chance be a lawyer, would you?"

"No," he said. "That would be my partner." He indicated the phone on the ground.

"Your partner is a lawyer and you're not?"

"No, my partner has a law degree. I'm just a simple captain."

"So he has a law degree and isn't a lawyer?"

"She."

"She?"

"My partner, to whom I'm referring, is a she," he said, grinning. "And no, she's not a lawyer—she's a Chief of Police."

Jordan nodded. "So that would make you a captain of…"

"Vice," he supplied.

"As in Miami?" She grinned.

"As in San Diego," he replied, grinning too.

"I meant—"

"I know what you meant," he said, interrupting her with a smile. "I'm in charge of the narcotics, homicide, and diversion units."

"I see," she said, nodding. "So you are a cop."

"I am indeed," he replied, inclining his head.

"That was one of the rumors."

"What were the others?" he asked. "Perhaps I can further dissuade or convince you."

"Let's see… drug dealer was one."

"Nope, never have been. I've played one, though."

"Victim."

"Of?"

"They say your parents were murdered."

"They were."

She hesitated. "Some say you did it," she said softly.

"In some ways, I did," he replied seriously.

"Excuse me?" she asked, stunned.

He gave her a long look. "I was the reason they were murdered."

"Why?" She was horrified.

Joe looked back at her for another long few moments, not sure why he was having this conversation with a total stranger. He found himself drawn in by her quick responses though. He still wasn't sure why he was answering her, but he was.

"I was the leader of a gang. Another gang leader wanted me dead. He got my parents by mistake," he said evenly.

Jordan stared back at him for a long moment. She wished she could see his eyes. She had a feeling that what he had just said meant a lot more than his tone had belied.

"My God," she said, shaking her head. "I'm sorry."

Joe nodded, having heard a similar sentiment from so many people over the years.

"I would say, though, that the other gang leader's skewed priorities were the reason for your parents' murder, not you," she said, surprising him.

"Perhaps," he acquiesced.

Their conversation was abruptly interrupted when a Nerf ball hit Joe on the shoulder. He glanced down at it, then searched for the culprit. Jordan looked over her shoulder and saw the boy Joe had identified as his. JT was all blond hair and blue-eyed innocence. He stood staring at his father with an impish grin on his face.

"You throw this?" Joe asked.

His son nodded slowly, his eyes still on his father.

"You meant to hit me with it?" Joe asked, his tone ominous now.

Again the boy nodded, even as his eyes widened.

Jordan looked at Joe, wondering if she was about to see this outwardly affable man's temper.

Joe nodded to the boy, looking thoughtful.

Jordan was about to say something about kids being kids when Joe leapt out of his chair, vaulted the stone railing, and ran toward his son. The boy squealed in obvious delight and turned to run.

Jordan watched in shocked amusement as Joe grabbed his son, swinging him up in the air and twirling him around, then set him down. He was promptly attacked by all the other children. He held his own, grabbing Nerf balls and throwing them at escaping kids. He even got ahold of a can of silly string, covering his daughter in the green stuff. At one point, he had a child clinging to each leg and one in his arms. He wrestled one to the ground, only to be jumped on by another.

A number of minutes later, he walked back over to the terrace. Throwing a leg over, he moved to sit on the rail, looking at Jordan with a grin. He was only slightly winded. Jordan found that his grin was quite endearing. She also found herself feeling more affection toward him, having seen him being so silly with his kids.

"Feel vindicated?" she asked.

"Oh yes," he replied, smiling.

"You're good with kids."

"I work around them all day long."

She laughed.

He reached up then, taking off his sunglasses and wiping his blue eyes. When he looked back at her, she found she couldn't speak. It must have shown on her face, because he commented on it.

"What?" he asked, sounding very English.

She shook her head slowly. "I... umm..." she stammered, not sure what she should say. Blowing her breath out, she shook her head, deciding to be honest. "You have the most beautiful eyes..."

He grinned at her. "So do you."

"Well, thank you," she said, perversely pleased that he'd even noticed them.

His reaction to her hadn't been what she was used to. She'd begun to wonder if he had even been paying attention. It wasn't that she was conceited—she was far from, knowing all of her flaws intimately—but she'd gotten so used to men commenting on her looks first and foremost. It almost seemed insulting that he hadn't said anything, as if he was purposely avoiding comment.

Joe stepped down off the railing, moving to pull another chair over. It was an invitation to join him, and Jordan grabbed the opportunity.

They spent the next several hours talking. They discussed art, religion, music, police work, politics, everything they could think of.

Before they knew it, it had grown dark. The children had long since gone inside.

They went in, settling in the living room and continuing to talk. Eventually a woman came in. "Joe?" she queried.

"Deb, hi," Joe said, getting to his feet. "Deborah, this is Jordan Tate. Jordan, this is Deborah Debenshire."

Jordan stood, taking the other woman's extended hand.

"It's nice to meet you," she said.

"Nice to meet you as well," Deborah replied, her English accent very proper. She looked at Joe. "The kids are getting sleepy. Would you like me to take them upstairs and put them to bed?"

Joe grinned. The kids had come in and out of the living room during the last few hours, many times climbing up on his lap, at others asking questions or wanting his opinion on a picture they'd colored. He'd indulged their every bid for attention.

"I'll be right there, Deb," he said, smiling. "Thanks."

"You're very welcome," Deborah replied, smiling back. She turned and left the room.

"I'll be right back," Joe told Jordan.

"I'll stay right here."

"Good," he replied, winking at her.

While he was gone, Jordan started reflecting on her feelings. She was very definitely attracted to Joe Sinclair. She'd never met a man quite like him before. He was undeniably attractive. Her eyes had frequently dropped to the small amount of bare skin at the neckline of his shirt. What she saw looked tanned and nicely defined. She admitted to herself that she was dying to see more.

Her eyes had connected with his a number of times during the evening. Although she was sure she saw desire there, he had made no moves to get more intimate with her. She wasn't sure what that meant. Of course, she'd noticed the wedding band on his left ring finger. But he hadn't mentioned his wife thus far. Nor did there seem to be a wife in residence, that she'd seen. He seemed to be on his own with the kids, and comfortably so.

On the one hand, it was unnerving that they'd spent so much time talking but he hadn't made a move on her. On the other, it thrilled her no end to find a man that could not only carry on a highly intelligent conversation but assumed her capable of the same. Over the years she'd actually gotten used to being talked down to. Everyone she dealt with assumed she was just "fluff" because she was a singer and pretty. Only people who actually knew her found out that she was actually quite intelligent. Having grown up throughout Europe, she'd been educated in many of the best schools. But what was Joe's story? Did he want her or not? Was he just entertaining himself with her? Was his wife joining him later? Was that why he hadn't touched her? She knew she was becoming fixated on him. She'd stared at his lips so many times, wondering how he kissed. She'd been let down so often in that arena. A guy that couldn't kiss just didn't make it with her. She thought it was an important point in the attractiveness of a man.

"Oh God, Jordan, relax!" she said out loud.

"What?" Joe asked from the doorway.

He'd been standing there watching her for the last couple of minutes. He had been trying to figure out what she was thinking about.

"I, uh…" she said, grinning self-consciously. "Nothing."

Joe nodded, grinning as he walked over to her.

"You hungry?" he asked.

She nodded, realizing that she hadn't really eaten all day.

"Come on," he said, gesturing with his head.

He led her to the huge kitchen. There they rummaged through the fridge, picking through all the catered food that had been brought in for the party. In the end he made them sandwiches while she cut up cheese and got them each a beer.

"You want to eat in the dining room?" he asked.

She grimaced, shaking her head. "Too formal."

"Here then?" he said, indicating the kitchen.

She grinned, nodding.

Reaching out, he took her by the waist and lifted her up onto the low island in the center of the room. She shivered slightly at the contact, even if it was through the material of her blouse. She forced that thought aside, not wanting to spoil the camaraderie they'd already built. They took their time eating, once again talking about anything and everything. Joe sat on the counter across from her. She watched the way he gestured, the way his eyes lit up when he talked about a subject he obviously liked—police work, cars, rock music. They spent hours there, lingering over a couple more beers and dessert, which they joked about being the "sugar high" they both needed at that point.

They rounded out the time with Joe giving her a tour of the house. Again, they talked about art and antiques. Joe told her stories about how his parents had acquired this piece or that piece. He had her laughing so many times her sides hurt. His wit was the dry, subtle type, which she had always liked about the English. He was intelligent enough to convey his meaning without ever denigrating her by explaining himself unnecessarily.

They were up on the second floor, in the hallway, when the distinct ringing of a phone could be heard. Joe glanced at his watch, making a disgusted noise in the back of his throat.

"I'll kill her," he said to himself, grinning all the same. "Come on." He took her hand and led her to a door at the far end of the hallway.

Joe was staying in the bedroom he'd grown up in. He refused to stay in his parents' room, especially now that he was sleeping alone again. Inside, he let her hand go, and she stopped in the doorway, watching as he strode over to the bedside table. He picked up the phone, glancing back at her and smiling.

"Night, you really need a life, babe," he said into the phone without preamble. He laughed a moment later, shaking his head. "Who the hell else would call me at four a.m.?"

He glanced over at Jordan again, gesturing for her to come in. She stepped inside, looking around. He had the classic Union Jack up behind his bed, and various rock bands on posters on the wall. The furniture was heavy-looking dark-wood antiques. She walked over to his dresser and looked at the pictures there, glancing back at him. He was watching her, even as he listened to the person on the phone.

"Night, you really need to learn to relax," he said, grinning. Then he nodded. "Fine, I'll tell Rick he needs to stop working late. It gives you way too much time to think of ways to bug the shit out of me." He winked at Jordan as she laughed softly.

Jordan sat on his bed, putting her back to the headboard. She was on the opposite side from where he stood.

"Midnight, if you want to wait, I'll be there to run it." He listened for a minute. "Well, look at it this way. They can come up on their Christmas break. You do the ride-alongs the week before. After

58

the first, I'll be there." He listened again, grinning. "I'm just tired, Night. I haven't slept yet." He grimaced, his tongue sliding over his upper lip in agitation as he shook his head. "How did I know I shouldn't have told you that?" he said, his grin appearing a moment later. He listened again, looking up at the ceiling, the grin widening. "No, I don't particularly want to tell you anything, because there's nothing to tell currently, okay?" He paused. "Gad, will you leave me alone, woman!" he growled. He looked then like he was getting chastised. He stood staring straight ahead, his grin widening slowly to a smile. "Fine, fine, I will, when I have something you actually need to know." He looked down at Jordan and saw that she was still watching him. He rolled his eyes, quirking his lips in a sardonic grin. He sat down on the bed, still listening to the apparent tirade going on on the other end of the line. Finally he lay down, glancing up at Jordan. "No, you don't know her," he said. "No, I'm not telling you 'bout her either." He grinned as he bent his knee, reaching one hand down to unlace his boot, then doing the same with the other. "Face it, Night, sometimes your babies grow up and move out of the house," he said as he kicked off his boots. "And I'm currently being rude, so I need to go," he added, glancing up at Jordan. "Okay, fine, I'll talk to you soon. Bye," he said, hanging up. He tossed the phone aside.

"I'm sorry," he told Jordan.

"It's okay," she said, turning to look down at him. "They seem to really need you."

"Yeah," he said, grinning. "And the degree of that need seems to be in direct proportion to the distance between us."

Jordan laughed, then looked at him seriously. "Can I ask you a question?"

"Sure," he said softly.

Jordan looked down at his left hand, which now rested on his chest, focusing on his wedding band.

"You're married?" she asked gently.

"Currently," he replied, his light blue eyes watching hers.

She nodded, still looking a bit unsure.

"My wife has filed for divorce," he said.

"Oh…" she said, grimacing. "I'm sorry."

He shrugged, pursing his lips. "Does that bother you? That I'm still married…"

Her eyes were on his lips again. *My God, I'm becoming obsessed.* Then she suddenly realized he'd asked her a question and was waiting for an answer. It had happened a few times that evening. She tried to formulate a reply, but she couldn't even remember the question.

"Jordan?" he said, bemused.

"I, um…" she said, shaking her head.

"Does it bother you?"

"I, uh…" she stammered. "No, it doesn't bother me. I mean, that you're married… no." She was trying desperately to cover her preoccupation, and she knew she was failing miserably.

"Uh-huh…"

"What?" she asked, smiling.

"I believe that would be my question."

Jordan pressed her lips together, knowing she'd been caught. She started grinning self-consciously. Joe turned over on his side, looking up at her.

"Where did you go a minute ago?" he asked, his eyes searching hers.

His voice sounded gravelly now. She wondered if there was any significance to that. She knew, however, that it sounded very sexy to her, all rough like that. Was that how he sounded during sex? She wanted to know. She came back to reality suddenly, seeing that he was watching her closely. He was waiting for an answer, but what to say? Finally she thought, *Oh, fuck it.*

"Are you ever going to kiss me?" she asked, staring directly into his eyes.

Joe laughed outright at her bold question. "Is that what you want?" he asked, raising an eyebrow.

"That's what I've wanted all night."

His light blue eyes widened, even as a grin played at his lips. He moved to sit up, his lips capturing hers as he did, kissing her softly at first then deepening in intensity as his hand slid through her hair to the back of her neck. His other hand touched her waist, pulling her closer to him as he continued to kiss her.

Jordan moaned softly against his lips. God, the man could kiss! His lips moved over hers sensually, sucking gently, then kissing almost hungrily again. There was just enough heat to make her want more. She pressed forward, pushing him back. Using her momentum, he pulled her with him as he lay back. She ended up lying half over him, his lips still connected with hers. She groaned at his action, pressing closer to him, her hands on his chest. She flexed her fingers, her nails grazing his skin through his shirt. Joe groaned, grasping at her back. They continued to kiss, their lips meeting hungrily.

His hands slid up her back, skimming her sides. His thumbs brushed over her breasts, moving over already hard nipples. Jordan gasped, biting his lips in reaction to the thrill that had just gone through her. Her reaction prompted him to become more aggressive, wanting more from her. He moved his hands to cup her breasts, caressing her nipples, making her ache suddenly.

"God, Joe!" she gasped, pressing closer.

She moved her hand down his chest, past the waist of his jeans. Moving lower, she pressed her hand against him, feeling his hardness. Joe groaned loudly.

"Jesus… Jesus!" he chanted against her lips.

His hands moved down her body, sliding up under her tunic-style blouse. She shuddered at the feel of his hands on her skin. Wanting more, she reached up to unbutton her blouse. Joe pulled back, watching her as she exposed more skin. His hands slid up her body, unclipping her bra in the front, brushing aside the material as he touched her bare breasts.

Jordan felt frenzied at that point, wanting him so much, but he was taking his time. He touched her skin, leaning up to kiss her, then her neck, moving down. She grasped at his shoulders as his mouth claimed an extremely sensitive nipple.

"God, Joe, please…" she moaned. "Please, please…"

She moved her hand under his shirt, touching his skin, causing him to moan against her. Shifting her to his side, he sat up long enough to pull his shirt off and toss it aside. As he lay back, she moved over him to kiss his chest. She pulled back to gaze at his body, his face, his eyes. Her eyes connected and stayed on his.

"God, you are so gorgeous," she said, lying back down to cover his body with hers.

She kissed his chest again. Then, moving to one of his nipples, she kissed, then sucked, making him moan. His hands were in her hair instantly, guiding her.

She kissed down his chest, moving lower to his stomach. She heard his breath quicken and grow heavier, and it excited her more. Unbuttoning his jeans, she moved lower, gazing up at him. He watched her, and he thought she looked very much like a tigress perched over her prey, with her gold eyes.

"Jordan…" he breathed, shaking his head.

He wasn't sure how much longer he could control himself. He was fairly sure that if her mouth touched him where she was hovering at that moment he would lost all control. She grinned, enjoying the power she held. He narrowed his eyes at her, silently threatening retribution if she proceeded.

Jordan laughed softly, realizing that she was dealing with a man who liked to hold on to his control. She knew at some point she'd want to see if she could make him lose it, but not now, not this first time.

Raising an eyebrow at him, she grasped the denim at his hips, curling her fingers around the waistbands of both his jeans and his underwear. She pulled them down slowly, driving him closer to the edge as her mouth moved so close to him he could feel her breath. He closed his eyes, willing himself not to lose it. Then she moved lower. He groaned when her lips touched the inside of his thigh and moved downward. When she'd gotten his clothes off, she gazed back up at him as she pulled off his socks. He laughed softly, shaking his head. Leaning down, she kissed his big toe, even making that sensual.

"Jesus." He was stunned at how she was making him feel. "Come here," he said, his voice husky and deep.

Jordan smiled, raising herself to her knees, pushing down the silken material of her pants. They slid down her hips, Joe's eyes tracking every inch. *My God, she's beautiful,* was all he could think. Her skin was golden, smooth, and absolutely perfect. A moment later she tossed aside her own clothing, taking off the shirt and bra that were half off already.

"Jordan," Joe said, his voice more urgent now. "Come here."

She moved back to him, sliding back over his body, enjoying the feel of his skin against hers. As soon as she was close enough, his hands were on her skin, pulling her to him, claiming her lips again. He began caressing her, taking his time, making her writhe against him. She was sure she was going to explode before he even made love to her. Her body was so alive with nerves screaming for release.

She moved her mouth to his neck, kissing it, biting it, sucking at his skin.

"I need you, Joe," she said fervently. "I need you inside me."

She felt him groan deeply, and his hands pulled her up to him, her body directly over his. He kissed her deeply as he slid his hands down her body again.

Jordan gasped out loud as he grasped the back of her upper thighs, his long fingers sliding between them, brushing tantalizingly against the wetness there.

"Please, Joe, please…" she moaned against his lips.

His hands spread her legs slightly, moving his body upward and sliding inside her.

Jordan cried out as he filled her finally. She found that he filled her completely, and her body responded immediately. Her nails bit into his shoulders as she grasped at him.

"God…" he moaned against her neck, nipping at her skin.

He reached down, holding her, pressing her against him, stilling her movement. "Wait, wait," he whispered against her ear.

She bit her lip, trying desperately to do as he said. Wanting so much to move on him, her body begging her to do just that. She dropped her head to the hollow between his neck and his shoulder, breathing heavily. He slid his hand through her hair, pulling her head up, kissing her lips again, slowly, sensually. She kissed him back, trying to concentrate on his lips instead of his body literally pulsing inside her. She could feel his heartbeat inside her.

He took what seemed like forever to allow them to calm down just a bit, kissing her, caressing her gently.

"Joe, please," she said.

"I want this to last," he said huskily.

"I need you now," she countered, biting his earlobe gently. "Please, Joe… now."

He groaned, unable to resist her half demand, half plea. Putting his hands at the back of her thighs again, he began moving her body on his, caressing the sensitive area of her inner thighs as he began kissing her again. Within moments, she was moaning against his lips. He moved one hand to her shoulder, the other down to one of her knees, pulling her knee upward and pushing her shoulder so she sat up, her body straddling his. She settled on him, feeling him slide just a little bit deeper inside her. She groaned, putting her hands to his chest to steady herself.

He put his hands to her hips, guiding her movements. His hands slid up her body as they moved into a rhythm. He caressed her nipples, making her moan over and over, then one hand slid down to where their bodies met, touching her. It was all she could take.

"Joe!" she literally screamed. "Oh God!"

Her heat washing over him made him lose his control. They came together in a thunderous explosion, both of them crying out loudly. He clutched her hips, holding her to him.

Afterward, Jordan found that she was literally shaking with the fervor of what they'd just experienced. She lay down against him, feeling his hand move to caress her back. His breathing was just as labored as hers.

"My God," she said, amazed.

"Mmhmm…" he murmured, smiling tiredly.

She moved her lips to his neck. "You are incredible."

"You are fantastic."

She smiled against his neck. She felt drained. The fact that she hadn't slept all night wasn't as much a factor as the incredible orgasm she'd just had. Her head was still spinning from the intensity.

Jordan fell asleep against the warmth of Joe's body. She didn't feel him pull the covers up over the two of them. She didn't feel the soft kiss he placed on the side of her head as he gathered her closer, allowing himself to relax too. They were both asleep minutes later, feeling extremely sated and comfortable.

CHAPTER 3

Nick and Mikeyla's second date took place three weeks after the first. It went resoundingly well. Nick came home that night feeling like nothing in the world could bring him down. He'd taken Rhiannon's advice and let Mikeyla pick the movie. It was a chick flick, to be sure, but in the end, Nick had actually liked it. He had noticed that Mikeyla was crying during a particularly sad part, when one of the main characters was dying. He reached over, putting his arm around her. She'd surprised him by reaching between them and moving the arm of the movie theater seat, cuddling closer to him. He'd been thrilled. He'd handed her a napkin from their trip to the snack bar, and she'd taken it gratefully.

When the cab stopped at her house that night, he got out and walked around to open her door, drawing on everything his dad had ever taught him about being a gentleman. He took her hand, helping her out of the car, and held on as he walked her up to the door. They stood on the porch, talking for twenty minutes while the cab waited, both of them reluctant to end the night.

"I had a really great time tonight, Nick," Mikeyla said, smiling up at him almost shyly.

"I'm glad," he said, grinning. "So am I forgiven for last time?" he asked, his head down.

Mikeyla laughed. "Maybe."

"Maybe?"

She laughed again. "I guess the fact that you didn't make fun of me when I cried at the movie should earn you extra points."

Nick shrugged. "I've seen women cry."

"Really?"

"Yeah."

"You're lucky—my mom never cries," she said, grinning.

"Your mom is too tough to cry," Nick said, laughing.

"She was a gang leader, you know."

"Really?"

"Yeah." Mikeyla nodded. "You didn't know that?"

"Nope," Nick said, shaking his head.

"She was the leader of a gang called The Vettes."

"As in Corvettes?" Nick asked, leaning comfortably against one of the pillars in front of the house, crossing his feet at the ankles.

He didn't realize how much of a man he looked at that point. Rick did, since he'd pulled up a few minutes before and was sitting in his car watching them talk.

"Yeah," Mikeyla said. "She said she always loved Corvettes, and she thought that was her only chance to have one—in a gang name."

Nick shook his head. "That's cool. But now she has one."

"Yep," Mikeyla said, grinning.

She glanced at the front door, wondering if her mom was going to come out soon. She'd noticed her dad wasn't home from work yet. She was relieved. Nick noticed her looking nervously at the door.

"I better let you get inside," he said, not wanting to get her into trouble. And certainly not wanting to have any kind of confrontation with either of her parents.

"Yeah…" she said, her voice trailing off as she bit her lip nervously.

Now came the uncomfortable moment. Would he kiss her? Would he not kiss her? Should she hug him? What should she do?

Nick reached out, putting his hands on her waist and pulling her to him. He leaned down, kissing her lips softly, then kissed her again, and then a third time. Mikeyla found really quickly that she didn't want to let him go. She put her arms up around his neck and kissed him back. They kissed for a full five minutes, and only stopped when they heard a car door slam. They pulled apart, glancing toward the drive. Rick strode up, carrying his gear bag and still wearing his Kevlar vest and dark blue jersey that said *POLICE* in yellow letters. His blue eyes were on them, but he didn't seem irritated at all.

"Good evening, Lieutenant," Nick said politely.

"Hey, Nick," Rick said as he climbed the stairs to the front of the house. He stopped behind Mikeyla, leaning down and kissing her on the top of the head. "Have a good time?" he asked her.

"Yes, Dad, I did," she said, glancing at Nick.

Rick nodded. "Good."

He looked at Nick for a long moment, canting his head slightly to the side, and Nick realized that Rick had indeed witnessed that kiss. He made a point of looking back at Rick, without any disrespect, glancing at Mikeyla, who was watching him. He turned back to Rick then.

"Thank you for letting me take her out again, sir," Nick said. "I needed to make up for the first date."

Rick looked at Nick for a minute, his eyes showing surprise that he wasn't very intimidated by him. He nodded, grinning slightly. "Well, I'm glad you apparently managed it."

Nick smiled. "Well, I better be going," he said, reaching out to take Mikeyla's hand. "I'll call you tomorrow, okay?"

"Okay," she said, smiling and biting her lip.

"Have a good night, sir," Nick said to Rick, then turned and walked down the steps.

Mikeyla stood and watched until the cab drove out of sight. She sighed.

"That good a kiss, huh?" Rick asked from behind her.

Mikeyla jumped, not realizing that her father hadn't gone inside yet. She turned to look at him, half afraid he was mad now. But he was smiling at her. She smiled back, and nodded.

"Come on," Rick said, gesturing with his head to the front door. Mikeyla followed him into the house.

That night she lay in her bed and dreamed about Nick Masterson.

Nick knocked lightly on his dad and Rhiannon's door. His father called out for him to enter. He opened the door. Kyle and Rhiannon lay on the bed. Rhiannon was wearing her sweats and a T-shirt; Kyle was in faded jeans and a cotton button-up shirt that was totally unbuttoned. Kyle leaned against the headboard and Rhiannon lay against him, her head on his chest. The television was on and they were watching the news. Nick knew this was a kind of ritual for them, spending the late evenings together to stay "connected," as his dad put it.

Rhiannon looked up. "Well?" she asked, grinning. "How did it go?"

"It went…" Nick hesitated, wanting to tease her but unable to hold in his jubilance. "Great—it went great," he said, smiling broadly.

He walked over to the bed, catching his father's smile.

"Rhiannon," Nick said, looking excited, "you were totally right. She seemed so different this time. She smiled all the time, and we laughed a lot."

Rhiannon nodded, moving to sit up. Kyle's hand stayed on her shoulders.

"So what movie did you get stuck watching?" Kyle asked, grinning.

"Oh," Nick said, rolling his eyes. "Total chick flick called *Roses of Tomorrow*."

Kyle made a face, to which Rhiannon narrowed her eyes. "Watch it, Masterson. I want to see that movie," she said, making him grimace.

Nick laughed. "Uh-oh, Dad!"

Kyle sighed, shaking his head. "Why do I even open my mouth?" he asked no one in particular.

"I have no idea," Rhiannon replied, grinning. Then she looked back at Nick. "So it went good?"

"Yeah," Nick said, smiling fondly. "It went real good."

"I'm glad."

"Me too, Nick," Kyle said.

Nick nodded as he stifled a yawn. "I guess I'd better get to bed."

He moved to hug his dad, then to Rhiannon's surprise hugged her too, giving her an extra little squeeze. "Thank you," he whispered.

Rhiannon had to hold back tears at the sincerity in Nick's voice. She simply nodded, not trusting her voice to speak at that moment. Nick straightened, looking down at her. She could see by the look in his eyes and the slight grimace he made that he could tell she was trying not to cry. In truth it made Nick see graphically how hard he'd been on her the last few months. It also made his mind up about something. He walked over to their door, then turned and looked at both of them.

"I love you guys," he said. "Goodnight."

"Goodnight, Nick," Kyle managed, even though his face reflected the shock his son had just given him.

Rhiannon was speechless. Nick had had a feeling she would be. He grinned and then closed the door behind him.

Rhiannon looked at Kyle. "Did I just hear what I thought I heard?"

Kyle grinned, extremely proud of his son at that moment. "Yeah, you did, hon," he said gently.

Rhiannon pressed her lips together in subdued excitement as she nodded. She blew her breath out a moment later, shaking her head.

"I never realized how good it would feel to hear a child say that to me," she said in wonder.

"Feels pretty good, huh?"

"Yeah…" she said, smiling.

Kyle reached out and pulled her to him, hugging her close. He knew she was feeling overwhelmed at that moment, and he didn't want to put her on the spot. He did sincerely hope she realized that she had made a huge leap with Nick. And he loved her all the more for having made the effort all along.

***

Five hours after they'd originally fallen asleep that first morning, Joe climbed carefully back into bed next to Jordan. He was wearing sweatpants and a white cotton button-up shirt open at the throat. He turned onto his side, watching her sleep.

She was undeniably beautiful, even with her makeup from the day before faded to almost gone. She had tanned, smooth skin, and long, dark eyelashes that brushed her cheeks. Her hair was a dark chocolate brown, shot through with reddish highlights that made it seem even richer. Her hair was long, but not as long as Randy's; it fell midway down her back, versus Randy's waist-length hair. Whereas Randy's was all the same length, Jordan's was cut in long layers so it fell to frame her face. Jordan was definitely the type of woman that spent time in the beauty salon, having her hair done, having her nails done, having her eyebrows waxed, everything. But she didn't seem in the least bit fake. Joe was used to natural beauty without any real enhancements, but he'd found that Jordan's enhanced beauty was quite attractive too. Even so, she was beautiful without makeup, and definitely without clothing.

He'd been attracted to her from the minute she'd walked up the day before. She had a quality about her that made a man react to her. He'd held tight to the control he'd cultivated over many years in law enforcement. More so when he'd found out she was a famous singer. It wasn't Joe Sinclair's style to act like the crowd. He always made a point of being himself. Also, he'd found that even though he found her highly attractive, it hadn't been easy to picture himself doing anything about it for a while. In truth, he hadn't been sure any pass he'd made would be received well. She was, after all, a star, and he was just some cop from California. In the end, he had sensed her desire for him, and had decided that he wanted her enough to go for it. He was happy he had; she'd turned out to be a very exciting lover. He knew he was probably just a diversion for her, which he decided was fine. At this point, he just wanted to forget relationships and enjoy himself. At least this woman wasn't dating, living with, or in love with any member of his family.

Jordan stirred, turning onto her side to face him. She opened her eyes, looking up at him. Her eyes were literally golden. They looked brighter than they had the day before, without her makeup making them seem darker. Her dark eyebrows and eyelashes framing them made the gold color seem to glow.

"Hi," she whispered.

"Hi," he replied, smiling at her.

He leaned down, kissing her softly. Her hand went to his neck and she kissed him back. She glanced down at his clothes.

"You're dressed?" she asked, realizing she'd missed something.

"Yeah," he said, grinning. "I got a little visitor this morning, 'bout an hour after we fell asleep."

"Oh," she said. "One of the kids?"

"Yeah," he said. "So I got up, made them some breakfast, and got them started for the day."

"Mmm…" she said, nodding. "What time is it, anyway?"

Joe glanced back at the clock. "Two o'clock."

"Oh…" she said, grimacing. "I guess I slept for a while, huh?"

"Yeah, I figured you probably needed it," he said, shrugging.

"I'm kinda spoiled, used to about nine hours a night."

He grinned. "I wouldn't know what to do with that kind of sleep."

"You don't sleep much?"

"Nah, don't need much. Gotten used to it over the years."

Jordan stared back at him for a long moment, then moved to sit up. She looked around her, then reached down and picked up his discarded shirt from that morning, pulling it on. It was big on her, and the open buttons at the neck exposed a fair amount of skin. Joe grinned. She lay back down, looking up at him.

"Tell me about you," she said.

"What do you want to know?"

Jordan looked thoughtful. "What about your partner, the Chief of Police—tell me about her."

"That's Midnight. She's one of my very best friends in the world."

"You're best friends with a woman?" she asked, not altogether surprised.

"Yep," he said. "Surprised?"

"No," she said, shaking her head. "I'm betting most of your friends are female."

"Nah," he said. "'Bout half and half."

"Wow, I'm surprised about that."

"Why?"

She shrugged. "A guy that looks like you, with money, a great personality and sense of humor, probably gets women like they're going out of style. Other guys tend to be jealous of that kind of stuff—doesn't make for friendships."

It was Joe's turn to shrug. "Well, the guys in the Gang are pretty secure with themselves, I guess."

"The Gang?" she questioned, noting from the way he said it that it probably wasn't just a regular use of the term.

"Yeah. The people I've been friends with for years, we're kinda called the Gang by other people in the department. We never knew about it till a couple of years ago, and when we did it just kinda stuck." He shrugged.

"Explain," she said simply, moving to lie against him, looking up at him.

He put his arm under her neck, pulling her closer and settling into a narrative.

"I met Midnight when I came to the police department. She was the reason I applied. She was running a task force that targeted gangs using ex-gang members and leaders. I thought she was pretty damned insightful to know that it would work. So I joined her. We ran the unit together for a long time. We worked together constantly, so eventually things between us became intimate."

"Okay…" she said, glancing up at him. "What happened with that?"

He shrugged. "We're too much alike, Midnight and me. She's a damned good cop, but she takes chances a lot. It's what makes her good, but it's also what made me paranoid as hell to lose her…" He trailed off for a moment. "Anyway, we ended up being best friends, and together when we needed each other. Eventually, Rick—my best friend from here in London—came to California to visit, and met Midnight. They fell in love, and I met Randy and fell in love with her. So that's how things worked out."

"Okay, and what about this 'Gang'—who are they?"

"The Gang is mostly the core members of the original gang task force. There's Spider, Tiny, Kana, Rick, and Dave, then me and Midnight. Over the years other people have become part of our group, either by way of being with one of the members or by relation. There's Donovan, who is Randy's younger brother and a cop now. His on-again-off-again girlfriend, Jeanie. There's Christian, who's my cousin, and Stevie, his now fiancée."

"Now?" she asked, noting the change in his voice.

"Long story there—I'll tell you that sometime… Anyway, there's Kyle, who is the Assistant Chief, who knew me and Midnight and the Gang a long time ago and has in the last couple of years joined us. There's his wife, Rhiannon. And there's Spider's wife, Tammy, Tiny's wife, Jess, who I met in Sacramento and came to see me after that, and ended up marrying Tiny. There's Susan, who is my kids' nanny and is now married to Dave. There's also Erin, who is one of the girls Donovan was dating for a bit, who turned out to be a pretty good kid…"

"Damn, you people keep things close, huh?" Jordan said.

"Well," Joe said with a shrug, "most of us don't really have any family to speak of, so this pretty much takes the place of that."

Jordan nodded. "And you and Midnight are kind of like the heads of the family?"

Joe grinned. "Yeah, pretty much. We joke all the time that we're like their parents, and sometimes the kids just aren't happy with us."

Jordan laughed softly. "Is that Rick?" she asked, pointing to one of the pictures on his dresser.

"Yeah, that's him," Joe said. "He and I have been best friends since I was seven."

"That's a long time."

"Yeah."

They were silent for a little while, then Jordan sat up, looking at him. "So how long were you married?"

Joe looked at her for a long moment, not sure if he wanted to talk about his marriage with her. But then he shrugged.

"Thirteen years."

"That's a long time."

"Yeah, it is," he agreed again.

"So what happened?" Jordan asked. She knew she was prying, but she wanted to know what could happen to make a woman that had been married to this man for thirteen years want out. He'd said she'd filed for the divorce.

Joe thought about his answer for a long minute. Jordan moved to lean across his lap, draping her arm over his knee and waiting. Joe touched her shoulder, sliding his hand down over her arm then putting it at her waist.

"I guess we just outgrew each other," he said finally. "When we got married she was twenty years old. She was very shy, very innocent, and very sweet," he continued, his eyes taking on a faraway look. Jordan watched him as he talked. "When we met, things were really crazy in my life. She was my secretary. She had this whole way about her. A kind of naiveté that was highly attractive to someone as jaded as me. And she needed me."

"Needed you?"

"Yeah. It was just her and her two brothers—her parents had taken a powder when Randy was only fourteen. Her older brother, Darrell, had kept the three of them together. She was like this beautiful, homeless orphan to me. I guess at the time, I kind of seemed larger than life to her, because she'd always been so sheltered."

"No," Jordan said. "I think you're larger than life too, Joe, and I haven't been sheltered in the slightest."

Joe looked back at her for a moment, but didn't comment on what she'd said. "Anyway," he went on, "I fell in love with her innocence, with her sweet way. With her undying faith in me." He shrugged. "Eventually she grew up, and I guess now we've grown apart."

Jordan nodded, thinking there had to be more to it than that. "Were you really in love with her?"

"Yeah, I was," he said, nodding. "She was my life for a long, long time."

Jordan nodded again. "So you think her needs changed?"

Joe considered that. "Yeah, I think she didn't need me as much. She grew up. I mean, I'm not saying she didn't love me—she did, and maybe still does—but it's not the same now."

"So maybe your needs changed too," Jordan pointed out.

Joe stared back at her for a long moment, looking like he'd just been struck by lightning. "God, maybe you're right," he said, shaking his head slowly. "I never even thought about it that way."

"People change, Joe," Jordan said. "And sometimes those changes are so subtle that you don't realize they've changed till all of a sudden they're not who they used to be."

Joe nodded, remembering thinking that about Randy a few times. That she wasn't the woman he'd married anymore.

"God…" he breathed. "I don't know if that helps or hurts more," he said honestly.

Jordan looked back at him for a few moments. "Are you going to stop her from divorcing you?"

Joe thought about that, then shook his head. "I don't think I have a choice. Even if I did, I don't know if I want to. Things just haven't been..." He trailed off as the words came to him. "What I need anymore."

He was amazed at that. It hadn't really occurred to him till then that while he'd been so caught up in Randy not wanting him anymore, maybe in truth he really didn't want her anymore either, that he had been feeling that the marriage lacked something now too. So maybe neither of them had failed. Maybe they just stopped being what the other person needed. They'd grown together for a long time, and then grown past the point of being together. Was that possible? Was that it?

Jordan watched him go through the possibilities, wondering if she'd really just made him aware of something he hadn't thought of before. It was amazing, sometimes, what an outsider's view could do. They could see things more clearly than someone who was so deep in the relationship that they couldn't think past it.

His eyes connected with hers again a few minutes later. "So," he said, his tone more upbeat. "When do you have to be back in town?"

"Well, I was going back with my friends..."

"And when were they going back?"

"Last night," she said, grinning.

"Oops," he said, grinning back at her.

"Uh-huh..."

He leaned forward, kissing her softly. "I can take you into town whenever you want to go."

"I could play hooky from my life for another day," she said, then looked embarrassed. "I mean, unless you have plans..." she added, realizing that he might actually have other things to do than spend time with her. She couldn't believe she'd just assumed so much.

He grinned, seeing that she was appalled at her presumption.

"I do have plans," he said.

"Oh," she said, feeling even dumber.

He leaned forward, kissing her deeply. "My children have gone with Deborah for the day, so I plan to first make you something to eat. I then plan to lounge around the house all day with you. And finally I plan to make love to you a few times during the course of the next twenty-four hours."

"Mmm…" she said, leaning forward to kiss him again. "I think I like your plans."

"Good," he said, smiling down at her.

"I'm going to take a shower."

"Okay."

"Okay," she repeated, kissing him again.

In the end they spent the day relaxing in the den Joe had converted over the years. He'd had a large plasma screen TV put in, with a Bose home theater system. They lay on the oversized leather couch watching movies, TV, whatever came on. At one point, she leaned over to kiss him on the lips. He pulled her closer, deepening the kiss until they were both breathless.

"God," she said in a heated whisper. "You drive me so crazy."

"Mmm…" he said in response to her hand touching him, closing his eyes then opening them to stare up into hers. "You make me feel damned good too, babe."

"Make love to me," she said, moving to lie directly over him. It wasn't a request.

He did as she asked, taking them both to dizzying heights again.

Afterward he pulled his sweats back on, but left his discarded shirt on the floor. She put the clean shirt that she'd borrowed from him back on, lying against him, her back to the couch, her leg over his. She reached across him, stroking his left arm.

"Have you ever thought about getting a tattoo?" she asked.

He looked at her. "Why?"

She glanced up at the TV, which was still on. One of the men on the screen had a tattoo, which was what had made her think of it. She shrugged.

"You have the most incredible body," she said. "I just think you'd look really cool with a tattoo."

"Hmm…" he said, his expression thoughtful. "Where do you think I'd get one?"

Jordan scanned his body, her hand tracing over his chest, down to his stomach, making him shiver at the contact. Then she moved her hand back up, stopping at the lower part of his upper arm.

"I think a band right here would look really good on you."

Joe glanced down. "A band?"

"Yeah, you know, the tattoo that goes around your arm, like a band?"

"Hmm…" Joe said. "If they're so cool, how come you don't have a tattoo?" He'd seen every inch of her body, and she definitely didn't have one.

"I want to get one," she said. "I've just never been able to decide what to get."

"I see," he said, nodding.

"I've thought about it a lot. I've even come up with some designs of my own, but I just don't know what I want." She looked over him again, then at his arm. "In fact…"

"What?" he said warily.

"I have this really cool design that I came up with for a band tattoo, but it's really too masculine for me. I think it might look really awesome on you though," she said, biting her lip.

"What's it look like?"

"Well…" she said, trying to think of a way to describe it. "It's kind of a tribal design."

"Tribal?" he asked, mystified.

"Uh…" She hesitated, trying to think of a way to explain it.

Finally, she got off the couch and went over to the computer. Joe followed. He sat in the chair in front of the computer and Jordan sat on his lap. He put his chin on her shoulder, watching as she got on the Internet and searched some sites for what she wanted to show him. She pulled up a tattoo that was all done in black. It was about an inch wide, and it was literally a band that went around the arm. The pattern was like a series of jagged pieces spaced around the width of the tattoo.

"Now, see, what I did—and I can show you the sketch some-time—is I replaced these sections with fragmented sections of the Union Jack, so this area had the red, white, and blue and pattern of the Jack, without being too corny-looking." She pointed to the center section of the tattoo.

Joe tried to envision what she was saying. He was really starting to see it. The idea wasn't a bad one—but still, a tattoo?

"How about this," she said, turning around and straddling his lap. "If you get one, I'll let you pick out one for me."

Joe looked back at her for a long minute. "Anything I want?"

"Anything."

"Anywhere I want to put it?"

She hesitated for a moment, but then nodded. "Anywhere."

"Hmm…" he said, the idea more appealing now.

He had no idea what it was about this woman that made him want to try something he'd never even considered before, but she definitely had a way about her.

In the end they left the house in the early evening and went to hers to pick up her sketch. They went to the best tattoo house in London, and Joe got her design put on his left arm, including her initials, JT, worked in carefully so as not to take away from the design. He looked through book after book to find the one he wanted her to get. In the end he designed one of his own, taking ideas from the book. The tattoo went on the small of her back. It was a butterfly with sapphire, teal, and golden wings outlined in black. It had slanted lines of curled flames of orange, gold, and red that spread out from the butterfly in a V, completing the design.

The owner of the shop begged them to allow him to buy both designs, but they refused, wanting to keep them exclusive between the two of them. They left grinning like kids who'd just broken all the rules. They had dinner at a Hard Rock Cafe in London, then went back to his house and made love half the night. Joe fell asleep feeling like something had very definitely changed in his life. He didn't know if this thing with Jordan was permanent. He did know that he enjoyed her, though, and that was what he was going to do for the amount of time that he could be with her.

***

Dave walked into his house sensing something different. He went into the kitchen and opened the refrigerator, pulling out a beer. He glanced at the clock on the stove; it was noon. *Not too early for beer,* he thought with a grin. Tuning in to his surroundings, he still detected something different, but not necessarily wrong; his senses weren't warning him, just giving him a heads-up.

He walked down the hall toward the bedroom, and that was when he heard voices. English-accented, female voices. Pushing open the door, he saw Susan sitting on the bed and the backs of two familiar heads. He leaned against the doorjamb with an amused look on his face.

"David!" Susan exclaimed happily. "You're home early."

"Yeah, got done sooner than I thought."

Susan's eyes went to the beer bottle in his hand, but she said nothing about it. "David, you remember Terry. And of course you know Liz," she said, indicating the women sitting on the bed with her.

"Ladies," Dave said, inclining his head to each as they turned to look at him.

He drained the bottle of beer and walked over to drop it in the trash in the bathroom. Then he went around the bed and crawled onto it, leaning far over to kiss his wife on the lips. He lay down on his stomach, putting his head in her lap and wrapping his arms around her waist. Susan smiled fondly, reaching down to stroke his hair and back.

Terry and Liz watched in fascination. It was obvious this was common practice, since Susan didn't seem the least bit surprised. Dave moved his feet around, kicking off his shoes. Then he nuzzled Susan's abdomen, and was still.

After a couple of minutes, Susan resumed the conversation

they'd been having when Dave walked in.

"As I was saying, I think we need to go out to Horton Plaza for the…" She trailed off as she noted that both women were looking down at Dave and then back at her with surprise on their faces.

"Is he asleep?" Terry asked in a whisper, sounding doubtful.

Susan glanced down at Dave, brushing his hair back from his face. She looked back at Terry.

"Oh yes," she said, grinning. "He falls asleep rather easily like this."

"And we won't wake him talking?" Liz asked quietly.

"Oh no," Susan said, shaking her head. She smiled as she realized neither woman believed her. "David has this uncanny ability to turn off everything around him. He's like this computer. He can mentally turn off all the noises around him, and tune in to only one thing. Right now, I'm sure he's tuned in to my body and my emotions. If I get upset, or scared, he'll sense it and wake up. Otherwise he's fast asleep and nothing will wake him, unless I want him to wake up."

"Liar," Terry said, grinning. "I'll bet he'd wake up if there was a loud noise."

"Only if it frightened me," Susan said confidently. Again she could see that neither woman believed her. She shrugged. "Well, it's true."

Liz and Terry still insisted on talking softly. Susan's hand continued to smooth over Dave's hair and his back. She knew the beer he'd had meant that his case wasn't going the way he wanted it to, that he was on edge about it. She was worried about that, but she kept her concern to a minimum. She knew that if Dave sensed her worry, like she'd told her sister and friend, he'd wake up, or at least toss and

86

turn.

They were just discussing where else they could take Susan shopping for her birthday when a gust of wind blew the bedroom door closed with a slam. Liz and Terry jumped, but Susan had noticed that the breeze in the room had been toying with the door, so she wasn't surprised. It was, however, a loud noise. And Dave didn't even twitch. Susan looked down at him, then back up at her friend with a grin.

"Good lord," Terry said, shaking her head. "But you say he'd wake up if you were scared or nervous or something?"

"Yes," Susan answered simply.

Terry looked skeptical, but kept her disbelief to herself this time, lest she look like a fool for a second time that day.

Terry and Elizabeth had shown up to surprise Susan for her birthday. They'd heard that Joe Sinclair was in London with the children, so they figured she would have some time off. They were very right, and Susan was just getting desperate for something to do when they showed up.

"Let's go have lunch somewhere and get started on that shopping spree," Elizabeth said.

Their mother had sent a credit card with Susan's name on it for her birthday. The card had a line of credit that, as Deborah had instructed in her letter, Susan was to use for herself to buy anything and everything nice she wanted. Elizabeth was quite eager to help her out with that. Susan was always the careful sister, and Elizabeth was determined to make her loosen up.

"I don't know," Susan said, glancing down at Dave.

"Susie, didn't you tell me that he sometimes sleeps for twenty-four hours at a time when he comes home?" Terry asked.

"Well, yes… but…"

"But what?" Liz asked.

"If he wakes up, I want to be here."

"Good lord, Susan," Elizabeth said, unable to fathom being that much in love with any man in the world.

Sure, Susan's husband was good-looking. And he had that whole bad boy, dangerous thing going on too. But Jesus, get real! The man was gone all the time, so just because he happened to come home a day early didn't mean Susan had to drop everything.

"Elizabeth, I don't even know how long he'll be home," Susan implored. "Sometimes he only comes home for a day if he's in between meetings."

"So you miss a little time with him," Liz said, shrugging.

"Yes, Elizabeth, I miss time with the man I love, and that's important to me."

"What's the big bloody deal?" Liz asked, exasperated now. "So, what? He comes home in a few more days and you can be with him all you want."

Susan narrowed her eyes at her sister. "The big bloody deal is that what my husband does for a living is very dangerous." Tears sprang to her eyes as she continued. "And if something were to happen to him the very next time he goes out to do his job, if I lose him…" Her voice deepened with emotion. "Then I will have lost my last few moments with him, *shopping*, Elizabeth."

True to what Susan had said, Dave detected that she was upset. He began stirring and a moment later opened his eyes, moving his head to look up at her.

"What's up?" he asked, glancing back at Liz and Terry.

"Nothing, David," Susan said softly. "Go back to sleep."

Dave shook his head, moving to sit up, watching Susan's eyes. She looked back at him unhappily. She wasn't pleased that she'd managed to wake him up with her emotional outburst.

"What is it, hon?" he asked, ignoring the fact that anyone else was in the room. His eyes were solely on her.

"It's nothing, David, really," she said. "Elizabeth and Terry want to take me shopping, but I wasn't sure how long you'll be home, and I didn't want to leave while you were asleep..." She grimaced. "I didn't mean to wake you."

"It's okay," he said, grinning. "You know me—I can go back to sleep in a matter of minutes. But you don't need to worry, babe. I'm home till after your birthday now."

"You are?" she asked, her face lighting up like he'd just given her the best birthday present ever. It meant he'd be home for a week. It was a large block of time to share with him.

"Yeah," he said, grinning. "So go, shop, have fun." He smiled as he leaned forward to hug her.

Both women had watched with stunned looks on their faces. It was very obvious that no matter what was said, Susan was going to listen to her husband. But there was no denying the dazzling joy that had lit her face when he'd told her he'd be home until after her birthday. The question was, did David E. Dibbins warrant such awesome devotion?

They saw graphically over the next few days how sweet Dave was with Susan. They also saw how close the couple really were. When home, they were constantly touching, not necessarily in a sexual way, just tenderly. Many times Dave would simply stare at her as she talked, the look on his face reflecting his love for her. It was almost painful to see sometimes, because one wanted to be part of something so deep and apparently abiding.

When Dave accompanied the ladies on shopping excursions, he spent a great deal of time waiting around as they tried on clothes. He'd sit outside the dressing room with seemingly endless patience. When Susan would ask him for his opinion on something, he'd cant his head to the side and tell her what he honestly thought, but nothing negative ever came out of his mouth. If he didn't particularly favor an outfit he'd say something like, "I think that blue one was prettier," or "I lose you in that color," or "I want to see you, not the dress." He never said anything negative about her.

He was just as complimentary of the other two women, but there wasn't the light in his eyes that he had when he looked at his wife. When they had lunch, Dave sat with his back to the wall, his eyes constantly scanning the area even as they all talked. Terry noticed it, and commented on it.

"Dave, are you looking for someone?" she asked.

His blue eyes went to her, and he grinned. "No, just being a cop."

"How so?"

Dave just kept grinning. Susan answered instead.

"That disconcerted me too, at first," she said, reaching over to take Dave's hand. "Our first date, he told me he liked to see what was going on around him, and not leave himself open from behind." She grinned. "I was terrified we were about to be accosted by drug dealers." She looked over at her husband. "But he just likes to be safe."

"What could possibly happen here?" Liz asked, glancing around.

Dave looked back at his sister-in-law, raising an eyebrow. "You think drug deals and shootouts only happen in seedy, low-income neighborhoods?"

Liz stared back at him. It was apparent from the look on her face that that was exactly what she thought. Dave grinned. "Don't worry, Liz, that's what most people who grew up watching cop stuff on TV believe."

"So drug dealers do things in malls?" Terry asked, leaning forward in her interest.

Dave nodded. "Usually they like public places. That way, if anything goes wrong, they have a better chance to get away in the crowd."

"Do you arrange deals in the mall?" Liz asked, raising an eyebrow at him.

"If I did, I wouldn't be here right now."

"Meaning?" Liz countered.

"Meaning that if I thought one of the dealers I'm working would show up here, I wouldn't be here with my wife."

"Because they don't know you're married?" Liz asked, scornful.

"Because I don't want them to know anything about the people I love," Dave replied, his tone direct but without any kind of anger. "They use people you love against you. I won't allow anyone or anything, including my job, to endanger Susan."

Liz and Terry were taken aback by his words. One look at Susan showed that she knew exactly why he did things the way he did them. It was obvious they'd had discussions about this before. Indeed, they had. Susan understood every aspect of Dave's way of doing things. He took the time to explain everything to her, never leaving her to her own thoughts. It was so comforting to be able to understand his every action. There was no guessing. And if he did do anything she didn't understand, she knew all she needed to do was ask him.

Dave never got angry with her for questioning him. He never felt that something she asked about was none of her business. The time she'd mentioned worrying about him telling her it was none of her business, his comment had been, "My life is yours, and that means that everything about it and me is and will always be your business, Susan." It had warmed her heart no end. It still did, just thinking about it.

Later, on the way home from the mall, Dave had the radio on. He was listening to a Def Leppard album. At one point he glanced over at Susan as he turned the volume up. She knew that meant he wanted her to listen to the lyrics. He sang the words, and Susan found herself astounded; it was like the band knew them and had written the song for them. It talked about true love in all its aspects. It also referred to her as the sun and to him as the rain, and said that he'd love her for all the tomorrows. The song was very sweet, and it was obvious that Dave meant every word he sang.

Susan remembered well their wedding vows, ones they'd written themselves. Dave had told her that she was the sun to him. That she took him in and healed his soul. It had changed her whole way of seeing his need to be in the sun at the beach, surfing as he did all the time. It had also showed her his heart, and that he wanted to be healed from all the hurts he'd sustained over the years. Not only did he want her to heal him, he'd let her do just that. It was that concession that she was most grateful for. He allowed her to heal him. He allowed her to see his heart. It made her feel loved.

When the song ended he turned the radio back down, glancing at the two women in the back seat apologetically. They were both watching him. They'd listened to the words too, and it had only served to make them both feel bereft at not having a man that loved them that much in their own lives. Susan was indeed a lucky woman.

"What about that?" Susan asked as she pointed to a car they were stopped next to.

Dave looked over at the other vehicle. "Honda Civic?" he said, his tone indicating his distaste. "Good on economy, but kinda lacking in the style department."

Susan laughed. Like anyone could ever top his beloved car. She knew Dave considered his car his only child.

"You're looking for a new car?" Liz asked.

"We're looking for a car for *her*, yes," Dave said.

Susan looked over at him, narrowing her eyes, even as he started grinning.

"Don't you dare, David!" she said, starting to grin herself.

"What?" Terry asked.

Susan glanced back at her friend, then sighed. "David won't allow me to drive this car anymore."

Both women were shocked. There was something Dave wouldn't allow Susan? They had to hear this one.

"Why not?" Liz asked.

Dave glanced over at Susan, an amused smile on his lips. "Tell them."

"No," she said, crossing her arms in front of her and sticking her lip out in a pout.

Dave started laughing.

"David!" Susan cried plaintively. "Don't be mean."

"Mean?" he asked, raising an eyebrow at her.

She sighed, shaking her head. "No, you're not being mean." She glanced back at Liz and Terry, turning in her seat to look at them.

"David was gone on one of his cases, and he didn't take his car because it would be too easily recognized in the area he was in. He'd told me I could use it if I needed to. I usually drive Joe's old Jaguar to squire the children about." She glanced over at Dave, noting the grin he still wore. "Anyway," she said, looking at her husband pointedly, "I had to use it to go to the store, because Joe had dropped me off. I wanted to make sure there was food in the house for when David got home. So I used his car…" Her voice trailed off as she bit her lip.

"You wrecked his car?" Liz asked, her eyes widening.

"No, I didn't wreck it," Susan said, too quickly. "I just dinged it a little bit."

"A little bit?" Dave asked, his eyebrow raised once again. Susan looked back at him, narrowing her eyes. "I had to replace a headlight, and pad out a fairly nasty dent in the front-left fender, sand, prime, re-sand, re-paint…"

"Alright, alright," Susan said, looking embarrassed now. "I'm not used to the power of his car—I accelerated too much when I pulled into the garage."

"You ran into your own garage?" Terry asked, already holding back laughter.

"Yes!" Susan said, starting to grin too. She looked chagrined. "I do have to say that David handled it very well."

Liz glanced at Dave, seeing that he was pointedly looking out the front window, a subdued grin on his face.

"How did he handle it?" Terry asked.

"He drank an entire bottle of Jack Daniels in the garage, staring at the dent," Susan said, her lips pressed together so she wouldn't laugh.

Terry lost her composure then and started laughing, as did Liz. That had Susan laughing, and eventually Dave too.

"So what kind of car is this anyway?" Liz asked, receiving a scowl from Dave.

"English women!" he said, rolling his eyes and shaking his head.

"Oh, stop," Susan said, giving him a sour look. "Not everyone is as well versed on vehicles as you are, David."

Dave gave a long-suffering sigh, then glanced back at Liz and winked at her. "It's a 1970 Dodge Charger, with a 426 Hemi."

"And that means what?" Terry asked. "426 Hemi," she repeated, the words sounding very foreign to her.

"That's the engine," Dave said. "The 426 puts out about 450 horse power." He could see he wasn't getting anywhere with that description. He looked at Liz.

"Hold on to something," he said.

He down-shifted and pushed the gas pedal. The car shot forward like a rocket. Susan put her hand on the dash but gave no indication of being nervous at all. She trusted Dave's driving implicitly. After a few minutes, a number of cars on the freeway left in the dust, Dave slowed down.

"My lord!" Liz said, laughing all the while. She'd always loved speed.

"Indeed," Terry said, grinning.

"So now you're trying to find a car for Susan to drive?" Liz asked.

"Yeah, one she can handle," Dave said, winking at his wife.

She reached over and swatted his arm, making him laugh again.

Two days later was Susan's birthday. That morning Dave didn't go on his usual trip to surf; instead he woke his wife with soft kisses on her lips.

"Happy birthday," he said, smiling down at her.

"Thank you." She smiled back. "I'm so glad you could be home with me, David," she said softly.

"I'll always be here for your birthday, and our anniversary, honey, come hell or high water," he said sincerely. "Now, when do you want your present?"

"You got me a card?" she asked sweetly.

"Yeah."

"Whenever you'd like."

"Alright," he said, grinning like a kid with a surprise. He got up, taking her hand and pulling her gently with him. He waited while she pulled on her robe; he already had his sweats on. He'd been waiting for her to wake up since 4:30 a.m. He picked up a scarf.

"Turn around," he said.

"What?" she asked, looking up at him.

He reached out and turned her back to him. He put the scarf over her eyes and tied it. He then led her through the house. Liz and Terry were already awake, having been told by Dave that if they wanted to see Susan's birthday present and her reaction to it, they'd better be up early. They followed. Dave led Susan outside and then took the scarf off with a flourish.

Susan stood staring, dumbfounded. He'd bought her a car. Not only had he bought her a car, but he'd bought her a Mercedes E320. It was silver, and absolutely beautiful. Susan couldn't even think of words to say. She turned to him, and everything she couldn't say was in her eyes and on her face.

"David…" she breathed, shaking her head in amazement.

"Happy birthday, honey," he said, smiling at her.

She threw her arms around his neck and hugged him, kissing his face, his lips, his neck. Liz and Terry were stunned too, both staring in awe. For Liz, seeing a Mercedes wasn't new, but she realized that Dave wasn't rich like her family was, so for him to buy Susan a car that ran in excess of $60,000 was a very big deal.

Susan turned back to the car, scanning every inch. She shook her head in wonder. "David, David…" she said, over and over again, not able to believe what he had done.

She didn't know how he'd afforded it, and she was worried that he'd spent far too much, but she wasn't about to chastise him right then. She could see that he was very happy at that moment, and she didn't want anything to spoil it for him. He'd bought her a Mercedes!

What she didn't know was that Dave had taken out $30,000 in equity on his house, using that as the down payment for the car. He'd taken out a loan for the rest. The way he saw it, his car was paid for, his house was almost paid for, and his wife deserved the best he could afford for her. And Mercedes just seemed like Susan. She was the epitome of sophistication, and Mercedes said that too. The E320 was a nice mid-range model, with a V6 engine to give it some power but not too much, with only 221 horsepower. He'd made sure to get the leather interior, CD changer, and every little gadget they made. He wanted her to have the best, because he felt that in having her, he had the best.

After spending literally an hour sitting in the car discovering every single one of the gadgets Dave had made sure to include, Susan ran into the house to shower and dress so she could drive it. Dave sat drinking coffee at the kitchen table.

"Very nice present, Dave," Liz said.

"Ya think?" he asked, grinning.

"I do believe so," Liz said, smiling at him.

She really did like her brother-in-law. The more she knew him, the more she liked him. He had a very easy way about him. And she couldn't deny the fact that he loved her sister.

"Can I ask how you afforded it?" Liz asked, never having been one to observe privacy.

Dave stared back at her for a long moment, his look saying he was surprised that she'd been bold enough to ask. Finally he shook his head, grinning. Elizabeth certainly was nothing like Susan. Susan wouldn't have dreamed of asking him where he'd gotten the money for the car. She would trust that he knew what he was doing.

"I borrowed some money on the house," he said calmly. "And I financed the rest."

"You took out a second mortgage?" Liz asked, sounding concerned.

"No, I took out some of the equity I have built up in the place," he said. "I've been paying on this house for about fourteen years now. And house values in this area have quadrupled in the past ten years."

"How much equity is still left?" Liz asked, raising an eyebrow. She was concerned about her sister getting stuck paying for his house if something happened to him.

"More than enough to pay the original loan off three times over."

"Oh…" Liz said, surprised.

It was a nice enough home, but certainly not what she was used to, having grown up in a mansion.

"Perhaps I should buy here in San Diego," she said, contemplating the idea.

Dave rolled his eyes, shaking his head. He wasn't sure what he'd do if his far too spirited sister-in-law was in town all the time. She was in constant trouble in England. She couldn't seem to avoid a scandal if her life depended on it. Then again, it might be better for her in America, where "scandal" was basically commonplace.

Susan walked into the kitchen a few moments later, saving him from further comment. She put her arms around him and kissed him softly.

"Thank you for my present, David. You are the most wonderful man…" she said, her voice trailing off as she kissed him again.

He smiled down at her, happy that she obviously liked the present. He'd debated on a number of cars, but had decided she needed something that represented her sophistication. He knew it was a bit cliché, but it made him feel good to be able to buy his wife a Mercedes. Little old Dave Dibbins from the Imperial Beach Trailer Park bought his wife a Mercedes Benz for her birthday. Who would have ever thought? Maybe it really was true that good things came to those who waited. He'd waited all his life to find a woman that would make him so deeply happy. He'd found her, and he would hold on to her with everything he had.

CHAPTER 4

Christian drove up to the college in his sapphire blue Dodge Viper. He turned a number of heads, including Rosa Delario's. He got out of the Viper wearing all black, including Predator 2 Ray-Ban sunglasses. His black hair glistened in the sunlight, waving back from his face and down to just past his collar. He walked to the front of his car looking at his watch, a very expensive piece. Leaning on the right fender with legs crossed at the ankles, he reached into his long leather jacket's inner pocket for a cigarette. Lighting it, he looked up just as Rosa was walking past. His eyes tracked her very obviously. Rosa glanced at him and saw a jet black eyebrow go up, even as a very sexy-looking grin spread over his face, extremely white teeth showing against his tanned complexion.

"Careful, Collins," came Stevie's voice from the ear piece he wore, which was so small it was totally undetectable. "She'll hurt herself tripping over the hooker heels."

Christian had to hold back a laugh. He could hear Stevie's disgust in her voice. In truth, Rosa Delario was the type of woman he'd normally find attractive, even if she was a bit obvious in her sex appeal. Christian liked women who weren't subtle about their sexuality. It made it easier to fuck them and then leave. Unfortunately, or fortunately, as the case may be, he'd been caught by the one he just couldn't leave. So women like Rosa really didn't appeal anymore. He had something much deeper now, and he wasn't going to screw it up again for some pretty piece. He had the whole package in Stevie, and he knew that now.

Pushing off the car, he stubbed out his cigarette. He reached into the back seat and pulled out the black leather case holding his laptop. Looping it over his shoulder, he armed the alarm on the car and pocketed his keys. He walked in long strides toward his first class. Interestingly enough, it was Rosa Delario's. He caught up to her in the hallway, simply because his strides were longer than hers in her four-inch heels. He could tell she got nervous when she heard his footfalls behind her, his boot heels resounding on the tile floor of the hallway. She fidgeted more. He grinned. This was going to be too easy. Reaching past her, he opened the door for her. She caught a whiff of his cologne as he moved past her—he smelled fantastic!

Inside the classroom, he followed her to her desk, putting down his laptop case and reaching into his pocket, handing her his add sheet. She read his name.

"Christian Sinclair?" she asked.

"That's me," he replied, his English accent clear.

"I see," she said, sounding very officious. "Well, Mr. Sinclair, when you're in my class you'll remove your sunglasses. I want to see people's eyes. I don't like people to sleep through my classes."

Christian's lips curled in a derisive grin. "Are you boring?" he asked, his tone bordering on sexual.

Rosa was taken aback, her eyes widening slightly, but she regained her composure. "No, Mr. Sinclair, I'm not boring. I just deal with a great deal of immature adults who feel that this course is too challenging for them." She drew herself up, throwing her shoulders back.

Christian's eyes, still hidden by the sunglasses, dropped to her

101

breasts, stuck out at that moment in her huff. Again the sly, derisive grin started, the white-white teeth showing just slightly. He took off his sunglasses, his luminescent light blue eyes looking directly into hers.

"I'm sure you're a challenge for everyone," he replied, his tone screaming a come-on.

Rosa was stunned into silence, both by his words and by the effect his eyes, set in such an outrageously handsome face, was having on her nervous system.

Christian pocketed his sunglasses, picked up his laptop, and walked to the back of the class, sitting down. He saw that she was still watching him.

"You are such a flirt!" Stevie said in his ear.

Christian had to put his hand in front of his mouth to hide the grin that her comment caused. Once again, he could hear her disgruntlement. He found it very endearing. As he looked up the other students starting walking into the room, but Rosa was staring at him like he was the only person there. His eyes connected with hers and stayed on them, even as he leaned back casually in his chair, the look on his face one of smug assurance.

Rosa had an impossible time keeping her mind on topic that day. Every time she'd look toward the back of the class she couldn't miss the black-haired, blue-eyed devil watching her. His eyes never seemed to leave her. It made her feel warm and excited and nervous all at the same time. While she was having the class read a section of the textbook, she sat down, purposely keeping her eyes off the back of the classroom. She thought about him though. He was driving a very expensive-looking car. He had a very streamlined laptop on which he was taking notes. The watch he wore looked expensive too, along with the gold flat-linked bracelet on his wrist. The leather jacket was also expensive. She knew leather, and she'd made a point of walking behind him, running her hand over it. It was butter soft, meaning it was probably Italian. And it fell to his mid-thigh, so it was probably very expensive. Who was he? Some rich kid? Did she dare? She wanted to, there was no doubt about that. Would he even accept? She thought he might; he'd been watching her almost hungrily all during the class. She just wasn't sure how to approach this one.

Christian gave her the perfect opportunity at the end of class. He sat tapping away at the keys on his laptop for an extra few minutes as the rest of the students filed out. When everyone was gone, he closed the screen and stood. He stretched, and Rosa couldn't help but watch. He looked too incredible to be real. Reaching down, he slid his laptop into its carrying case. He pulled on his jacket, then looped the laptop over his shoulder again. He glanced up, and when his eyes found her, they stayed on her as he walked toward her.

Rosa found she was holding her breath. He walked straight up to her, stepping just a bit closer than would be normal for a student and teacher.

"I'd like to find out what I've missed," he said simply, but his eyes said something totally different.

"Well, we're a few weeks into the semester," Rosa said, stammering just a bit, showing she was indeed affected by his closeness. "It could be a lot…"

Christian nodded. "Do you have some material I could read over?"

"I don't have anything with me," Rosa said, thinking quickly. "If you want it right away, you could come by tonight and pick it up."

Christian nodded, his lips curling slightly. "Sure, sounds good."

"Fine," she said, doing her best to keep the tremor out of her voice.

She reached into her desk and took out her card. She handed it to him. He took it, his index finger pointedly sliding down the length of hers. Rosa couldn't stop the shiver that went through her. Christian noted it, and the grin became a brilliant smile. Rosa was well and truly hooked.

"What time?" he asked.

"Seven?" she said, her voice shaky now.

"I'll be there," he said, his light blue eyes staring into hers.

Rosa nodded, unable to think of anything but that night.

"Jesus, the poor woman never had a chance," Jeanie said, grinning.

Christian grinned, shrugging.

"You're lethal, Collins, face it," Stevie said.

They were sitting in the surveillance van, parked at the back of the carpool at the department.

"Only for you," Christian told Stevie, leaning over to kiss her neck.

She smiled. "Yeah, me and the entire female population."

"Only the ones that can see," Donovan put in.

"Nah, he smells damned good too," Stevie said.

Donovan laughed at that, shaking his head.

"Yeah, you do smell good, Blue," Jeanie agreed.

"Hey now…" Donovan said, narrowing his eyes at her.

Jeanie leaned down. Donovan was sitting in front of her on the floor of the van, where she was up in the seat. "You smell better, babe," she said in a stage whisper.

"I see how you are…" Christian said.

Jeanie laughed. "Shh!"

"Okay, I won't tell them about our affair," Christian said in a louder whisper.

That had the four of them laughing.

"What's going on out here?" asked Midnight, who had come down to find out how things had gone.

"Oh, um, nothing," Donovan said, straightening up first.

"We're having an orgy," Christian said, insubordinate as ever. "Want to join?" he asked hopefully. Which got him elbowed by Stevie. He "ooffed" and grinned.

"I think I'll pass this time, Blue, but make sure you invite me next time," Midnight replied, winking at him. "So how did it go?"

Christian nodded.

"Oh, she's so hooked," Jeanie said.

"Yeah, she's definitely interested," Donovan said.

Stevie smiled sweetly. "She touches him, I'll kill her."

Midnight grinned at her. "Okay, my new fab four, what's next?"

"Fab four?" Christian queried, raising an eyebrow.

"Yeah…" Midnight said.

Christian made a face. Jeanie shook her head. Donovan grimaced. Stevie stuck her tongue out in a "gag me" parody.

"A-Team?" Midnight said, getting the same general reaction.

"Angels?" she tried.

"Angels?" Christian raised a jet black eyebrow at her.

"Not since the day you were born, Collins," Stevie put in.

"That's my point, love," Christian said, winking at her.

"Rogue Squadron?" Midnight threw out then.

"Hmm…" Christian said, nodding. "That has some merit." He glanced at the other three then looked back at Midnight. "That would make you Rogue Leader though."

Midnight looked thoughtful, then nodded. "That pretty much fits," she said, grinning.

The other four laughed.

"So, what's next?" she asked again.

"Blue has a meeting with Rosa tonight. I'm sure she'll try to dose him and get him in bed," Donovan said, giving Stevie an apologetic look.

Midnight nodded. "Okay, so how are we going to avoid him getting the X?"

"I have a plan," Christian said, winking at her.

"Oh good," Midnight said, rolling her eyes.

"Trust me."

Midnight looked at Stevie. She shrugged, a half-grin on her face.

"So it's a surprise?" Midnight asked.

"Yeah…" he said, trailing off as he glanced back at Donovan and Jeanie. "And this way, if it doesn't work, I won't look like a total idiot," he added, grinning.

They all laughed.

Christian drove up to the house wearing black chinos, a crisp white shirt with onyx buttons, and black ankle boots. What Rosa couldn't see was the holstered gun strapped to his ankle—he had no intention of being too confident. He started up the stone walkway, saying "Got me?" to test the wire that was inside the button at the top of the shirt.

"Loud and clear, handsome," came Stevie's purr.

Christian had made a point of taking her home that afternoon and making love to her repeatedly. Both to rid himself of any need to react to Rosa in the slightest and to assure Stevie that she was the only woman that turned him on constantly. It was obvious to Christian that Stevie was still feeling the satisfaction. He grinned to himself as he stepped up to the front door, reaching up to knock.

Rosa answered much as she had for Donovan, wearing a sexy, clingy, low-cut dress. Donovan saw it from across the street in the van.

"Boy, the MO doesn't change much," he muttered.

Jeanie glanced over at him and saw the look on his face. She leaned over and kissed him softly on the lips.

"She found you sexy enough to want, Donovan," she assured him.

"Uh-huh…" he said, unconvinced.

"I find you sexy enough to keep forever—how 'bout that?" Jeanie asked, grinning.

"That works for me," he said, grinning back.

Stevie glanced at them, smiling. They were a cute couple. And Donovan Curtis was definitely a good-looking guy, though no one compared to Christian in that department—no one. Donovan was far too clean-cut for Stevie's tastes. She liked Christian's wild side; it fit her perfectly. But Donovan and Jeanie seemed to have a pretty good thing going on, if they could just keep it together for more than a month at a time…

Rosa led Christian into the parlor. Her husband was not in evidence. In truth, Rosa hadn't wanted Larry to see this one. This young man was just too handsome to share at all. And she knew Larry would have a fit to see that Rosa had picked out someone who was very obviously not easy to control, like the others had been. She was still irritated about losing Donovan Curtis, but he just hadn't gotten with the program. He'd been one hell of a good lay, though; it was a shame.

"Would you like something to drink?" Rosa asked.

"You got a beer?" Christian said, his light blue eyes all over her.

"Sure, we've got it on tap," she said, smiling to herself. This was too easy.

"Ah, I hate that shit. You got anything else? A Corona or Tequiza, maybe?"

"I have Heineken," Rosa said, thinking fast. "Would you like a shot?"

Christian looked like he was considering it, thinking she'd just made it easy on him. "Yeah, you got tequila?"

"Of course."

"Make it a double," he said, purposely turning to look at the room, giving her time to do whatever she had to to lace the shot.

He knew he'd just screwed up her plan, but he'd also given her another avenue. He was risking it that she wouldn't put some in the beer bottle too. Rosa walked over, handing him a beer and setting a shot on the table next to him. She also had a salt shaker and a lime. Her expression told him she was getting a little wary of him. Christian knew he needed to get rid of her suspicion. He could only think of one way to do that; he also knew he was about to get himself into trouble with his lady, but what could he do? He had to play the game Rosa was playing if he wanted to make this case.

Taking the beer, he drank a third of the bottle, making sure to keep his hand covering the top. Rosa handed him the salt shaker, looking into his eyes. Christian looked back at her calmly. He leaned forward, sliding his tongue over her neck, tasting perfume, even as he heard her moan softly. He tipped the salt shaker, dropping grains on the wet spot at her neck, praying to God Stevie hadn't just heard Rosa's moan and was headed into the house with her gun to shoot them both. He licked the salt off her neck, then picked up the shot, tossing it back and chasing it with a drink from the beer bottle. She handed him the lime as she took the shot glass from his hand. He ran it over her lips, then turned it rind-side in, sliding it between her parted lips. Stepping forward, his hands on her waist, pulling her body flush with his, he moved his lips to hers, sucking at the lime and kissing her at the same time. She reached up, pulled the lime away, and kissed him back with an almost frenzied hunger. As he kissed her, Christian chanted in his head, *Not now, not now,* still hoping his girlfriend was keeping her cool.

In the van, Donovan had purposely but discreetly moved to block any exit from the vehicle. He and Jeanie had exchanged a look when the first moan was heard, and both knew that Stevie was likely to jump out of the van and go throttle the woman Christian was with. Donovan was sure he knew what Christian was doing, it was just going to be his job to keep Stevie from letting her jealousy get the better of her judgment.

Just then, Stevie threw off her headset and moved toward the door, finding it blocked.

"Get out of the way, Donovan," she growled.

"Now, O'Neil, let's remember we're making a case here…"

"Case my ass—she's making it with my man!" Stevie said, narrowing her eyes.

"Stevie," Jeanie said from behind her. "He's doing what he needs to so she won't be suspicious. This chick is very jumpy. She cut Donovan off cold turkey because he didn't accept her first offer. We can't lose this. Christian is just trying to calm her down."

Stevie glanced over her shoulder, her look wry. "You've kissed him, Jeanie. Did that ever calm you down?" she asked, raising an eyebrow at the other woman.

Jeanie stared back at her for a moment, stunned. She hadn't realized Stevie knew about her and Christian's minor dalliance a few years before. Then Jeanie saw the humor in what Stevie had just said, and started to grin. Which had Donovan grinning too. Stevie eyed them both murderously, then couldn't help but grin as well. She shook her head and sighed deeply, looking heavenward.

"The man is going to be the end of my career, I can just feel it," she said.

"Or one hell of a partner someday," Donovan put in pointedly.

Stevie looked over at him, canting her head to the side. "Hmm…" she said thoughtfully. "It's not a bad idea…"

"No one would ever take him for a narc," Jeanie put in, still listening in on the wire.

"Not in a million years," Donovan said.

Stevie nodded, moving back to her seat and picking up her headphones. Just in time to hear Rosa murmur, "Let's go upstairs."

She grinned. "You're paying for that, Collins," she said into the mic very softly. She could almost feel him grin back.

Inside the house, Christian did indeed grin. Rosa was leading him upstairs. He'd purposely set the beer bottle on the side table out of sight as she'd taken his other hand. Once upstairs she turned to him, sliding her hands up his chest. Christian obliged her by reaching up to unbutton his shirt, pulling the shirt tails out of his pants and taking it off. He laid it aside, careful to keep the side with the wire up. Her nails grazed his chest and she grabbed at him. He took her hands in his, holding them away.

"I run this show, doll," he said firmly. "Or there is no show. Got me?"

Rosa shuddered in response. She hadn't ever had a man talk to her like that. She'd gotten so sick of being the dominant one, and she was willing to play the submissive role for now. Later she'd bring him to heel. Christian shook his head then, as if to clear it, blinking a few times, mimicking the signs of X kicking in to perfection. He sat on the bed, looking around.

"This is pretty nice," he said, looking at all the antiques and expensive wall coverings and accompaniments.

"I like nice things," she replied haughtily.

"If you're good, you might get more," he said, his voice low, almost throbbing.

Rosa knelt down, actually getting on her knees in front of him. She put her hand on his thigh. "I can be very good," she said, staring up into his eyes.

"Who all did you fuck to get this much?"

"What?" she asked, shocked.

"Come on, they don't pay professors this much," he said, grinning. "You must have fucked a few rich guys like me to get all this."

"Actually, I make my own money," she said indignantly.

"Of course you do," he said, smoothing his hand over her hair, his eyes searching hers. "Don't matter to me, doll. You're gonna fuck me now—that's all that matters."

"I didn't fuck anyone to get all of this," she replied angrily. "Are you rich?" she asked then, curious in spite of being mad about his presumptions.

"I make my money," he replied mysteriously.

"How?"

"Not in a way a sexy little professor would, honey."

Rosa caught his meaning and moved to get up. His hand on her head held her down.

"Where do you think you're going?" he asked, a jet black brow raised.

Rosa was feeling very weak, considering the position she was in, on her knees in front of him. With his hand on her head, the connotations were so clear. He seemed to sense that, because his other hand reached down to touch her hair, before he put a hand on either side of her head suggestively. Rosa looked up at him. He was watching her closely. She closed her eyes, trying to regain something of her control. This man was making her insane. All she could think of was fucking him. She was willing to do anything, say anything at this point. She wanted him.

"S-so…" she began, stuttering in her desperation to get her mind off her thoughts as his hands tightened on her head. "How do you make your money?" she asked, managing to look up at him with some semblance of defiance.

Christian stared down at her for a long moment. He shrugged.

"I'm in import/export," he said simply.

"What do you import?"

"Oh, all the colors of the world," he said, grinning. "You know, reds, blues, blackies…"

"You deal drugs?" Rosa said, sounding appropriately aghast.

"I give people what they want," Christian replied, looking offended.

"Do you sell a lot?"

"Do you think Viper grows on trees?"

Rosa shook her head slowly. "Do you ever deal in X or roofies?"

"Why?" he asked, grinning. "You looking to score?"

"No," she said. "But I might be able to help you score."

He looked back at her for a moment, doubtful. Then his expression changed. "You are gonna help me score, doll—you're gonna get yourself up here and fuck me."

Her hand lashed out, and her long, talon-like nails left bloody trails across his chest. Christian hissed in pain, snatching her wrist up and pulling her hand away from him, squeezing it painfully.

"That wasn't very smart," he said, narrowing his eyes.

She winced in pain as he applied pressure to her hand.

"I meant," she gasped out, trying to get her point across but having a hard time because while part of her was in pain, the other was getting extremely excited at the violence he was showing. "I meant," she began again, "that I could help you score a new source for those." She gasped as he pulled her closer.

"What source?" he growled.

"Me," she said, staring back into his eyes.

He pushed her away, shoving her back to her knees. He sighed,

113

rolling his eyes. "Just stick to what you're good at, little teacher."

"I'm telling you," she said, sounding hurt, as she reached up to rub her wrist. "I have the best quality at the lowest cost you're going to find anywhere."

"You sellin' me a car?"

"No," she said, looking back at him haughtily. "I'm offering you a chance to tap into a source that makes the best product out there, and won't cost you anything to get into."

Christian looked back at her for a long moment, then glanced down at his chest. Blood was actually sliding down in drops in some places. He narrowed his eyes at her. "This better be good," he said, his voice heavy with an unspoken threat. "And you'd better be better in the sack." He sat back, bracing his arms on the bed behind him, placing his foot on her thigh and moving it up under the dress meaningfully, making her breath come faster. "I'm listening," he said.

"My... my husband, he's a chemist," she said, stammering at first, then rushing on, wanting to get the business over with so she could take him in any number of ways she could only begin to imagine. "He makes the drugs. He got the formulas for Rohypnol and X from some kid that was in his class who thought it would be good extra credit years ago. Larry has perfected it, and made it stronger so you can sell it cut with lower-end stuff, making the profit higher. Plus, Larry does anything for me, so we just share the profit. I can get you more than you ever dreamed, and we can get rich together."

Christian looked unimpressed. "Roofies and X are pretty low end. And I'd have to set up a whole new distribution for those—they aren't mainstream in the real world."

"I've already got part of that covered. I have the market here at the college and at two others," she said triumphantly.

"How?" he asked. "You don't strike me as the type to sell," he said derisively.

"I'm much smarter than that," she chided him, enjoying that she was about to show him how smart she was. "I take young men that show promise in, and get them to sell it for me."

"Promise?" Christian asked blandly.

"Well, they have to be fuckable, of course," she said with a smug grin. "I bring them here, give them a taste of the product, fuck them a few times, then send them on their way. They come back like dogs to a bitch."

"And you'd be the bitch," Christian said, his voice a growl.

Rosa had the temerity to smile confidently.

Christian shook his head slowly, his face showing disappointment as he said, "Hit it."

"What?" Rosa said, even as the door to the bedroom was kicked open.

Jeanie and Stevie walked into the room. Jeanie moved to pull Rosa up off her knees as Stevie went to Christian, who was standing.

"Jesus…" Stevie breathed, reaching up to touch the bloody welts on his chest. Her head whipped around to Rosa as Jeanie started to read her her rights.

"Rosa Delario, you are under arrest for the manufacture and distribution of narcotics. You are also being charged with assault on two peace officers as well as reckless disregard for the health and safety of a peace officer. Do you understand the charges against you?" Jeanie asked as she put cuffs on the stunned woman.

"Peace officer?" Rosa said, glancing back at Christian.

Stevie handed him his badge, and he held it up to show her.

"Two peace officers?" Rosa queried next, right as Jeanie turned her around to walk her out of the door.

Donovan leaned against the doorjamb, holding up his badge.

Rosa paled significantly, shaking her head in disbelief as she was marched out of the room.

Luckily, Larry was even easier to take down. They walked into his night class at the college and arrested him in front of his students. Donovan did the arrest, with Jeanie helping him. Stevie and Christian stood near the door. Christian wore his white shirt with spots of his own blood smeared on it, but he looked pleased.

Later that night, Stevie straddled his waist as she cleaned the scratches with antiseptic. He was leaning against the headboard of their bed, bare-chested, with a bottle of beer in hand. He hissed as she touched a particularly deep section, pulling away from her ministrations.

"I'm sorry, babe," she said, looking sincerely so. "I need to clean them, though. No telling what that bitch had under her nails." Her eyes narrowed on the last part.

Christian grinned at her angst. "Easy now..."

"Easy, my ass," she said. "That broad is so lucky Jeanie took her into custody—I would have dragged her down those stairs by her hair, given the chance."

"She did Jeanie's man a lot more damage than she did me, babe," he pointed out.

"True," Stevie said, realizing he was right about that.

Rosa had endangered Donovan's life, dosing him with Ecstasy when she had no idea if his body could handle it. She'd been playing a very dangerous game with people's lives. Christian had begun to wonder if she'd ever managed to actually kill someone with her little play. He'd set Midnight to thinking, and she'd set Tiny on the trail. If there was anything to be found, Tiny would find it.

When she'd finished cleaning his wounds, Stevie reached over to pick up the Neosporin.

"Gad, no," he said, holding up his hand as she unscrewed the cap.

"Bullshit, Collins," she said, shaking her head at him even as she started applying the ointment. "If you get an infection you'll scar for sure. I don't want a trace of that woman on you."

Christian took a drink of beer as he watched her. He put his hand back on her hip, where it had been before he'd protested at the medicine she was applying to his skin.

"We make a pretty good team," she said, smoothing more ointment over a welt.

"Yeah," he said, nodding.

"Ever consider getting into narcotics?" she asked, glancing up at him through the veil of deep red hair that had fallen across her forehead.

He looked back at her for a moment, narrowing his eyes. "I'm a geek, remember?"

"Computer geek," she qualified, grinning.

"Ah, yes."

"You did really good in there tonight, babe," she said, trying to adequately convey her admiration for the way he'd handled himself.

"Thanks," he said, looking back down at her hands as she continued applying ointment.

Her finger reached up to touch him under the chin, bringing his eyes up to look into hers. "No, Christian, I mean it," she said. "You have a talent for this." She shook her head, blowing her breath out. "I've had a ton of training, and some experience, a lot more formal stuff than you, and I can't even come close to what you have. You have the instinct."

Christian looked back at her for a long moment, then made a face. "I don't have anything, babe, just a knack for bullshit."

"That's what every good narc has." Stevie sat back, looking down at him. "I think you should seriously consider a career here…"

Christian looked almost disgusted. "I never wanted to be a cop."

Stevie shrugged. "You make a damned good one all the same, Christian."

"You think so?" he asked, feeling like what he'd done earlier that night was a simple case of bullshit and who was better at slinging it.

"Yes, I think so," she said, leaning down to kiss his chest, just above one of the scratches.

He put his hand to her head, pulling her up gently with a handful of hair and kissing her lips. He looked into her eyes.

"I liked having you there as my backup," he said.

"I liked being there to be your backup."

"If I did this full time, would you be there with me?"

"You would want to partner with me?" she asked skeptically, thinking of Dave and his solo ways.

"You think I want to be like Dibbins and be away from my lady all the time?" he asked, knowing what she'd been thinking.

Stevie shrugged. In truth, yes, she had thought that's what he'd want. Finally she nodded.

"And you still pointed out the idea of me changing careers?" he asked, thinking that would have been suggesting something that was bound to leave her lonely, a lot like Susan was.

"Yeah," Stevie said, then shrugged again. "I just want you to be happy doing what you're good at. If you're happy doing the computer thing, then I want you to do that." She looked down at him. "I just think you're meant for more."

Christian stared up at her for a long moment, then pulled her to him, kissing her deeply.

"Wait, wait, wait!" she exclaimed, knowing he was getting amorous and not wanting to wipe off all the ointment she'd just put on him.

Grabbing the roll of gauze, she then wrapped it around his chest a few times and tied off the ends. She had to ignore his hands sliding over her body the entire time. As soon as her task was complete, however, she reached up and pulled off her shirt, pressing against him. They made love, and lay afterward feeling sated and tired.

"If I do this," he said in the semi-darkness of the room, stroking her back as she lay over him, "I want you with me."

She kissed his neck. "You want me, you got me, babe," she said, grinning.

That same night, Donovan stood at his cutting board, chopping up chicken. Jeanie sat on the low island, watching him.

"She should be here soon," she said.

"Good."

"You're making her favorite, aren't you?"

"Yeah…" he said, grimacing. "Think it'll help?"

"Couldn't hurt," Jeanie said, making a face.

They'd called Erin and asked her to come to dinner. They thought they'd better tell her about them being back together before it became common knowledge.

"So I don't get one thing…" Jeanie said.

"What's that?" Donovan asked, not sure what she was talking about. She had a habit of jumping from one topic to another without warning. It was always a challenge to keep up with her.

"How did Blue avoid drinking the X?" she asked.

Donovan nodded, getting mentally on the same page as her. "He spit the shot into the beer bottle."

"That's why he asked for beer that was bottled," Jeanie said, grinning. "He's good, huh?"

"He's damned good."

"You're damned good too, Donovan," Jeanie said, knowing that he was still feeling really dissatisfied with himself for his mistake.

"Yeah, yeah…"

"Donovan…"

"I know, Jay, I know," he assured her. "I'm just saying, Blue's instincts are dead on. He knew exactly how to handle Rosa, and he nailed her inside of an hour. That's incredible work."

"Yeah, but he knew what he was up against."

"True," Donovan said. "But he was still able to roll with it when she got mad."

"Yeah, he was. Think he'd consider becoming a narc?"

"I think he should."

"I think Stevie's gonna talk to him about it," Jeanie said, grinning.

"Really?"

"Yeah. Her and I talked about it while you boys were booking our friends."

"Does she think he'll go for it?"

Jeanie shrugged. "She doesn't know, but she thinks exactly what you just said, that his instincts are too good to be wasted." She gave him a pointed look then. "I think we'd make a pretty good team, the four of us, don't you?"

Donovan narrowed his teal eyes at her. "Maybe… Why?"

Jeanie shrugged again. "I'd just like to work with you guys again. I think we all have pretty different takes on the job, and I think we'd help each other improve a lot."

Donovan nodded, accepting her answer. Jeanie wanted to be the best at whatever she did. She was still fighting her own demons for quitting Alcoholic Beverage Control the very first time she got hurt. It wasn't so much that she'd gotten hurt, but the fact that she really hadn't had the street time she'd needed. She knew Donovan had been right when he'd pointed it out before she'd taken the job in the first place. It was for that reason that she had decided to come back to the department and put in the time. That and wanting to be near Donovan again to try and win him back. And she finally had, thank God.

They heard the front door open then, and glanced at each other.

Erin walked into the room a few moments later.

"Hi, guys," she said, walking over to hug Jeanie, and then Donovan. He turned his head, kissing her softly on the lips.

It was something they'd always done. He wasn't going to change it, unless she wanted him to. They were still friends, and he still loved her for everything she'd done for him.

"So, how did it go?" Erin asked, moving to sit next to Jeanie on the low island.

"It went great," Jeanie said.

"Yeah, it did," Donovan said, selecting an oil and pouring it into the pan he had heating on the stove. He picked up his glass of wine and took a drink before glancing at Erin.

"What kind is it?" she asked.

"A merlot, new one we're trying. Want some?" he asked.

She hopped off the counter, taking the glass from his hand and sipping it. Then she nodded, and turned around to reach for a glass. Jeanie handed her one. Donovan poured her wine.

"So, Blue is okay?" Erin asked, concern in her voice.

"For the most part," Donovan said, grinning.

"Oh boy. What happened?"

Jeanie grinned. "Oh, he got a little scratch."

"Let's just say Rosa has a propensity for using her talons," Donovan said.

"She scratched him?" Erin asked, aghast.

Donovan nodded, reaching up to pull his shirt off to show where he still had two distinct lines from when Rosa had clawed him.

"Oh shit," Erin said, her eyes wide. "Donovan... are you really okay?" she asked, having understood what Christian had been telling Stevie that day in the car.

Donovan nodded. "Yeah, I still get headaches now and again, but for the most part I'm fine. Those first few days were brutal, though... Jay took care of me."

Erin nodded. "I'm glad you're okay."

Donovan looked at Jeanie, and she shrugged, not sure how to

start either.

Erin glanced at Jeanie, then back at Donovan. "Hey, you two can relax. I know you're back together."

"You do?" Donovan asked, thinking Christian might have told her.

"Yeah, Donovan," Erin said. "It's so obvious."

"It is?" Jeanie asked, surprised.

"Yeah. You two are glowing like a pair of headlights."

Donovan looked at Jeanie, and she stared back at him. They both made an embarrassed face that had Erin laughing.

"Oh God, you two…" she said, shaking her head and rolling her eyes.

"You're okay with this, Erin?" Donovan asked, stepping over to her, concern clear in his teal blue eyes.

She looked up at him for a long moment, then nodded. "Yeah, I am, now. I wasn't at first, but I know that you two belong together—you always have."

Donovan took her into his arms, hugging her to him.

"We'll always be here for you, Erin, no matter what, okay?" he said against her hair.

Erin nodded, tears coming to her eyes.

Jeanie hopped off the counter, moving to hug her from behind, laying her head on Erin's shoulder. Erin laughed through her tears.

"We'll find you Mr. Perfect," Jeanie said.

"Yeah," Erin said. "Too bad Darrell isn't anything like Donovan…"

"Eww…" Donovan said, which got Erin laughing. Jeanie laughed too.

Darrell was Donovan and Randy's older brother, and he was far from like Donovan. He was and had always been a construction worker. Just because he'd been running his own company for almost twelve years didn't mean he wasn't still as gruff as he'd always been.

They had dinner a while later, eating in a companionable atmosphere. Donovan and Jeanie felt better, and Erin found that she did too. It was obvious they both cared enough about her to want to spare her feelings. That was important to Erin. She knew her Mr. Right was out there somewhere, she just hadn't met him yet. She held on tight to that thought that night.

***

The top tabloid news story of the day was all about Joe and Jordan Tate.

Jordan Tate and her new man, one Joseph Michael Sinclair IV, were spotted in a London tattoo parlor. The shop owner stated that Jordan and her man designed each other's tattoos, each getting the initials of the other put into the design. Is this true love? It's well known that Jordan Tate has moved from one man to another. Last year she dated rock star BJ Sparks, and the year before that, she was seen out with any number of stars. While Mr. Sinclair isn't famous in the commercial way, he is quite famous in the law enforcement community. However, Joe Sinclair is married. Is Jordan Tate going to wreck a home with her wild, party-girl ways?

Nick heard it first, telling his dad as he was drinking his coffee that morning. He was waiting for Rhiannon.

"Joe's dating who?" Kyle asked.

"Jordan Tate, Dad," Nick said. "She's like this incredibly sexy singer. Oh my God, she is like the top of the charts right now. Wait, wait, I'll get you her picture." He ran off to his room and came back with the magazine he'd been ogling for the last week, opening it to the page with the story on Jordan Tate.

Kyle couldn't stop the natural physical reaction to the picture. The woman was blatantly sexy. She wore all black, her blouse cut so low you could see the curve of her breasts. She was standing with her head down, but looking back up at the camera. Her eyes sparkled like polished gold, outlined in a sooty liner, with long, dark lashes and perfectly curved eyebrows. Her cheekbones were high. Her dark hair framed her perfectly smooth, tanned face. Her body was a whole other story. She was petite, but there was nothing skinny or bony about her. It was obvious from the form-fitting blouse and short skirt that she had no fat to hide, and plenty of assets to show off, but not in false-looking proportions. She wore sheer black stockings and ankle-length, high-heeled calf-skin boots, and a long leather duster that fell to the backs of the heels. Everything about the woman screamed sex appeal.

"And you say that woman said Joe is dating her?" Kyle asked, wanting clarification.

"Who?" Rhiannon asked, walking into the kitchen.

"Nick says there was a report that Joe's dating this woman," Kyle said, handing her the magazine.

Rhiannon looked at the picture. "Holy shit…" she said, then grimaced as she realized she'd said that out loud.

Kyle nodded. "Exactly."

"He's in England, though, isn't he?" Rhiannon asked.

"Yeah, Rhi," Nick said. "The report said that he and Jordan Tate were in a tattoo parlor getting tattoos."

"A tattoo?" Rhiannon asked, raising her eyebrow.

"Mid-life crisis is a bi—" Kyle started to say, but stopped himself. "Bad," he finished, grinning.

"I guess…" Rhiannon said, shaking her head.

She scanned the story about Jordan Tate.

"It says she's basically pop culture's bad girl. She's always going from one party to another. I wonder if Joe has any idea who he's hooking up with… It even says here that she was in drug rehab for a while for alcohol and drug abuse," Rhiannon said, concern coloring her voice. Joe was their friend—did he know what he was getting himself into?

Kyle looked at his wife for a long moment, then shook his head. "I'll talk to Midnight."

Later that morning he went to Midnight's office. She was, as usual, inundated with messages. She had no idea what today's were about. She'd gotten in late and was just picking up the phone to make the first call when Kyle walked in.

"Good morning," he said, glancing at her desk and the pile of messages there.

"Hiya," she said, grinning.

"You might want to know what you're about to step in before you make any calls."

"What do you mean?" she asked, looking wary.

"Uh…" Kyle tossed the magazine opened to the picture of Jordan Tate on her desk. "Joe's dating her."

"What?" Midnight said, looking at the picture, then scanned the article, her pen in her hand moving more and more in agitation. "Jesus Christ…" she said, glancing up at Kyle. "And you know he's dating her how?"

"It was apparently on *E* this morning," Kyle said. "Nick saw it and told me. They've been seen in London together."

"Okay, but that doesn't mean they're dating," Midnight pointed out.

"They were getting tattoos together."

"Oh," Midnight said, her eyes widening. "Joe got a tattoo?"

"Apparently, with her initials in the design."

"Oh good, Sinclair, make it permanent," Midnight said, rolling her eyes. "So you're saying this is what all these messages are about?" She indicated the pieces of paper that had scattered when he tossed the magazine on the desk.

"More than likely. They knew his name, and they knew that he's 'famous in the law enforcement community.' Probably didn't take long to figure out where he works."

"Oh boy…"

"Uh-huh…" Kyle said. "I think we're about to become famous again."

"Great…" Midnight said, with the beginnings of a grin on her lips.

"Problem is, if that story's true, Joe's dating someone that's a pretty wild child. Should we warn him, or do you think that's what he's after?"

"Hard to know at this point," Midnight said. She grimaced. "He's reeling pretty bad right now."

"What?" Kyle asked, detecting that she'd just said something she wasn't supposed to say.

"I have the biggest mouth…" she said, shaking her head.

"Yes, you do," Rick said from the doorway. He walked in. "Joe's dating a rock star."

"You're late," she said, grinning and holding up the magazine. "How did you hear?"

"Our daughter," Rick replied, then looked at Kyle. "From your son, apparently."

"He does make the rounds."

"So what are we gonna do?" Rick asked.

"Wait, wait, wait," Kyle said, holding up his hands. "Reeling from what?"

Midnight looked at Rick. He stepped back, closing the door.

"Randy filed for divorce," Rick told Kyle.

"She did?" Kyle was stunned.

"Yeah," Rick said, nodding. "My dad handles Joe's legal issues, and he called us thinking we'd know. Apparently Randy didn't ask for anything but shared custody of the kids."

"Nothing?" Kyle asked.

"Nope, not one red cent," Midnight said, looking unhappy.

"So what's Joe going to do?"

"Apparently Joe countered, settling a rather large amount of money on Randy. My dad said he was very generous—he couldn't tell us any details, of course. And we can't tell Joe that we know."

Kyle nodded. "Well, that explains his need to let loose then."

Midnight nodded, looking at Rick. "We have to stand behind him on this one," she said, her tone no-nonsense. "I don't want to hear any shit about Jordan Tate, okay? If Joe is with her, then we have to assume that either this press is bullshit or that she's different now. I'm not going to doubt my best friend again."

Kyle nodded, understanding that Midnight was making an edict that she expected to be fully supported by him and the rest of the Gang. There would be no denigrating Joe's judgment this time. He was a full-grown man whose wife was divorcing him after thirteen years of marriage. If he wanted to go out and have a good time, get wild, go crazy, even get a tattoo, that was his business. As his friends, they would support him regardless. And if Jordan Tate hurt him, they'd hunt her down and kill her.

Joe took Jordan back to her flat in London the morning following their trip to the tattoo parlor that had become so famous all of a sudden. She kissed him before she got out of the car, promising that someday she'd invite him up when she knew it was clean. He grinned at that. She didn't strike him as the type of woman that cleaned too often.

"I'll call you as soon as I have a handle on my week," she said as she leaned down on the driver's side.

"Alright."

She kissed him again, loath to leave him. His hand went to her hair, then slid to the back of her neck as he kissed her deeply.

"Mmm…" she groaned against his lips. "I gotta go…" She didn't sound like she really wanted to.

"I know," he said, grinning, his lips still very close to hers. "You gotta go."

"Uh-huh…" she said, leaning in to kiss him again. The kiss deepened, and she had to drag herself away from him, sighing. "You kiss too good, Joe. You're like a drug," she said, her voice chastising him but her grin spoiling the effect.

"Uh-huh…"

"But I gotta go."

"I know," he said, smiling.

"Don't do that either," she said, wagging a finger at him as she stepped back from the car, knowing if she didn't take a step away from him she'd never go inside.

He nodded, looking appropriately apologetic.

"I'll talk to you soon," she said.

"Okay."

"Bye."

"Bye." He put the car in gear and drove off, knowing one of them had to leave.

Jordan stared after the car, already missing him. She shook herself mentally as she went inside. She could tell she was already addicted to him. He made her feel too good. Climbing the stairs to her flat, she felt the twinge at her back where the bandage covered her tattoo. She grinned to herself. She couldn't believe she'd finally done it. And to allow someone she really didn't know to design it and choose where it went was just insane, but it seemed really right for some reason. Just like having the tattoo she'd designed put on his arm. It just seemed right.

She opened the door to her flat and stepped inside. She glanced around the apartment. It wasn't too bad. Not spotless by any means, but was it ever? She walked into the kitchen, thinking she needed to plan to go shopping for some food pretty soon. She was surprised to see dishes in the sink. There were a couple of glasses and a plate. She didn't remember having left any dishes when she'd left the flat two days before. That's when she got the feeling in her stomach. Tightening her lips, she walked toward the bedroom.

She opened the door and there he was, lying in her bed as if he lived there. He was awake, looking at her.

"Finally decided to come home?" he asked mildly.

"Mark," she sighed. "What are you doing here?"

"Waiting for you—what else?"

"Don't I pay for a flat for you on the other side of town?" she asked, then grimaced. It was a mistake, starting off like that. She saw it on his face instantly.

She turned and walked toward her closet, planning to change clothes. Second mistake—that took her right past the bed. His hand whipped out, grabbing her arm in a vice-like grip. He pulled her to him, down onto the bed.

"Who the fuck is he?" Mark seethed.

She winced as he tightened his grip on her wrist. "Mark! Stop!" she yelled, trying to pull away from him.

"You stay gone for two fucking days and you think you're just going to ignore me?"

"Mark…" she said placatingly. "He's just a guy, okay?"

"Just a guy? A guy that put his fucking mark on you," he said, his hand pressing painfully against the bandage at the small of her back.

"How did you know about that?" she asked before she thought to stop herself.

"Ever hear of the media, Jordan?"

"They... heard?"

"Jesus fucking Christ, how stupid are you? They watch you constantly—you give great headlines."

"I wasn't thinking about that," she said, shaking her head, just trying to placate him in any way she could.

She knew Mark's temper well; she'd known it since she was fifteen. He was a very handsome man, with light brown skin and dark honey eyes with just enough brown in them that they weren't gold like hers. Funny that they weren't really related at all by blood. Just by marriage—their parents' marriage.

"You never fucking think, Jordan. That's why I have to do it for you," he said cuttingly.

He pulled her over him then, pushing her down on the bed on her stomach, yanking her pants down and off to look at the tattoo, ripping away the bandage with no care at all. Jordan winced painfully.

"You let him mark you like his territory, you stupid bitch," he growled.

She started to get up, but his body moved to pin her down. He was behind her. She knew him well enough to know she needed to get away from him now. She tried to get out from under him, but it was too late. She felt him press closer.

"Mark, no..." she said, hating the begging in her voice.

"Why?" he asked, sliding his body up closer to hers. "Because you fucked him?"

"You know that's not why," she said, gasping painfully as he slid into her. "No!" she yelled, but it was too late. But she fought him this time, and that made him mad.

When he left an hour later she had the bruises to show for trying to defy him.

His parting words were vicious. "Don't ever forget that I own you, you stupid cunt."

Jordan lay on her bed, staring at the ceiling. She felt vile. She knew it hadn't hurt as much as it could have, because she'd still been under the effects of kissing Joe before she'd come up to the flat. It had been the only thing to save her from being ripped up badly. She knew how vicious Mark could be sexually.

As she climbed into the shower, she let her mind go over the whole thing.

Mark O'Brien had been eighteen when her father married his mother. His mother was a beautiful woman. Mark's father had been a famous NBA player, and Mark had inherited his mother's looks, some of his father's height, and definitely his build. Mark stood six foot three, weighing an easy 240, and it was all muscle. He was a good-looking man, there was denying that. It was his vicious streak that made him less attractive. But you didn't see that when he was playing the part.

Jordan had never realized when she was fifteen that her step-brother had designs on her from day one. He'd seen in little Jordan all the potential she was going to attain when she was a woman. He'd primed her from the very beginning. Mark had befriended her, and since they were now "brother and sister," she finally had a friend that she wouldn't move away from. They spent lots of time together, and he was always just the sweetest, nicest guy. What Jordan didn't know was how many nights he jerked off thinking about her. Mark played it smart though, knowing that his little teenage sister wouldn't go for that just yet.

Over the course of the next six years, Mark had his girlfriends, and his toys, but Jordan was always bound to be his, and he knew it. Eventually he'd worked it so they lived in the same flat in London. Then in LA, when she went to The Musicians Institute, he'd gotten her an apartment. He had to be in LA a lot, conveniently enough, and it was there that he'd finally nailed her the first time.

He'd just broken up with his long-time girlfriend in London. She was cheating on him. At least, that's what he told Jordan when he climbed into her bed, to be consoled. Jordan, of course, consoled him. How many times had he consoled her when a relationship she'd been just sure was love had gone to shit? She talked to him for a long time, telling him that the woman just didn't deserve a great guy like him, saying all the right things. Eventually, they'd fallen asleep. Jordan woke to feel his hand on her breasts. She was shocked at first, but he whispered to her that he had always loved her, and that she was his very best friend. It took a little coaxing to get her to remember that they weren't really related, that this wasn't some kind of sick incest thing. They were a man and a woman, and it wasn't so bad if they got together, was it? Jordan had given in, letting him make love to her. For Mark it was heaven; for Jordan it was the beginning of the biggest mistake of her life.

They'd been a couple for a few months, but they didn't tell their parents. Jordan was adamant about keeping it a secret. She knew it was wrong, no matter that they weren't blood related, and she was determined to keep from hurting her father. She wanted out of the relationship, but didn't want to hurt Mark. For those first few months he was so sweet. He kept telling her that this was what they had been meant for. They'd been meant for each other. But Jordan knew it was wrong, and she knew she couldn't keep doing it. Sex with him did nothing for her. He held no attraction for her that way. He'd always been her big brother, and he would never be anything but that to her.

After four months she'd broken it off, saying she just couldn't do it anymore. That was the first time he'd beaten her. His mother had left his father because he was physically abusive, putting her in the hospital the last time before she left him. Jordan realized in horror that night that Mark had inherited a violent streak from his father. She'd stayed with him a few more months after that, but things were different then. Any time she voiced her own opinion he would slap her if he didn't like it. In the end, she knew she needed to get away from him. She graduated The Musicians Institute and ran back home to London, to her father's house. There she was safe from Mark. He couldn't touch her with her father there.

A year later she'd finally gotten her music on track. She'd joined a small bar band to gain some singing experience. She'd hung out in the clubs in London since she was old enough to manage to get in, so getting into a band hadn't taken much. She'd spent a lot of time trying to figure out what she wanted to do. After two years she was finally sure, so she started doing demos, but nothing really hit. She knew she hadn't found her niche yet. But then she'd finally done a demo she thought was really good. And her father got her the meeting with a good agent, and suddenly she was being signed.

The day she came home to her father's house to tell him about the deal she'd made with the agent was the first time she'd seen Mark in three years. There he was. She hugged him like a good sister would, and recoiled when he hugged her too close. Her father had come in then, and she told him her great news. Her father said that Mark had a great idea that he wanted to share with her.

"What is it?" she asked, her tone a little too cool.

"I've made some great connections in LA, Jord," he said, winking at her. "And I've decided I'm going to manage you."

Jordan felt sick. "But I have an agent."

"Jordie," Mark said, shaking his head at her like she was still a child, even though she was twenty-seven by this time. "An agent works for lots of talent—I'd only be working for you. I'd have your concerns in mind all the time."

Jordan looked at her father, who was smiling happily. How could she tell him she didn't want Mark as her manager? *Because we slept together, Dad, and he's not so great in bed, but he'd make a great boxer.* She smiled wanly and thanked Mark for being "willing" to use up his time managing her, all the while gritting her teeth.

That night, Mark had come to her room, and she'd told him in no uncertain terms that this was strictly a business arrangement.

"There won't be any sex, or any relationship of any kind," she said, her chin raised, daring him to hit her in her father's house. "You will manage my career, not me."

Mark had narrowed his eyes at her, but had also realized that he couldn't do anything at that point. He had no power. But that was when he decided she'd never have any power over him. Little Jordan could kiss her career goodbye—he'd make sure she never made it.

In the end it had taken six years, during which there had been a few notable fights between them. He'd forced himself on her a few times, usually when he was feeling threatened or needed to prove who had the power in the "business relationship." The guilt had taken its toll on Jordan so many times, she'd turned to drinking and taking anti-depressants like Skittles to keep away the horrible, dirty feeling she had inside. Mark made her feel that way. He made her feel like she was nothing but trash, that she didn't deserve the fame she had.

When she had made it, despite all his efforts, he of course took the credit, and controlled her all the more. It was frustrating to the extreme, but she didn't see a way out.

She sat down in the shower, letting the water run over her, shivering and feeling so sick she could just scream. Instead she cried. The urge to start drinking was so strong. It made her mad. The last two days with Joe had been so great, she hadn't wanted to drink like she did a lot of the time. She'd wanted to be clear-headed, to engage in their fantastic conversations, and then she wanted to feel everything when he'd made love to her. Now she felt she was right back to the hell she usually lived in.

Jordan resisted the urge to drink, and instead took one of the Valium she'd been prescribed and slept for the next thirty-six hours. When she'd slept herself out, she got up, took a shower, and washed her hair, intending on getting on with her life. By the time she'd toweled off, gotten dressed, and blow-dried her hair, she realized she couldn't really face anyone just yet. She climbed back into bed and lay curled into a ball, holding on to a pillow, staring into space.

Joe called a couple of times. The answering machine was in the kitchen, though, so she didn't hear his voice. She just heard the phone ring next to her on the nightstand and refused to answer it in case it was Mark. She heard the intercom buzz at her front door, but she didn't get up to answer it—she just knew it was Mark.

Joe knocked on the door to the manager's flat downstairs.

The man answered wearing a bathrobe.

"Hey, man, I need your help," Joe said, smiling.

"What for?" the man asked in a cockney accent.

"Well, I lost the key that my girlfriend gave me, and I need to get into her place. I'm trying to surprise her for her birthday," Joe said, using his most entreating tone.

"Whose place?"

"Jordan Tate's."

The manager nodded. "Yeah, everyone wants to get in there. What makes you any different?"

Joe narrowed his eyes as the man scratched his belly, looking away but putting his other hand out. So that was the way of it, huh?

Joe handed him a £50 note. He nodded, looking pleased, before going over to a cabinet and withdrawing a key.

Joe shook his head as he walked up the stairs to Jordan's flat. She was going to have to do something about that—just about anyone could get into her place at this rate. Some people would pay a lot more for less.

He was worried about Jordan. She hadn't called as promised. He'd finally given in and phoned her, getting no answer. Another twenty-four hours had passed. His instincts were telling him something was wrong. Yes, he realized she could be blowing him off, but he wanted to know for sure. The cop in him made him have to know for sure.

Joe put the key in the door and opened it.

"Jordan?" he called out, not wanting to scare her. He got no answer. He walked inside and looked around. It was a nice enough flat, but it was obvious it wasn't her primary residence. It was too Spartan looking. He walked down the hall, calling her name again. His senses were working overtime.

He walked past the open doorway that led to her bedroom. He

saw her then, lying on the bed. Her eyes were open and she was staring at the wall.

"Jordan?" he said, standing in the doorway.

It took her a few moments to even react to the sound of his voice. Finally she looked over at him.

"Hey…" he said, walking in and looking down at her.

She smiled like a child that had just been given a present. He sat on the bed, reaching down to touch her on the cheek. She was lying on her side, wearing white cotton pants and a blue shirt. Her long, dark hair fell about her shoulders in a silken curtain. He brushed a few strands back from her face, and that's when he saw the bruise.

"What happened?" he asked, not realizing his tone was all cop just then.

She looked back at him for a moment, as if not sure what he was referring to. He touched her face where the bruise was, high up on her cheekbone.

"Oh," she said, moving to sit up, pushing her hair back as she did, not looking at him. "I fell."

"You fell?"

"Yeah," she said, shrugging, then grinned, her eyes still not connecting with his." I'm kind of a klutz."

"How did you fall?"

"I tripped on the stairs, didn't watch where I was going," she said airily.

He looked back at her for a long moment, his eyes searching hers. She looked away, glancing down at his left arm.

"Hey!" she said, reaching out to touch the tattoo. "It looks great."

Joe knew he was being diverted, but he went along with it. He looked down at his arm. "Yeah, I think so. How does your look?"

She looked contrite then. "You know, I haven't even checked."

"You haven't?" he asked, surprised.

She shrugged. "I've been really busy, didn't even think about it."

"Oh," he said, nodding. "So that's why you didn't call me, right?"

She bit her lip, realizing how that sounded and not wanting him to think she'd been avoiding him. She'd been avoiding the world, not him specifically. She reached up to touch his cheek.

"I'm sorry, Joe, really. Things have just been really crazy." She looked up into his eyes. "I've missed you, though," she said, realizing that she really had.

Seeing him walk into her bedroom a few minutes before had been like suddenly being able to breathe clean air again.

"I've missed you too," he said, leaning down to kiss her gently, his hand touching her cheek.

She put her arms up around his neck, moving closer to him, kissing him deeply. Joe slid his arms around her, gathering her to him. He felt her flinch, and moved his arms, reaching down to touch her waist. She relaxed again. When the kiss ended he looked down at her.

"So, can I see the tattoo?" he asked, grinning.

"You wanna?" she said, grinning too.

"Yeah, let me see. I'll tell you how it looks."

"You just want me to take my clothes off!" she said, shaking her head at him.

He laughed. "Damn, you figured me out."

She turned around and lifted her shirt, glancing back at him.

He moved her pants down so he could see the tattoo. His gaze also took in the bruises on her back. They were light—she probably didn't bruise easily with her darker skin tone—but they were very definitely bruises. He knew he was being lied to about her "falling." He'd seen enough abused women in his career to know when one was lying to cover someone else's crime. He also knew that at this point if he pushed her too much, she'd probably run from him. He didn't want that.

He slid his hands around her waist, moving to lean against the bed and pull her back against him. He kissed the side of her head.

"How does it look?" she asked, leaning back against him comfortably.

"Looks great."

She turned around. "I really did miss you," she said, reaching up to touch his lips.

"Good," he said, grinning. "So what have you been up to?"

"Well," she said, thinking quickly, "I've got this concert coming up—I needed to get that organized." It had been organized for three weeks. "And I've had some stuff to arrange for the tour." One of the few things Mark did well. "Just busy, busy, busy," she said, smiling up at him.

"And now?"

"And now," she said, moving up closer to him, kissing his lips. "Now I want to spend a little time with you, if that's okay."

"That's more than okay," he said, smiling.

"Good."

Joe leaned down, capturing her lips with his, and they kissed for a long time. Eventually she moved over him, straddling his waist and opening his shirt to kiss his chest. Before long, their clothes lay in a pile on the floor. He laid her back on the bed, her head at the foot of it, his body over hers as he kissed her deeply. As his body slid into hers, he felt her tense instantly. He pulled back, looking down at her.

"What?" he asked worriedly.

"Nothing," she said, reaching up to kiss him, horrified that she'd reacted to the twinge of pain that his entry had caused. "I guess I'm just still a little sore from our first two days," she said, grinning.

Joe nodded, knowing that was highly unlikely. Her body fit his quite well, nicely snug, but he didn't feel like he was too big for her, and there hadn't been any hint of discomfort from her while they'd made love the days before. Something was different, and it worried him.

Hiding his thoughts quite well, he leaned down, kissing her deeply, taking his time to excite her again. When his body began to move in hers again, the discomfort was gone. He brought them to climax soon after that. He had definitely missed her sexually; his body remembered hers well.

Afterward, he lay holding her against him.

"Jordan?" he said softly.

"Hmm?" she murmured, feeling so good at that moment.

"Why don't you come stay at the house with me?"

She looked up at him for a long moment. "Why?"

He shrugged. "I figure this way we don't have to miss each other, right?"

She looked thoughtful, outwardly thinking only of the possibility of being with him full time for the little while they had together. Inside she was also thinking that she didn't want to be in this flat alone if Mark came back. Spending time with Joe was definitely a plus, though. But she'd definitely incur Mark's wrath for disappearing on him.

"Joe, I don't know…" she said, with that thought in mind.

He leaned down, taking possession of her lips, kissing her so thoroughly and deeply it left her breathless, making her body come alive once again. Then he pulled back, heat very definitely in his eyes.

"Still don't know?" he asked huskily.

She bit her lip, her body screaming at her to do it. Her heart wanted the comfort of his sheltering arms, while her head warned her that there would be hell to pay. It was two against one, and her mind lost.

"Okay," she said, staring up at him.

"Good."

A little while later, he helped her gather some things and drove them back up to his estate. She got a message ten minutes after they walked in the door.

"I'll go check on the kids while you take care of that," Joe said.

"Okay," she said, grinning as she pulled out her cell phone.

Joe left her and she dialed Mark's number. She went into the study, closing the door. She didn't want anyone to hear her conversation.

"Yeah?" Mark answered.

"You messaged me?" she said coldly.

"Where the fuck are you?"

"I'm at Joe's house. Why?"

"I thought we took care of that the other day."

"Mark, what do you want?" she asked, sighing.

He was silent for a moment, then decided on a new tact. "I just got a call from Wembley about your concert," he said snidely. "We have a problem, Jordan."

"What's the problem?"

She'd been planning this concert for weeks. It was a benefit for an orphanage called London Society. Growing up mostly in London, she'd had a very good friend who had been housed at the orphanage. It was a really great place for kids, but it never had adequate funding, and now the house was in serious need of repair. It had always been Jordan's fantasy to present a huge check to them as a way of thanking them for the work they did. That's what this concert was for. She'd managed to score Bush and Red Dogg, a British band making a name for themselves lately, for the show, and she was still hoping to hear back from one of the big-name bands she'd asked as well. She hadn't heard anything yet. In truth, a couple of the bands had called Mark with an agreement to play, but Mark had lied and told them the show was booked already. Little Jordan was getting too big for her britches, and it was time to show her who was really in charge.

"The problem is, you promised them $50K for the stadium, and you promised to pay Bush and Red Dogg's expenses up front. Besides all the publicity you're running and all that," he said, sounding so official. "You just don't have the liquid assets for all that."

Jordan's mouth dropped open, then her eyes narrowed. "I just went double platinum with the new album and I don't have any money?"

"You have money, Jordan," Mark said. "You just don't have an unlimited supply."

"I haven't bought anything substantial in months, Mark," Jordan pointed out.

She could almost feel his temper rise. "What are you trying to say here?"

"I'm not saying anything, okay? But I want to do this concert." She glanced up to see Joe walk in the door.

"And I'm saying you don't have the cash," Mark replied hotly.

Jordan sighed deeply, having to tamp down on the desire to throw the phone across the room. "I want to see the books," she said, her voice very controlled.

"You what?"

"You heard me—I want to see the books. I know I have the money for this, and I'll prove it to you. I want to do this concert, and it's going to happen."

"Oh, listen to Miss Big Star…"

"Just make an appointment for me with my accountant," Jordan said. "I don't want to fight about it."

"Fine."

She could sense his anger, and she knew she was risking his wrath, but she also didn't want to get taken for a ride by him. There had to be enough money to do this concert; if there wasn't, something was wrong and someone was taking her for a lot of money.

Jordan hung up a few moments later, glancing over at Joe.

"Problems?" he asked.

"Yeah," she said, looking unhappy.

Joe sat down on the leather couch, pulling her down with him. "So what's up?" he asked.

Jordan looked back at him for a long moment, then shrugged. "I want to do this benefit concert, but my manager says I don't have the money to put up for it."

"What's the concert for?"

"It's for an orphanage called London Society," she said, leaning back against him, allowing his warmth to envelop her. "They do a lot of really good work. I had a friend that came from there. She told me about all the programs they have to try and get kids to feel like they're not cast-offs. I just think it's important."

Joe grinned behind her, thinking she sounded like Randy at that moment. His heart tugged a bit at that thought, but he tamped down on it.

"So how much money are we talking here?" he asked.

"A lot," she said, sighing. "About three to four hundred thousand."

"Concerts are expensive to put on, huh?"

"Kinda," she said, grinning, as she glanced up at him from her place against his shoulder.

"So, what if you could get funding elsewhere?"

"Elsewhere?" she asked, then shook her head. "The concert is set for next week, Joe. I don't have time to go out and solicit funds at this point."

"Well, I don't want you soliciting…" he said, grinning. "I kind of had a corporation in mind."

"Oh, really?" she asked, moving to sit up and turn to him, still within the circle of his arms. "Who?"

"Me," he replied simply. "Well, not me per se," he qualified, seeing her hesitant look. "But the publishing company I own."

"Joe…" she said cautiously, shaking her head.

"Jordan, listen," he said, holding up his hand. "The company has so much that they donate to charity every year. This will just be one of those donations, okay?"

She dropped her head to his shoulder, shaking it slowly. "I don't want us to be about money," she said softly.

He put a finger under her chin, tilting her head up so her eyes met his. "We're not about money—this isn't about money," he said, leaning down to kiss her softly. "But the London Society needs the money, and you need the capital to get it to them, right?"

"Yeah…" she said, still sounding reluctant.

"I'm not doing this for you, Jordan," he said. "I'm doing it to do something good, okay?"

She took a deep breath, then sighed, nodding. "Okay."

"I'll even have my lawyer draw up the paperwork to make it all above board, okay? So no one can say your boyfriend is paying for your shows now," he added.

"My boyfriend?" she asked, grinning up at him.

"God, I hope so," he said, rolling his eyes. "I have your initials tattooed on my arm."

"Well, I've got yours on my butt," she said, laughing.

"It's not your butt, love," he said, leaning down to kiss her again. "It's your back—get it right."

"Oh yes, you're right."

"I always am."

"Not with me, honey," she replied sweetly.

"Ohh…"

"Wow," she said then. "Now all I need to do is score one of the headliners I've begged to do the show and I'm set."

"You're not the headliner?"

"Nah," she said, making a face. "I'm not that big, Joe."

"Uh-huh…" he said, having heard quite differently since he'd started seeing her. He'd been told she was number one on the charts and that her album was climbing faster than a cat with its tail on fire.

"So who have you asked?" he said.

"Well, I've asked No Doubt, Matchbox Twenty, Dave Matthews, and the Goo Goo Dolls," she said, sighing again. "But we haven't heard from any of them yet."

Joe nodded, looking like he was thinking. "Well, I could try the one whole connection I have in the music world, if you'd like."

"Who?" she asked, surprised that he had a connection, although she realized she shouldn't be. He was rich, after all. Even if he was a cop, money still lent itself to stars.

Joe shook his head. "Let me see if they'll do it first," he said, reaching for the phone.

"Joe!" she said, her mouth open in shock that he was going to leave her hanging like that.

He grinned at her even as he dialed.

"Yeah, who's this?" he asked, staring at Jordan, who was watching him with narrowed eyes. "Maureen? Hi, Maureen, how are you? This is Captain Joe Sinclair, San Diego PD. Is Phil in today?"

He grinned as he waited, because he could see Jordan was really confused now. He'd identified himself as "captain" and not Joseph Sinclair IV—his connection was through law enforcement? That just did not jibe at all.

"He's where?" Joe asked when the woman obviously came back on the line. "Great, can you put me through? Perfect. Thanks, Maureen, you're a sweetheart."

Jordan shook her head. Captain Sinclair was definitely a

charmer. Maureen was probably panting over there, hearing his sweet English accent and sexy voice.

"Hey, Phil, it's Joe," he said, his tone changing again. "Yeah, can you get me in touch with SAS Harris up in the LA office?" He grinned. "No, not quite, man," he said, chuckling. "Although she does have potential…" He listened for a moment then laughed outright. "My point exactly! Can you give me her number? Great, perfect. Thanks, man."

He hung up then, looking at Jordan to see if she'd figured it out yet. She hadn't.

"Joe…" she said warningly as he started to dial another number.

"Shh," he said, lifting the phone to his ear and winking at her. She reached out and swatted his arm. "Yes," he said, his voice taking on its official tone again. "Captain Sinclair looking for SAS Harris, please." He waited. "She is? Fantastic, can you put me through? Thank you." He waited again, then smiled widely. "Nicolette, how are ya? Joe Sinclair," he said warmly. He listened for a minute, then laughed, nodding. "Tell me about it, I deal with it every day. So, how's the baby?" he asked. "Yeah? Damn, really? She's quick." He grinned, nodding. "So, what's your husband up to these days? Oh yeah? Perfect, do you think I can get ahold of him? He does? He won't mind if I call him there? Wow, great, thanks. Yeah, what's the number?" He listened, obviously memorizing the number.

He hung up again and then started dialing.

"Joseph Michael Sinclair IV, if you don't tell me who the hell you're calling I swear I'm going to have to hurt you," Jordan said, balling up her fist.

He put the phone to his ear, raising an eyebrow at her fist, tiny as it was. He grinned, his light blue eyes twinkling in amusement.

"Heya, Jerith, it's Joe Sinclair from San Diego," he said. "Yeah, hi. I'm doing good—and you?" He nodded. "Great, yeah, Nicolette told me. Hey, I was wondering, would you and the band want to come do a gig here in London?" His eyes settled on Jordan then. "You know Jordan Tate? Yeah, yeah, sounds right. She's setting this up, and she needs a headliner. Since you're the only rock star I know, I thought I'd give it a shot." He grinned, then laughed. "Yeah, gotta get my favors in early." He looked pointedly at Jordan. "So what do you say? You think Billy and the crew would be interested?"

That's when it clicked. He had called the person he was talking to Jerith, and now he'd said "Billy."

"Oh my God," Jordan whispered, unable to believe that he was really talking to Jerith "Kid" Michaels of Billy and the Kid.

Joe smiled, winking at her even as he nodded. "That's fantastic, man. The date of the concert is…" His voice trailed off as he looked pointedly at Jordan.

"Um, November twenty-ninth."

"Um, November twenty-ninth," he repeated, grinning when she made an indignant sound. "Yeah, let me give you to Jordan so you two music people can work out the details." With that he handed the phone to Jordan.

Her eyes widened as she took it.

"Mr. Michaels…" she said hesitantly.

"Hi, Jordan, call me Jerith," came the very cheerful voice of Jerith Michaels.

"Oh my God," Jordan said, sounding very much like a fan.

In fact, she was a fan of Billy and the Kid. She had watched with the rest of the world as Jerith Michaels had gone through the roughest time in his life. Billy Montague, the lead singer of his band, had a drug problem and had nearly gotten him killed one night when she'd leapt offstage into the crowd. Jerith had thrown off his guitar and dived in after her, just about getting trampled in the process. That had been when Billy and the Kid had broken up for a time. Jerith had put out a highly successful solo album, and had gone straight to the top on his own. Eventually, he'd gotten the band back together, and Billy and the Kid had become a household name after that. They were back stronger than ever with their third album since the reunion. They were a big, big band, and Jordan was actually going to get them to play at her little benefit?

"Jordan, are you there?" Jerith asked, grinning.

He never could get used to people, especially famous people like Jordan Tate, being starstruck by him. To him, he was still simple Kid Michaels from New Jersey.

"Yes, I'm here, I just got a little tongue-tied for a second," Jordan said, shaking her head at how dumb she sounded. "Joe said you needed details? I mean, duh, of course you do. London's kind of a big town..." *Oh shut up, Jordan,* she thought. "I'm sorry. Yes, it's at Wembley Stadium on November twenty-ninth. You tell me when you'll arrive and I'll set up your sound check. If you need me to, I can arrange your flight," she said, trailing off as she realized she was talking too much.

Jerith chuckled. He recognized nervous chatter. "Well, we'd probably fly in on the twenty-eighth. Can we arrange a sound check for the morning of the twenty-ninth? It'll give us a chance to acclimate to the time difference. And no, Jordan, you don't need to worry about the flight arrangements—we'll cover that."

"Okay."

Then it hit her—how was she going to pay them? She bit her lip, thinking if nothing else, she'd sell something to do this. She didn't care what Mark said.

"What will you need to cover your expenses?" she asked.

"Not a thing."

"I meant, well, I meant monetary," she said, trying not to sound too crass.

"I know, Jordan, and we don't need anything."

"But…" Jordan said, looking mystified.

"My wife owes Joe a favor—tell him I consider it paid up," Jerith said with a laugh in his voice.

Jordan laughed softly, nodding. "I'll do that."

"We'll see you November twenty-ninth, for a sound check at, say, nine?"

"Sounds good, Mr. Michaels."

"Jerith," he corrected.

"Jerith," she repeated, grinning.

They hung up a moment later. Jordan looked up at Joe with wide eyes.

"Jerith Michaels says his wife's debt is paid up," she said.

Joe grinned, nodding. "Yeah, I kinda figured that."

"Who the hell are you?" she asked, shaking her head.

Joe smiled. "I am exactly who I said I am, Jordan. I just got lucky with that connection."

"Right, sure."

"My best friend runs what is considered by a lot of agencies to be the biggest and best department in America." He shrugged. "It comes with some perks."

"Right, it's not you or anything," Jordan said, giving him a wry look.

He grinned, shaking his head. "Nope."

"Bullshit," she replied sweetly. "Oh my God, Joe! I've got Billy and the Kid playing at this thing! Oh my God… I need to do new publicity… change the posters… get radio time…"

Joe nodded. "I'll go start the kids' dinner while you make your calls."

He stood as she picked up the phone.

"Joe?" she said.

"Yeah?" he asked, turning to look at her.

She threw her arms around him, hugging him tight, reaching up to kiss him on the lips. "Thank you so much. You have no idea how much this means to me," she said, her voice colored with emotion.

He looked down at her, holding her in his arms. "You're very welcome. I'm glad I could help."

"You are incredible," she said, shaking her head as if unable to believe how much.

He shook his head. "Nah, I'm just me."

"Yeah, you are, and *you* are incredible," she said, kissing him again.

He grinned as he let her go, walking out of the room.

CHAPTER 5

"Guess who your cousin is dating," Stevie said, walking into Christian's office.

Erin and Christian looked up from the computer.

"Who?" Christian asked.

"Jordan Tate."

Christian looked mystified for a minute, then his brows furrowed farther. "You mean on-the-radio Jordan Tate?"

"Yeah, I mean ultra-famous pop-rock star Jordan Tate."

"Hmm…" Christian said. "What does she look like?"

Stevie gave him a sour look.

"She's drop-dead gorgeous," Erin said.

"Yeah?" Christian asked.

"Oh God, move aside, Collins," Stevie said, moving in front of him to take over his computer.

He laughed, pulling her down onto his lap as she started to tap on the keys. She brought up the Jordan Tate website and then leaned to the side so Christian could see the picture on the home page.

"Damn," he said, staring into the gold eyes of Jordan Tate.

"Not another word, Collins," Stevie said, raising an eyebrow at him.

Christian grinned. "Not another one?"

"No," she said, crossing her arms.

"Even if it was—"

"No."

"But what if—"

"No," she said, grinning.

"Even if I—"

"No."

"—said my cousin has excellent taste in women," he said, putting his hand in her hair and pressing her face into his neck so she couldn't interrupt him again.

She kissed his neck for that comment, then bit it gently for cutting her off.

Christian laughed. Then he looked concerned. "Think Donovan knows?"

"I don't know," Stevie said, shaking her head.

Donovan did know, and was headed to check on his sister. He caught her coming out of the house that morning.

"Hey, sis," he said, walking up and hugging her.

Randy looked up at him, knowing why he was there. She'd already gotten a call from Darrell first thing that morning.

"Yes, Donovan, I know Joe is dating a rock star in England," she said simply.

"Okay…" Donovan said, noting that she didn't seem too torn up. "I'm missing something here—isn't he still your husband?"

"Not for too much longer," she said quietly.

"What?" he said, surprised.

Randy looked up at him, her teal blue eyes so much like his, shining in the morning sunlight. "I filed for divorce."

"You did?" he asked, feeling like he was the last to know. Randy nodded. "I thought you were going to talk to him about it first... Or did you?"

"No, I didn't," Randy said. "And I only said I'd think about talking to him about it first, Donovan. In the end I decided it would be easier on both of us if I just did it. I know how Joe thinks, and he'd feel like he was abandoning me and the kids if he filed. So I did it."

"But, Randy," Donovan said, still reeling. "I mean, you two have to work out so much... Shouldn't you at least wait till he gets back?"

"There was nothing to work out. I didn't ask him for anything. I just asked for shared custody of the kids."

"That's it?" he asked, shocked.

"Yes, Donovan, that's it," she said, leaning back against her car, which in truth she hadn't asked for either. "I came into this marriage with nothing. I never contributed much financially, and in fact cost Joe a lot of money with my education. So I didn't think I had any right to ask him for anything when I decided to leave the marriage." She shrugged, as if it were so simple.

"What about the house? What about your center? How are you going to support yourself?" Donovan asked. He knew Sinclair House wasn't a money-making organization.

Randy sighed. "Well, I figured I'd just get my job back with the department, or maybe with another one. With my degree I can probably get a decent job. As for the center, I was hoping to rent the house back from Joe."

"How would that work?" Donovan asked. "Joe paid for the house in full."

"So I'd have to pay him back for it. I could maybe get a loan to buy it from him."

"Randy, he paid two million for the house," Donovan said, having asked Joe about it at one point.

Randy stared back at him for a long moment, stunned. "He what?" she breathed.

"He paid two million. It's a historic landmark, Randy."

"Oh…" Randy said, feeling a little sick all of a sudden.

Joe had paid two million dollars for what had been a Christmas present? My God!

"So that's roughly… um… $9K a month, sis…"

Randy shook her head, still shocked. "It doesn't matter, anyway," she said, embarrassed.

"Why?" Donovan asked, noting the look on her face.

"I got word from Robert," she said, feeling tearful again. "Joe insisted on paying me $5,000 in alimony, $2,500 in child support, giving me Sinclair House, this house, and a million dollars."

It was Donovan's turn to stare at her in shock.

"Wow…"

Randy nodded. She had been stunned when she'd talked to Robert. She'd tried telling him that Joe needn't be so generous, that she had no intention of causing trouble for him. Robert had gently told her that this was Sinclair nature and she'd be best to accept it, or she'd end up with half the estate in England too.

That was the very last thing Randy wanted. She'd never take half of what Joe's parents had left him. She had far too much respect for the memory of his parents to even consider taking anything from them.

"Did you accept it?" Donovan asked.

"Joe said he wouldn't sign anything if I didn't."

Donovan grimaced. "You have to admit, he's a helluva guy."

"I know he is. I still love him. I just think it's time that we move on with our lives. I don't make him happy anymore, and I'm seeing that he really needs someone with more fire than I have."

"Sis…" Donovan said, wanting to deny what she was saying.

"Donny, look at the women he's dated—Stevie, and now Jordan Tate. They both have more fire in their little finger than I have in my whole body," she said, matter of fact. "It's okay. I've come to understand a few things over the last month or so. I sincerely think that Joe needed me for a long time. He needed someone to help, to make better, to take care of. And he did, Donovan, he did so well. He loved me because he needed me, and I loved him because he was there for me, unlike our parents had been. But now I just think that he needs more. I'm much stronger now that I've ever been in my life, and Joe is the reason for that. He gave me the support I needed to become who I am. But who I am isn't enough to sustain him anymore. And that's okay. It doesn't mean that the world is over, it just means it's going to change. I love him—I will always love him. And I honestly think he still loves me. I just think he needs more, and I love him and myself enough to give us both what we need."

It was the first time she'd said all of that out loud to someone. And having said it, she felt more convinced of it. Those had been the thoughts swirling in her head for weeks now, but having said it to Donovan made it more substantial suddenly. And in a way, it made it okay. Yes, it hurt to see the man that she had loved for so many years with someone else. She knew it was going to hurt, but it was part of the healing process. Joe had always been good to her, and he'd never done anything to directly hurt her. She seriously doubted he even realized his relationship was being publicized. Joe didn't think like that.

She knew him so well, and she knew he was just enjoying himself and doing his best not to think too much at this point. She was actually relieved that he didn't seem to be drinking heavily. She'd been worried about him when she'd heard about Christian's suicide attempt, knowing exactly how Joe thought and that he'd blame himself. She'd been in close contact with Midnight, making sure Joe was okay. It had been why she hadn't protested him leaving to go to England, understanding that he would heal better there, where he didn't have to deal with regular life all the time.

Donovan was staring down at her. "You're really okay with this, aren't you?" he asked, astounded.

"Yeah, Donny," she said. "I think I am." She reached up and hugged him.

"Do you want me and Darrell to hate him?"

"No!" Randy said, then saw his grin. "He's been nothing but good to you two too. So no, absolutely not. In fact, I'll kick your ass if you do."

Donovan was relieved, because he had always liked Joe, and it would be very difficult if he had to split his loyalties.

"You hear he got a tattoo?" Randy asked, grinning.

"Yeah," he said, rolling his eyes. "I think I should too."

"I think I'll really kick your ass then. So how are you, anyway?" she asked. "You don't call, you don't write…"

"I'm good. Me, Jay, Stevie, and Christian made a case yesterday."

"Christian is doing narcotics work now?" Randy asked, surprised. Christian had always said he didn't want to be a cop.

"Well, he was helping us out. We needed a ringer," Donovan said.

"A ringer?"

"Yeah... long story, sis," he said, grinning. "But he did damned good. Stevie is going to talk to him about changing over to narcotics."

"He's that good?"

"He's got the instinct for it. The kind most of us would pay anything for."

Randy gave him a dirty look. "Donovan, you're good too. Spider has said so a billion times."

"Yeah, maybe. But trust me, Blue would be great. He'd be another Dibbins if he got into it."

"Wow, that's pretty interesting."

"You did hear that Stevie and Christian are getting married, right?"

"Yes," Randy assured him. "Christian called me himself."

"Oh, good," Donovan said, worried that he'd forgotten to include her on something.

"Yeah, really," she said, poking him in the ribs. "Since my brother doesn't tell me anything..."

"Ohh... that's low," he said, laughing, as he pulled back out of her reach. "I'm glad you're okay, sis," he said then. "But you know if you ever need me, I'm here, right?"

"Yes, Donovan, I know."

He hugged her to him. She hugged him back, feeling good, and very glad he'd come by.

"Thank you," she said.

"That's what family is for, Randy."

She nodded, smiling at him. It was good to have family.

***

The next morning, Christian and Stevie were driving to work. They were going in together for a change, since she needed to be in the office to work on the report for one of her cases. They'd just pulled up to get coffee when she pointed to his cell phone.

"You need to call your mother," she said.

Christian grimaced. He knew he was going to catch hell from his mother for not calling her sooner to tell her about the engagement.

"Collins?" she said, raising an eyebrow. "You're not afraid of your mommy, are you?"

"You ever dealt with an extremely irate Englishwoman?"

"Can't say I have," she said, grinning.

"Trust me, you don't wanna have to."

"Call."

Christian sighed deeply. "Fine, fine, fine." He set the phone on the holder and hit the hands-free.

"Hello?" answered a very English-sounding woman.

"Mum, hey, it's me," Christian said.

"Would that be my only child?" Josephine Collins queried sweetly, but with enough of an edge to make Christian grimace.

"Yes, Mother," he said, shaking his head already.

161

Stevie watched in fascination, never having seen him talk to his mother before.

"The only son that I labored—"

"Thirty-six hours to bring into this world," Christian said, finishing her usual litany. "Yes, Mum, that would be me. The unruly, ungrateful wretch of a child you bore."

Stevie grinned, getting a vile look from Christian for it.

"Just so I am sure who I am talking to," Josephine said, none of her steam having been deterred.

"Yes, I know I haven't called in a long time, okay? I'm sorry. So how've you been?" he asked, hoping to steer the conversation to a better place, but inadvertently backing into another bad one. It was not going to be his day, obviously.

"Oh, just fine," she said smoothly. "Got to work a few days ago and ran into that very sweet Robert Debenshire, who was ever so kind as to congratulate me on my own son's engagement…"

"Fuck," Christian said, without thinking.

"Christian Joseph Collins!" Josephine exclaimed. "Don't you dare use profanity in my presence. You aren't too old to take over my knee, young man."

That had Stevie about to burst with laughter. She had her hand covering her mouth and her head turned to the passenger window.

"Mother, please?" Christian all but begged. "I'm sorry I didn't call you. Things have just been extremely hectic here…" His voice trailed off as he sighed.

Josephine was silent for a long moment, then said, "I know you have your own life now, Christian," she said, sounding hurt, all anger gone.

Christian winced as if she'd physically hit him.

Stevie spoke up then, her tone placating. "Miss Collins, please understand that Christian has been thinking about calling you, but every time he'd remember it would be too late to call. I know he didn't mean to hurt your feelings."

Again there was silence. Christian looked over at Stevie, his expression telling her he appreciated the effort, but he didn't think it would work.

"Who are you?" Josephine asked softly.

"Mum, that's Stevie—she's the woman I'm marrying."

"Stevie?" Josephine queried, obviously waiting for her to answer.

"Yes, ma'am?" Stevie said, suddenly feeling like the pupil that had talked out of turn.

"Do you love my son?"

"Yes, ma'am, with everything I have," Stevie said without hesitation.

The conviction in her voice made Christian close his eyes for a moment, enjoying the feeling. Josephine felt it too, all the way in England, and her heart was warmed.

"Mum, I want you to come out early for the wedding," Christian said, his voice still a bit affected by his feelings. "Maybe a couple of weeks?" he asked, glancing over at Stevie, who nodded.

"Oh, Christian, I don't want to get in the way."

"You're not in the way. I want you to get a chance to meet Stevie and get to know her. Besides, I haven't seen you in forever."

There was a sigh at the other end of the phone.

"Come on, Mum, I'll send you the ticket. What do you say?"

163

"I say I'll pay for my own ticket," Josephine said, smiling.

"Not bloody likely," Christian replied. "I'm paying for this, and don't argue with me."

"Did I raise my son to talk to me this way?"

"No," Christian said. "You raised your son to love his mother and take good care of her. Just tell me what date you can come."

They went about figuring out dates, and set it so she would arrive exactly two weeks before the wedding. Christian hung up feeling better.

"Thanks for that," he said, glancing at the phone.

"For what?" Stevie asked.

"For what you said to my mother. When you tried to explain why I hadn't called…"

"Oh," Stevie said, grinning, then shrugged. "No problem. It's my job to back you up, right?"

"Right," he said, grinning too, then grew serious. "She doesn't know about the… um… you know."

"About the attempt to check out?" Stevie asked gently.

"Yeah," he said. "Fortunately, no one thought to call her till afterward, and then it didn't really matter, since I was okay."

"Christian, she really should know about it, don't you think?"

"Why? So she can worry herself sick?" He shook his head. "No, she was too worried when I got shot. I don't want her going through that again."

Josephine had been absolutely devastated about him being shot two years before, but Joe had assured her that he was fine, that they'd take good care of him. At that point, Josephine had worried herself to the point of being so sick she couldn't even travel to see Christian

164

to make sure he was okay. He'd been careful to call her and let her know that he was fine. He'd mentioned Stevie then, but never really said much to his mother about his love life. It always started the questions about when he'd settle down and make her a grandmother. He was glad he could finally at least put that first part to rest. Grandkids? That was a whole other story he wouldn't even think about yet.

"Yeah, but you're fine now," Stevie pointed out.

"Yeah, so what's the point in telling her?"

"What if one of the Gang slips at the wedding, or before, and says something?"

Christian grimaced. "I'll warn them not to."

"Uh-huh…" Stevie muttered, unconvinced.

"Steve…"

"I know, I know, she's your mother—I'll let you handle it."

"Thank you."

"Any time," she replied, grinning.

***

Joe had the interesting experience of attending a sound check. He then got to watch Jordan on stage that night at the concert. She only did four of her songs, but she had him enchanted from the minute she opened her mouth. He watched the way she moved when she danced, seeing in every move the way she was with him. There was no question about how sexy the woman was.

A number of times during one particular song, she looked straight at him while she sang, talking about being taken to his bed and kept there forever in his arms. It served to remind him of how

165

easy it would be to get wrapped up in her. Jordan Tate had an incredible magnetism that was almost impossible to resist. She was like a force of nature, pulling people into her. He could see easily how she had made it. While people responded to the sexy, sultriness of her look, her voice was just as enchanting. It had a smoky, sexy sound. Sometimes her tone was clear and sweet, other times hard and grinding, almost as if she was having sex, then still other times it made you feel everything she said.

Joe found himself watching her every move, every look on her face, every flip of her long hair. Everything she did was so much a part of her, so consistent with what he'd seen of her. There really was nothing fake about her. There was no denying how beautiful she was. She wore a clinging skirt of gold silk that was low-slung on her hips and stopped pretty high on her shapely thighs. She wore a matching gold top that skimmed her shoulders, exposing more skin there than hiding it, and was cut off just past her breasts. It exposed the new tattoo that had captured so many people's attention in the entertainment news. She'd picked the outfit specifically for that purpose. Let them all see it. She wore black silk stockings and black heeled ankle boots. Her hair was loose and wild, framing her heart-shaped face. Her makeup was darker than he'd ever seen before too, but done in such a way that he couldn't put his finger on it. He wouldn't have believed she could be any more beautiful than he'd already seen, but she just glowed.

When she was finished, she came out to take her bow. Joe was in the front of the audience, but off to the side, not wanting to deny anyone a good seat. When Jordan had taken her bow, she turned specifically to him, bowing and inclining her head to him. She then knelt down, picking up a bunch of red roses that had been thrown on stage for her. She pulled one rose out, putting it to her nose, then walked to the edge of the stage, kneeling demurely in front of him and hand-ing him the rose. Without stopping to even think, Joe took the rose, reaching up to stroke her cheek with his finger, staring up into her eyes. She bit her lip and smiled at him. The entire stadium went wild. No one could resist a love story in the making.

Later, in Jordan's dressing room, Joe sat on the couch. He was waiting for her to get changed; they were going to an after party. She'd already showered by the time he'd gotten backstage after watching Billy and the Kid play. When he'd walked in, calling her name, she'd called out from the bathroom that she'd be out in a minute. She was listening to music, as he found she did a lot. The band she was listening to was an eighties rock group called Vixen. Joe vaguely remembered that every woman in the band had been really hot.

He was thinking back over all the bands he'd listened to over the years, and musing that he'd never been backstage at a concert like this one, when she walked out. He was sure his heart stopped then.

She was mostly dressed. She wore a pair of thigh-high stockings with the line up the back, black heels, and a rich burgundy velvet dress that started at her mid-thigh. The killer part of the ensemble was that under the dress she wore a black lace short-skirted corset. The dress wasn't buttoned, and the corset was totally on show. It molded to her perfectly shaped body, pressing her breasts upward, and it was so sexy he could barely breathe. She still wore her stage makeup, making her eyes sultry, and her hair had been washed and blow-dried, but framed her face in a way that made her look like she'd just climbed out of bed. She leaned against the doorjamb to the bath-room, putting one heel up against it, staring at him as she sang.

The song on the CD had changed and she was now singing it to him. The music was a hard, driving beat, and the words just about had him on his knees. The song was about rocking her world. As she continued to sing, Jordan walked over to the couch, looking down at Joe. She grinned, watching his eyes and enjoying her power. She straddled his lap, kissing him deeply as the song continued. When it finally ended, Joe eyed her with pursed lips.

"You're gonna be the death of me yet," he growled.

He took possession of her lips then, kissing her with more heat than he had since that first night. She'd pushed him beyond even his limits, but he managed somehow to rein himself in long enough to unfasten the top four hooks of her corset, freeing her breasts, and leaned down to move his mouth over her skin.

"Joe," she groaned, her hands burying themselves in his hair, holding his head to her.

He pulled her closer, caressing her everywhere, reaching up to pull off the velvet dress, exposing her arms. He kissed her skin, sucking at it, pulling her to him. She pressed down against him, making him groan.

"I need you, Joe, I need you."

In the end, they made love sitting on the couch, without even bothering to remove all their clothing. She straddled his body, kissing him deeply and crying out as he filled her. When they reached their climax, Jordan screamed his name over and over again, not stopping to think that anyone might hear. Joe's lips silenced her, even as he groaned in his own release.

As they both panted, trying to catch their breath, Joe raised an eyebrow at her.

"Does this dressing room even have a lock?" he asked.

"Oh shit," she said, grimacing and laughing at the same time.

Joe shook his head, grinning. "You are going to ruin my reputation, Ms. Tate."

"Oh yeah, right."

She moved off him enough so that he could pull his black jeans back up and fasten them, not bothering with his belt for the moment. Jordan pulled the skirt of the corset back down to cover her backside. At that very moment, Mark walked in.

Jordan's head snapped around, her gold eyes narrowing at him.

"Mark, you could knock," she snapped.

"Oh, so sorry," he said, not looking like he was in the slightest.

Jordan looked back at Joe and saw that he was watching the other man, his face calm. She did, however, feel his hands tighten on her hips, which she took to mean, Don't move.

"Um, Joe, this is Mark O'Brien, my manager. Mark, this is Joe Sinclair."

Joe inclined his head.

"I know who he is, Jordan," Mark snapped. "His face is all over the papers, with yours." His tone indicated that he thought it was some kind of design of Joe's.

Jordan looked at Joe and saw his lips curl in amusement. She was happy to see that Mark's barbs weren't hitting.

Mark waited for Joe to comment, then realized he wasn't going to say anything.

"I understand you're the reason this concert happened," Mark said, managing to make even that an insult.

"I suppose," Joe said. "But Jordan's the reason they're here."

"Yes, and you paid a bargain price of $400,000 for your front-row seat."

"She's worth ten times that," Joe replied mildly.

"Yeah, she's a pretty good lay."

Jordan could have killed him. If she'd had a knife she would have thrown it at his heart, or jumped up and slit his stupid throat. She was waiting for Joe to shove her away from him and storm off. She was almost afraid to look at him, but when she did, she saw that Joe's eyes were shards of ice but his face was still calm as could be.

"I was referring to her talent," Joe replied. "I thought as her manager you'd know that, but I can see I overestimated your intelligence."

Jordan's eyes widened as she did everything she could not to laugh. In the end, she coughed as a way of relieving the need to laugh her ass off. She glanced back at Mark and could see he'd literally been rendered speechless. There was anger in his eyes, and she couldn't help but enjoy his impotent fury. Mark turned and left, slamming the door.

Jordan turned back to Joe, and saw that he was looking at her.

"Joe, I'm sorry," she said, biting her lip.

He nodded, his face reflecting his chagrin at having learned something he didn't really want to know.

"Does he always treat you like that?" he asked after a few moments.

She shrugged. "Mostly when he's feeling threatened."

"He's lucky you were sitting here," Joe said calmly.

"Why?"

"Because if you hadn't been between us, he'd be on the floor right now."

Jordan's eyes widened. Somehow she seriously doubted that

was an empty comment. She'd seen Joe's body, and could sense easily the strength that was housed in that frame. He was easily able to lift her, moving her to where he wanted her when they made love, even when they were just lying in bed together. If he wanted to move and wanted to keep her with him, he simply picked her up and moved her, like a doll.

She didn't address the issue about sleeping with Mark, knowing that if Joe wanted to talk about it, she'd have to, but hoping he'd avoid it. He did, and she was relieved.

Joe's thinking was that it was Jordan's business who she slept with. He had no say, and wouldn't try to control her. He had a feeling she had enough of that from Mark. It nagged at him, making him wonder if Mark had been the one that had given her the bruises. He was big enough to be brutal, and he certainly was possessive of Jordan. He decided that he needed to have Mark O'Brien checked out.

They went to the after party.

Billy walked up to Joe, pulling him out on the dance floor during a slow song. Jordan knew that Billy Montague was married to another cop named Skyler Kristiani. All the same, she watched Billy like a hawk, feeling quite proprietary about Joe. Joe and Billy talked on the dance floor, her arms draped around his neck. Joe laughed a few times, shaking his head. Jordan seethed.

"She's fairly harmless," Jerith said from behind her.

Jordan jumped slightly, then glanced behind her. "Yeah, well, till she gets off my man, I consider her a threat," she said, grinning.

Jerith laughed, nodding. "Her own man should be here soon."

"Whose man?" asked Nicolette as she came up.

Jerith nodded toward Joe and Billy.

"Oh God." Nicolette rolled her eyes. "She loves to stir up trouble," she said, looking at Jordan.

Jordan nodded. "She's about to stir it up too much," she said, seeing Billy reach up to kiss Joe's lips softly.

"Oh, that was calculated," Jerith said, seeing Skyler walk into the club.

Jordan looked at Jerith, who nodded at Skyler, who was walking over to the dance floor, intent clear on his face. Jordan took a step toward the floor, but Jerith's hand on her shoulder stopped her.

"Just wait," he said.

As Jordan watched, Skyler walked over to Joe, extending his hand. Joe took it, grinning at the other man as they shook. They looked like they were discussing Billy; Joe shook his head, holding up his hands, nodding toward Jordan. Skyler looked toward her, then nodded and started to walk toward her. Jordan wasn't sure what was going on, but then Skyler was there standing in front of her. She had time to note that he was a very handsome man. He leaned down, whispering, "Sorry about this," then kissed her lips softly.

"Skyler James Kristiani!" Billy yelled from behind him, smacking him on the ass.

Skyler started laughing, looking down at Jordan apologetically. She stared back at him, canting her head to the side. "Revenge?"

Skyler nodded. "Yup."

He turned then, grabbing his wife by the hand and dragging her back out to the dance floor. Jordan looked to see Joe standing at the edge of the space, his eyes on her. He beckoned her with his finger. She grinned and walked over to him.

"Hi," he said, grinning.

"Did you give him permission for that?" she asked, raising an eyebrow.

"I'm not in the business of telling people whether or not they can kiss you, Jordan."

Jordan nodded, then reached up and pulled him down to her, kissing him deeply. "Thank you."

"For what?"

"Everything," she said. "I'll thank you better later."

"This was good enough."

"You don't want me to thank you later?" she asked, only partially kidding.

"Oh, you can make love to me later, but it won't be to thank me—it'll be because you want to."

"Oh, I'll definitely want to."

"Then I'll definitely let you," he replied with a grin.

She pulled him onto the dance floor, looking at Billy as she walked by, holding Joe's hand. Billy stared back at her a moment, then stuck her tongue out. Jordan laughed and did the same. Joe and Skyler glanced at each other and shook their heads.

Later that night, after she'd made love to him, they lay in bed talking.

"So how much longer do you have until your tour?" Joe asked, still caressing her arm as she lay on his chest.

"I have a week and a half."

Joe nodded.

"How much longer till you go back to the States?" she asked.

"Well, I've got to be in Vegas on the twenty-fifth of December, so by then at least."

173

"What's in Vegas on Christmas Night?"

"My cousin's wedding."

"Oh," she said, nodding. She grinned. "The one that's engaged to Stevie 'now.'"

Joe laughed softly, surprised that she remembered that little detail. "Yeah, him."

"So, what does the 'now' mean?"

Joe grimaced. "I kinda dated her."

"Kinda?"

"Yeah... Problem was, she was living with my cousin at the time."

"Oh..." she said, grimacing too. "What happened?"

"Well, it's hard to explain. But basically things were shitty with me at home, so I moved out. Things were shitty for her with Christian because of this house she was buying... and things just happened between her and me." He shrugged, looking unhappy. "In the end it was a mistake, because it really hurt my cousin. Almost fatally so."

"Fatally?" she asked, surprised.

"Yeah..." Joe said, looking quite ashamed of himself. "Christian tried to overdose on painkillers right before I took off to come here."

"Is that why you came here?"

"That was part of it," Joe said. "The other part was having Randy serve me with divorce papers out of nowhere." He shrugged. "I just felt the need to get away."

Jordan nodded, understanding that need quite well. She did it often enough. And she always came running home to London and Daddy.

"But your cousin and his girl obviously worked it out," she

pointed out. "I mean, if they're getting married now."

"Yeah," he said, still looking chagrined. "One more of my screw-ups covered."

"I don't think it was a screw-up."

"How do you come up with that?

"Well, when you said things were shitty with them, what did you mean exactly?" Jordan wanted to make sure she wasn't making too many assumptions.

"She was buying a house, and he'd made no moves about moving into it with her," Joe said. "Plus there was this woman in Seattle that she thought he was screwing around with."

"Seattle?"

"Yeah, he travels for the department as kind of a computer consultant."

"Okay, so why do you think he didn't want to move into the house with her?"

"I figure it was a commitment issue. Christian's really paranoid about getting tied to one woman. Long story there."

"Okay, so he's commitment phobic," she said, grinning. "Like most men."

"No, he's worse than most. He pretty much gets any woman he wants, so I tend to think it's a major thing for him to give that up."

"He gets any woman he wants? He look a lot like you then?"

Joe laughed, shaking his head. "Well, he does some, but he's a very dark version of me. All black hair, and dark skin color. But he does have my family's eyes, the blue."

Jordan nodded, thinking that yes, this Christian probably was handsome. "But he's not you," she said, smiling up at him.

Joe grinned, shaking his head again.

"Okay, so he was basically not appreciating what he had with her, right?" Jordan asked.

"I guess, yeah."

"And if she was getting with you, then she didn't apparently appreciate him too much either, right?"

"Okay…" Joe said, trying to figure out where she was going.

"So, her being with you made him wake up and see what he was losing by playing," she said. "And him trying to kill himself made her realize that she could lose him for good. That's why they're getting married now. They both figured it out."

Joe gave her a considering look, then shook his head slowly. "How do you do that?"

"Do what?"

"See things like that? I mean, that wasn't really a big leap there, but you don't even know these two."

"No, Joe, but I've seen how you are. I've heard about your friends. I can only imagine how intense these people are in person. I think people like that need bigger shocks to make them change their minds. I'd say attempting suicide would pretty much be the be all and end all."

Joe had to agree with her there.

"Okay, so you're going to their wedding on Christmas Night," Jordan said, as if they'd never left that conversation. "Then what?"

"Then back to work, babe."

She nodded, grinning.

"And what's after the tour here in Europe?" Joe asked.

"America."

"How long is the tour?"

"Three months."

"And America?"

"Little over six months."

"Wow…" he said, shaking his head. "That's a lot."

"Yeah, but I don't have to get up and go to an office every day, and I get to sing for people," she said, smiling. "It's a great trade-off."

Joe smiled. "Yeah, I can see that you love performing."

"Can you?" she asked, grinning.

"Uh-huh…" he said, leaning down to kiss her.

She reached up, pulling him close. Their conversation was forgotten a few minutes later as he made love to her again. Jordan found that she was really quite addicted to him. Of all the lovers she'd had, Joe just seemed to be the best. She'd had good lovers before, but Joe had a way about him. She wondered if it was just the idea that they had so little time together that made things seem more intense. At this point she wasn't ready to analyze her feelings. All she wanted to do was enjoy the time she had with him.

They spent the entire week and a half enjoying being together. During the day, Joe spent a lot of time with the kids. Jordan joined them a number of times. Joe found quickly that Kat liked Jordan. He thought it was probably that Kat was missing the female influence in her life at that point. Which, of course, made him feel bad for having the kids away from their mother and even Susan for so long. But he sat one day watching Kat and Jordan talk. Jordan had gone to join Kat, who was drawing a picture. Joe couldn't hear their conversation, but he could see Kat's face light up when Jordan pointed to something on the page. Kat was his consummate artist. And it was obvious that she was connecting with the artist in Jordan.

There were a few games of ball played with the kids on the days when it wasn't too cold outside. There were also a few sessions of video watching and going to the movies with the children. Joe found that he appreciated Jordan's willingness to spend time with them all. He knew that he could never date any woman that didn't accept his kids. They were a very large part of his life, and there was no way he could care about someone that didn't understand that and try to share it with him. He'd been hesitant with Jordan, since she didn't have any kids of her own, and he'd assumed she wouldn't be able to adjust to them. He also didn't want anyone faking it with the children for the sake of being with him. They deserved better than half-assed attempts.

To Joe's surprise, neither of the kids questioned who Jordan was. It was as if they understood the situation. He wondered at that, but didn't know what all they'd been told. He knew Randy was very honest with them, and that she'd always be fair with her explanations, never blaming him solely for anything. It was quite possible that Randy had explained the situation to the children. It dragged at him. What had she told them? He found the need to ask.

"Kat," he said one morning when she'd crawled up onto his lap while he was drinking coffee at the dining room table.

"Yes, Daddy?" she asked, her blond hair, the same color as Randy's, all tousled from sleep.

"Did Mommy talk to you and JT about what's happening?" he asked, trying to phrase it so he wouldn't say something she didn't know.

Kat nodded.

"What did she tell you?"

"She said you and her were going to be friends now."

"What?" he asked, surprised.

"Mommy said that you and her weren't going to live in the same house anymore, but that you were always going to be friends."

Joe looked at his daughter for a long moment. So Randy had planned on divorcing him for a while.

"Did Mommy say why?" he asked.

Kat nodded again. "She said that you needed more."

"More?" Joe asked, glancing up as he noticed Jordan standing in the doorway, her expression one of concern.

Kat nodded again. Joe nodded too, not sure if Kat comprehended what that meant, but thinking he probably did.

His eyes met Jordan's for a long moment. She gave him a small smile, not sure what she could say at that point.

The day before Jordan was to leave for her European tour, Joe arranged for them to have the entire day together alone. He took her driving in the country, stopping anywhere and everywhere she wanted to. He found that she had a thing about taking pictures, and she took a lot of the countryside and a lot with him in them. They even found someone to take a picture of them together sitting on the rocks overlooking the ocean. As they drove back toward the house, Joe stopped in London proper. Jordan was surprised when he actually parked near Piccadilly Circus. Taking her hand, he led her down to Tower Records.

"What are we doing?" she asked, raising an eyebrow at him.

"I need something," he said, grinning.

He led her over to the pop/rock music section. He stood looking over the artists' names until he came to the *T*s. He picked out both of her CDs, the new one and the first.

She grinned. "I could get you those for free."

"Nah, I have to support my girlfriend's clothing habit."

He'd found that she was basically a clothes fanatic. She had tons of clothing. He didn't think he'd seen her in the same outfit twice in the two and a half weeks they'd been together. And with that went all the shoes. "Imelda Marcos eat your heart out" was her favorite phrase. She loved boots, so those were what she owned the most of, in all lengths, styles, and colors.

When they walked up to the register, the counter person recognized her. The young man, whose name tag read Brent, looked like he'd died and gone to heaven. Joe just grinned as he drooled. When the clerk finally managed to get the sale rung up, Joe handed him his credit card. The other guy read the name.

"Hey, you're that dude that's dating her," Brent said.

Joe looked back at him for a moment, thinking, *Not too bright, this one,* then nodded. He glanced at Jordan, who was doing her best not to laugh.

"Did you really get a tattoo that Jordan Tate designed?" Brent asked.

Joe looked mystified, then remembered that apparently that little trip had been documented by the local gossip mill.

"Yeah."

"Can I see it, man?" Brent asked, his face alight.

Joe looked back at him for a long moment, not sure why anyone would really care. But then he reached over and pulled his shirt sleeve up.

"Too right!" Brent said, giving Joe the thumbs up.

Joe simply smiled, thinking this whole fame thing was already getting annoying. He looked at Jordan, and she just grinned at him.

They finally made it out of the store, but not before she had to sign about ten autographs. Joe stood by watching, his look wary, his eyes keeping track of everyone around them.

"You okay?" she asked when they got back to the car.

"Yeah, why?" he asked, glancing at her over the roof as they got in.

"You just seemed pretty tense back there with the crowd."

"Not tense, honey, alert—there's a big difference."

"So you were doing the cop thing?"

He laughed at the term, then nodded. "It's a habit."

"I imagine," she said, then gave him a sidelong look. "Ever consider personal security?"

He looked over at her for a moment, then shook his head. "I'll guard your body for hours at a time, any time you want me to," he said, his look suggestive. "But you couldn't pay me enough to do bodyguard work."

"Why not?"

"I don't deal with pampered, over-paranoid attention junkies."

"Is that what we are?" she asked, grinning.

He grinned too. "Some of ya."

Jordan nodded.

He handed her the discs, pointing to the top one, which happened to be her latest album. "Put it in."

"Eww…" she said, making a face.

"Put it in."

"I don't listen to my own music."

"You do today."

Halfway through the first song, he looked over at her, noticing that in spite of herself, she was singing with the words.

"So tell me about this one," he said. "What was the mind-set here when you wrote it?"

"Oh," she said, grinning, "this was just me giving my theory about life and the meaning of it."

He listened, smiling a few times at her lyrics.

Once they got to the house, Jordan went in to take a shower while Joe continued to listen to her songs. By the time she'd gotten out, dried off, and blow-dried her hair, he was listening to her first album. She went to lie on the bed, singing along with the song that was playing.

Joe moved to prop himself up on one elbow, looking down at her. It was a song that talked about not being able to enjoy anything without this person there with her.

"Who's this one about?" he asked, grinning, thinking he already sounded like a jealous boyfriend.

"My daddy," she said, smiling.

"Oh," he said, grimacing. "I thought it was some other guy."

"Well, he's a guy too."

"Smartass."

She laughed.

When that song ended the next one started. Joe could see a

change in her instantly. She moved to sit up, like a physical manifestation of becoming very wary all of a sudden. Reaching over, he picked up the CD cover. The song was called "Damaged."

"What's this about?" he asked, before the words began.

She shook her head, not looking at him. "I wrote it when I was right out of The Musicians Institute," she said. She picked up a pillow and set it in her lap, like she needed something to put between them. She hugged the pillow as the words began.

Joe was riveted. She wouldn't look at him as she sang. She turned away, her face showing the pain of what she was singing. Her hair, usually tucked back behind her ears to get it out of her face, was like a curtain she was hiding behind. The lyrics spoke of sadness and a feeling of being alone. They also spoke of being afraid and "damaged." Joe suspected there was a lot more to this song than Jordan wanted to admit.

He felt something in his heart give then, and he knew he was falling for her. This was the first time he'd really seen her vulnerable. Even the morning he'd found her in her flat, when he was sure she'd been hurt, she'd put on a pretty brave front. The look in her golden eyes when she sang those words went straight to his heart.

"What does that song mean, Jordan?" he asked softly.

It was basically the same question he'd asked about every song. This time she wouldn't look at him, or answer him. After a long time, she shrugged.

"It's just a song."

"Bullshit," he said gently, moving to sit up. "You were able to tell me about every other song. Why is this one different?"

She shook her head, still not looking at him. Her fingers picked nervously at the pillow in her arms.

183

"It was about a relationship I had," she said finally, hoping to placate him.

"He hurt you, didn't he?"

Jordan's lips tightened, as if trying to keep herself from answering. Finally she nodded.

"Why do you let him?" Joe asked, his words not really phrased as a question.

Her head came up then, her eyes staring back into his warily. Then they slid away from him.

"I don't know what you're talking about," she said as her eyes narrowed.

"You know what and who I'm talking about, Jordan," Joe said, his voice still soft. She didn't answer. "It's Mark, isn't it?"

She couldn't stop the sharp intake of breath. It was instant. She was shocked and scared at the same time.

"No!" she almost yelled.

"Jordan…"

"No, Joe, okay—no," she said, her body tensing.

"Yes, Jordan," he said, touching her under the chin, bringing her eyes back to his. "And he's still hurting you."

Her eyes widened, and Joe could feel her begin to shake.

"What are you talking about?" she asked.

"That day I came to your flat," he said softly.

"I told you, I fell."

"I know what you told me. And I know you were lying to me."

"How?" she asked, her voice a scared whisper.

"Jordan, I've been a cop for a lot of years. I know the signs of abuse when I see them."

"But you didn't say anything..."

"No. Because I knew you'd run." He pinned her with a look. "Like you want to run right now."

Again he'd surprised her. How did he know she was trying to think of a way out at this very moment? What excuses could she make to leave?

"Jordan," he said beseechingly. "Why do you let him hurt you?" He tilted her chin up again, searching her eyes. "What does he have on you?"

She pulled away, turning her back to him. His hands shot out, taking her shoulders. He was afraid she was going to try to leave. He felt her tense. Sliding his hands around her shoulders, he pulled her back against his chest gently.

"I'm not going to hurt you, Jordan," he whispered against her hair. "I just want to help."

She leaned back against him, her head resting against the hollow of his shoulder.

"You can't help, Joe," she said, sounding so lost.

He kissed her temple, smoothing his hands over her arms. He held her like that for a while, then moved to lie back on the bed, pulling her down with him. She turned over, snuggling against him. He just held her, stroking her back and her hair.

Putting a finger to her chin, he tilted her face up to his, looking down at her.

"Just know that if you ever want my help, I'll be here for you, okay?"

She nodded, her eyes searching his. He pulled her closer then, kissing her softly, his hand cupping her cheek gently. She kissed him back, as if apologizing for her silence. When they made love this time, it was with a great deal more tenderness than passion. Jordan felt like Joe was trying to offset the hurt that had been done to her with his own gentleness.

Afterward they lay together quietly for a long time. He was on his side, she on her back. He stroked her skin under the covers he'd pulled up over the both of them.

"I'm going to miss you so much," she said softly.

Joe smiled. "I'm going to miss you too, babe."

She looked up at him. "Are you?" she asked, sounding doubtful.

"Yeah, Jordan. I will."

She bit her lip, grinning. "Good."

"Oh ho," he said, laughing. "She wants me to miss her."

"Of course I do."

"Of course."

She looked serious then. "Joe, I want to see you."

"You will."

"No, I mean, I really want to see you," she said, moving to sit up, looking down at him.

"You lost me, babe," he said, mystified.

She sighed. "I mean, I don't want you just saying, 'Yeah, yeah, we'll see each other,' and then we never do." She put her hand on his chest. "I need to see you, Joe."

He covered her hand with his as he reached up with his other to pull her back down to him, kissing her lips. "We will see each other, Jordan," he promised.

"When?" she asked, sounding almost desperate now.

"Babe, we will, somehow…" he said, not knowing what to say.

In three weeks they'd be on separate continents. She'd be on her tour; he'd be headed back to work. He had no idea how or when he'd see her. They wanted to, so they'd find a way. They had to.

CHAPTER 6

Two days after Christian helped to take down Rosa Delario, he walked up to Stevie's cubicle.

"Ready to go?" he asked, leaning against the doorway.

"Yep," she said as she logged off her computer.

She stood and stretched, then turned around to catch him watching her.

"What?" she asked.

"Nothing," he said, grinning.

He'd been watching her move, appreciating the way she looked in her jeans and emerald green silk tank top. There was no denying how sexy she was. Her hair was pulled back in a long braid, but the color of it, set off by the color of her shirt, just made it seem richer. She walked over to him, and he reached out, touching her jawline as he leaned down to kiss her lips. She held his waist as they kissed.

She glanced down then.

"What's that?" she asked, motioning to the envelope he had in his hand.

He looked down at it, then turned it so he could read the label.

"Well, let's see," he said with a grin. "It's addressed to Spider Nguyen, lieutenant in charge of narcotics…"

Her eyes widened hopefully. "You're doing it?"

He inclined his head. "I'm doing it."

She smiled brightly, then balled her fist and did a little "Yesss!" gesture.

Christian grinned, raising an eyebrow. "He hasn't approved the transfer just yet, babe."

"Yeah," she said, narrowing her green eyes. "And if he doesn't, I'm quitting."

"Like hell you are," he said, taking her hand and leading her out of her cubicle.

He stopped in Spider's office, dropping the envelope in his in-basket. Spider wasn't there.

They hadn't been in the car more than twenty minutes when Christian's phone rang.

"Yes?" he said, hitting the hands-free button.

"Blue, it's Midnight."

"Hi, Chief, what's up?"

"I hear tell that you want to transfer to narcotics," Midnight said, grinning.

Christian's mouth dropped open for a moment. He shook his head in amazement. "Jesus, I just put in for it like twenty minutes ago."

"Yes, well, news travels fast around here," Midnight said, winking at Spider, who sat in her office. "So, you really want to do this?"

"Well," Christian said, rubbing the bridge of his nose and glancing over at Stevie, "I'm told I'd be pretty good at it."

"That's what I've heard too," Midnight said, having spent the last ten minutes talking to Spider about it. "So you want it?"

"That easy?"

"That easy."

"Well, yeah."

"Okay, so who am I going to get to do my computer stuff now?" Midnight asked. "Got any suggestions?"

Christian nodded. "Yeah, use Erin."

"Really?" Midnight asked, surprised. She'd known Erin had been working with him, but she didn't know how much the girl had actually picked up.

"Yeah, she's actually really good on the computer, and she's got the best handle on the way it works. I can teach her the rest."

"That would be a pretty big promotion for her," Midnight said, thinking out loud. "But since it's a consultant position, I don't really have to advertise... Think she'd be interested?"

"Interested in making the kind of money I do?" Christian asked, as if it wasn't even a question. "Um, yeah, I'd say she'd be interested..."

Midnight laughed softly. "Well, she wouldn't make quite what you do to start with, Blue. I couldn't send her out to consult until I knew she could handle the projects."

"True, but it would still be more than she makes now, right?" he asked, concerned about Erin getting overworked without compensation.

"I take care of my people, Blue," Midnight chided.

"Of course you do," Christian said, grimacing. "Sorry, Chief."

"I'll let you live."

"Whew, good thing," he said. "Ah, speaking of pay... How much do narcs make?"

Midnight was silent for a minute, then said, "Well, it isn't consultant pay. You wouldn't get all the bonuses you've been getting..."

She trailed off as she thought about it. "But I think between base and the OT that you'll end up doing, you'll break about even to start with."

Christian nodded, glancing over at Stevie and seeing by the look on her face that she hadn't thought about that part. He looked thoughtful for a long moment.

"Alright, Chief, I'd say you got yourself another narc."

"Fantastic," Midnight said, smiling. "I'll set you up with a meeting with Spider and Dave—you'll need to do the usual run-through of training."

"Figured that much."

"Welcome to narcotics," Spider said from the other side of Midnight's desk.

"Uh-huh…"

Spider laughed, as did Midnight. They hung up a few minutes later.

Christian glanced over at Stevie.

"Trying to break me, financially?" he asked, grinning.

"Yeah, that was my goal," Stevie replied, smiling sweetly.

Christian shook his head. A one-time runner for a drug dealer was now going to be the one busting them. Would wonders never cease?

Two weeks later, Christian was knee deep in training. He was training Erin on the program, teaching her the ins and outs of loading it and testing it, trying to instill in her the confidence she'd need to go to other departments and load the program for them as well as modify it to their specifications. He was also into the first week of a drug recognition training course put on by LAPD. He was driving back and forth between LA and San Diego almost every day. He hadn't seen Stevie in a week either, since she was off working a case Dave had needed her help on.

Dave had asked to "borrow" his fiancée, citing that he needed a "wife" on this case for the time being. Christian had grinned and asked if in turn he could borrow Dave's wife.

Dave's response had been, "Touch her and I'll have to kill you, Collins," but his grin had spoiled the threat effectively.

Everyone knew by this time about the present Dave had given Susan for her birthday, and it reinforced what everyone already knew—that there was nothing Dave Dibbins wouldn't do for his wife. A number of the members had joked that Dave was going to have to do double overtime from there on out just to pay for the Mercedes. Dave took all the jokes in his stride; he knew his friends.

Christian was sitting at the computer with Erin when he got a call on his cell phone.

"Yes?"

"Christian?" said his mother.

"Mum, hi," he said, glancing at the clock. It was 5:00 in the evening there—probably not an emergency. He relaxed.

"I wanted to let you know when my flight is coming in," Josephine said hesitantly.

"Oh, yeah, great," Christian said cheerfully, cussing to himself. He'd forgotten about her coming to town early for the wedding.

"I'll be there on December twelfth at 9:30 a.m. Is that alright?"

"Of course, Mum, it's perfect," Christian said, thinking it was anything but, but he wasn't about to tell his mother that.

She'd be there in two days. Christian had no idea how he was going to handle this. He was supposed to be in LA when she arrived. He didn't know if Stevie would be back in town by then. After he hung up he tossed the cell phone on his desk.

"Shit!"

"What?" Erin said, worried.

He sighed. "My mother will be here in two days, and I haven't a clue what I'm gonna do to pick her up at the airport. I've got to be in LA, and Stevie may not be back yet…"

"I could pick her up, if you want."

He looked at her for a moment. "You'd do that?"

"Of course I would!" she said, giving him a look that said, *Duh!*

He grinned. "Guess I should have known that, huh?"

"Um, yeah," she said, grinning back.

"If you could, Erin… I'd love you for at least a week."

"A whole week, huh?" she said, laughing.

"At least."

"You got yourself a deal, handsome," she said, winking at him.

Two days later, Erin stood waiting at the gate for Josephine Collins. Christian had showed her his mother's picture, so she knew who to look for. She was still surprised by the little woman that walked off the plane. Josephine seemed so delicate, Erin wondered at her being Christian's mother. Christian just seemed so substantial, compared to this tiny woman.

"Hi, Ms. Collins, I'm Erin," she said, walking up to Josephine and smiling warmly.

"Hello, Erin," Josephine said, her English accent making her sound even more diminutive.

"Christian asked me to pick you up—he had a class he had to be at this morning," Erin explained as she gently took Josephine's carry-on bag from her, looping it over her shoulder then guiding her away from the gate toward the baggage claim.

"A class?"

"Yes," Erin said, smiling. "He's taking a drug recognition course from LAPD, and they had a test today, so he had to be there for the morning portion. He promised to be back by around noon."

Josephine nodded. "I hope I haven't put you to any trouble, Erin."

"Nope," Erin said, grinning endearingly. "Your son promised to love me for a least a week. I'm getting a good deal."

Josephine looked back at Erin for a long moment, obviously not understanding the joke.

"I work with him," Erin explained. "He's always teasing me about love because I'm a big-time romantic."

"Oh, I see." Josephine nodded, surprised that her usually staunch, serious son teased anyone. "My son actually teases?" she couldn't resist asking.

"Oh, all the time," Erin said. "Especially now—he's so much happier these days."

"Why is that?"

"Definitely because of Stevie."

"That's the girl he's marrying, correct?" Josephine asked, knowing her son's philandering ways.

"Yes," Erin said, grinning. "I was so happy to hear that they're getting married."

"Why is that?" Josephine asked as they reached the baggage claim.

"They're really perfect for each other."

"How so?"

"Well, I'm sure you know your son can pretty much get any lady he sets his sights on…" Erin said, wondering if she should be telling Christian's mom this stuff.

Josephine nodded, remembering well how easily her son got and discarded women.

"Well, Stevie is pretty different."

"How is she different?" Josephine asked, canting her head to the side in interest.

"Well, she doesn't really let him get away with much," Erin said. "I mean, she's not the type of woman to beg for his attention, and I really think that's something he needs." Erin bit her lip, wondering if she was overstepping here.

Josephine thought about it for a moment. "So you're saying that she keeps my son in line?"

Erin laughed softly. "Yes, she does. But she really loves him too," she qualified.

"And you know this how?"

"Well, when he was in the hospital a month ago—"

"In the hospital?" Josephine asked, alarmed.

Erin paled, realizing she'd just said the wrong thing. "Um…"

"Why was he in the hospital?"

"He… um… well…"

She hadn't realized Josephine didn't know about Christian's suicide attempt, and she knew that he would kill her if she told his

195

mother.

"Well?" Josephine asked, all mother lioness at that point.

"I'm sorry," Erin said, shaking her head. "You really should ask Christian about this. He'll kill me if I say anything else."

"Kill you?" Josephine queried, raising a black eyebrow at her, just as her son did so often.

"Josephine, Christian is a very private person—I'm sure you know that," Erin said. "And I just way overstepped myself. Please, for the sake of my friendship with him, don't ask me to talk about that."

Josephine was taken aback by Erin's earnest plea, and found herself acquiescing to the girl. She was, however, determined to find out what had happened.

To that end, she nailed her son with the question the moment they were alone.

"Why were you in the hospital a month ago?" she asked on the drive to the house that afternoon.

"What?" Christian asked, looking stunned.

"You heard me, young man."

Christian sighed. "Erin told you I was in the hospital?"

"Oh, no," Josephine replied. "You're not going to lay this at the feet of that sweet girl. You should have told me, Christian Joseph Collins. Why were you in the hospital? What happened?"

Christian blew his breath out in a deep sigh, his lips taut in his agitation. He shook his head. "I didn't tell you because I was fine, Mum."

"Why were you in the hospital?" she asked again, not willing to be put off.

"Because I took too many Vicodin."

"Were you hurt?"

"Yeah... I had cracked ribs."

"How did you crack your ribs?" she asked, sounding alarmed again.

Christian shook his head. He wasn't getting out of this no matter what, was he?

"Because I got into a fight, and my ribs got cracked."

"Who could possibly hit that hard? What were you fighting about?" Josephine knew her son well enough to know when he was hiding something.

"Someone had taken something of mine."

"What of yours could possibly be worth fighting over?" she asked, sickened by the idea of her son fighting over some piece of property.

Christian was silent for a long time, gripping the steering wheel of the Viper, his face set in a stubborn line.

"Christian?" his mother said. "I want an answer. I did not raise you to place so much value on possessions as to get yourself hurt to protect them. What did someone take of yours that could mean so much?"

"Stevie," he said, shocking her into silence for a few minutes.

When she recovered, she said, "Someone took her? You mean she was kidnapped?"

Christian gave a sardonic laugh, shaking his head and looking down. "No, Mum. Someone took her away from me."

"You mean, she went with another man?"

"Yeah."

"Well, Christian, if she wanted another man, how could she possibly be worth the effort?" Josephine asked, thinking her son deserved better.

"She's worth everything," Christian said, with more feeling in his voice than his mother had ever heard from him.

"Not if she fell for another man, she's not."

"She didn't fall for him," he said. "She just… I was pushing her away, because I was afraid of committing to her, and Stevie's nothing like any woman I've ever been with. She lets me push her away, and doesn't come begging me to take her back in. She walks. And she walked."

"Right into the arms of another man," Josephine said, still feeling defensive for her son's sake.

"No, Mum, that's not how it happened," he said, sighing. He knew how things looked on the outside, but also that he had to make her understand. "Look, Stevie is the kind of woman that doesn't take getting pushed aside. Her attitude is that if I don't want her, she'll leave and find something or someone else. And believe me, she could have a lot of guys, Mum. She's beautiful, sexy as hell, and as feisty as they come. Most guys couldn't hold on to her for long."

Josephine looked back at him, surprised to hear him defending this woman. "So why do you love her?"

Christian looked thoughtful for a long moment, then shook his head. "I don't know if I can explain it… She makes me feel so damned good… She's this incredibly strong woman, with more fire than I've ever seen in any woman I've ever dated. But at the same time, she has this vulnerability about her that she never shows anyone. But I've seen it, and it makes me want to be the one to be there for her when she's weak. She's been through so much," he said, shaking his head

198

as if he couldn't fathom it. "Her father was killed in the line of duty when she was eleven. Then when she was seventeen her older sister married a man that Stevie became extremely attached to. He was like the older brother she never had. He was killed in the line of duty when Stevie was twenty-seven."

Josephine's eyes widened as she thought how horrible it must be to lose two people that you loved that much. "My lord, that must have destroyed her…"

"You'd think it would," Christian said. "But it didn't, Mum. In fact, it was Stevie who went after the man who was responsible for her brother-in-law's death. She gave up everything to do it, too."

"What do you mean, she gave up everything?"

"She quit her job with the department, a job she'd wanted to do her entire life. And she basically infiltrated this drug dealer's operation, becoming his bodyguard. She got enough evidence on the guy to put him in prison, and eventually made the arrest with the help of another narcotics officer here in the department. But she could have gone to jail for what she did. She worked for this drug dealer for a year and a half, because she wanted to make him pay for what he did to her family. She risked her life and her freedom to do it. That's the kind of woman she is, Mum. She does everything all the way."

Josephine nodded, surprised by what she was hearing. "I need to know that she loves my son as much as he loves her."

"Well, the way to know that with her is simple. Nothing and no one makes Stevie react if she doesn't care about it or them. She left me when she thought I was sleeping with another woman. She came back when she knew she'd hurt me badly with the other guy. The fact that she came to me is one thing, but the fact that she literally begged me to forgive her, when she had literally nothing to gain by doing so, other than maybe my wrath, told me everything. She risked it to make sure that I was okay."

"Okay?" Josephine queried, catching the connotation of the word. "Why wouldn't you have been okay? You said you were alright when you went to the hospital."

"Well, I didn't die," he said. "Even though that's what I was trying for."

Josephine looked horrified. "You were trying to kill yourself, Christian?"

He closed his eyes for a moment as he nodded.

"Why?" she gasped.

"Because I'd lost her, because I was sure I'd never get her back," he said, shaking his head miserably. "Because she was with someone that I knew I could never compete against."

"Who?" Josephine asked in spite of herself.

Christian was silent for a long moment, then looked over at her. "Joe."

Josephine stared back at him, unable to fathom what had happened. "She was dating your cousin?" she asked tonelessly.

Christian nodded.

"I can't believe Joseph would do that," Josephine said. "What about his wife?"

"They're getting divorced."

"Oh my lord," Josephine said. "So this girl went after your cousin?"

"Mother, it's not as simple as that, and from what I understand, it was a mutual desire."

"All the same..."

Every time Josephine decided she might like this Stevie O'Neil, she heard something else that made her change her mind again.

"Mum, she could have stayed with him," Christian said. "You and I both know how much money Joe has. On top of that, he's got much more power in this department than I'll ever have. He's a bloody legend here."

"So what?" Josephine said defensively. "Either she loves you, or she loves him."

"She loves me. She didn't love him."

Josephine shook her head, thinking her son was making a mistake with this woman. She said as much.

"I think you're making a mistake, Christian," she said, reaching out to touch his arm. "I think you're blinded by this girl, because she's the first woman you've ever dated that isn't enthralled so much with you that you can walk all over her. That doesn't make it love. And if you love her more than she loves you, it will never work and you'll never be happy."

Christian looked at his mother for a long moment. He knew Stevie loved him—he knew it. But he didn't know how to convince his mother of that.

"Mum, if she didn't love me, why would she marry me?" he asked. "You don't know her. She is so far from the marrying kind, it's not even funny. But she's marrying me. And you have to believe that I know what I'm doing here."

Josephine looked back at him, not convinced. But she was definitely ready to meet this woman who obviously had her son's heart wrapped around her little finger.

Three days after Josephine arrived, Christian got a call from Dave while they were driving home from shopping. Josephine had decided she needed to at least buy a dress to wear to the wedding in case it actually happened.

"Yeah?" he said, answering on hands-free.

"Hey, Blue, it's Dave."

"Heya, Dave, does this mean I'm getting my lady back?" Christian asked with a grin.

"Yes, as a matter of fact it does," Dave said, smiling.

"Cool," Christian said. Josephine watched.

"Wanted to warn you, though…"

"Uh-oh… What?" Christian asked, his features clouding instantly.

"It's her shoulder again, man," Dave said, blowing out his breath.

"Bad?"

"Caught her throwing up a couple of times."

"Shit," Christian said, grimacing. "Okay, thanks for the warning."

"No prob. Take it easy."

"Yeah, you too," Christian said, hanging up.

He tapped his fingers on the steering wheel in agitation. Josephine could see that his mind was going a mile a minute.

"So what does that mean?" she asked.

Christian glanced over at her, as if just remembering that she was there. "Stevie's shoulder is giving her trouble again," he said, then, seeing that she was waiting for more of an explanation, he continued, "When she was shot over two years ago, it was one of the places hit. She's still having way more pain in it than she should."

Josephine nodded, thinking about what Dave had said about having "caught" her throwing up. "And she was throwing up why?"

"She probably did something that hurt it worse, and when she's in extreme pain, like most people, she throws up."

"But he 'caught' her?"

Christian gave her a wry grin. "Stevie isn't exactly the weepy, whiney type, Mum. When she's hurting she doesn't talk about it—she just deals with it. And I'm betting she was hiding out when she threw up so Dave wouldn't report it to me."

"Oh…" Josephine said, surprised.

But she didn't ask any other questions. They'd basically avoided the topic of Stevie for the last couple of days. She'd gotten the very definite impression from her son that he did not want to discuss Stevie if all she was going to say to him was that he was making a mistake. Josephine was doing her best to reserve her judgment until she actually met Stevie O'Neil, even though she was already fairly convinced that the girl was no good for Christian.

When they drove up to the house, Stevie's Trans Am was sitting out front. Christian got out of the Viper and walked inside, looking around. He spotted a bottle of water on the counter; glancing at the cabinet, he saw that it was half open. He nodded to himself and walked down the hall to their bedroom. Josephine followed at an unobtrusive distance. She peeked in the open doorway, seeing a young woman lying on the bed wearing a tank top and sweatpants. Christian stood next to the bed, looking down at her.

"Babe?" he said softly.

"Mmm?" she half-moaned.

Christian lay down carefully next to her, reaching out to touch her shoulder gently.

"Here, babe?" he asked.

She nodded, wincing.

"Okay, okay..." he said soothingly. He picked up the ice pack that was lying next to her on the bed. "Hold on to me," he said warningly.

Josephine saw a small, delicate hand reach up and take hold of a handful of his shirt.

Christian put the ice pack to a bare shoulder. She flinched, making the slightest sound of pain.

"I know, honey, I'm sorry," he said softly, his lips brushing her forehead.

She nodded in response.

"Okay, I gotta press here..."

She let out a hiss as he pressed against the shoulder, her foot moving in what was obviously reined-in pain.

"I know, babe, I know..." he said, his voice soothing. His fingers brushed at her cheek. "So how did you do? You bust a lot of little bastards today?" he asked with a grin.

Stevie laughed slightly, obviously still in pain, her breath coming in short gasps even as she nodded.

"Yeah?" he asked. "How many?"

"Five," she said in a gasp.

"Five? Wow, impressive... bet I can do six in one takedown."

"Bullshit," she said, grinning.

"So you get any good drugs?"

"No, just three pounds of meth."

"That all?" he asked. "Kiddie stuff."

"Fuck you, Collins."

"Any time you want, O'Neil," he replied, smiling.

She sighed, moving her head against his shirt.

"Painkiller kicking in?" he asked gently.

"Mmhmm."

"Good," he said, reaching down to stroke her hair, his lips pressing against her forehead. "You'll be okay, babe."

She sighed, and relaxed against him. Christian looked up then, and saw his mother standing in the doorway watching them. His eyes connected with hers, then went down to Stevie, lying against him. Leaning down, he kissed her forehead again, keeping his lips pressed against her skin. Josephine went off to leave them alone. It was definitely a surprising scene she'd witnessed. Seeing her usually cavalier son taking such tender care of this woman made her realize how much he really did seem to love her. Once again, Josephine told herself she'd do her best to give this girl a chance.

An hour after they'd gotten home, Christian wandered out into the living room to find his mother sitting in the chair next to the couch, reading a book. Josephine looked up when he walked in.

"She's asleep," he explained.

Josephine nodded. Christian sat down on the couch, turning on the TV with the remote. They sat in companionable silence for the next couple of hours. Christian got up every so often to go and check on Stevie.

They were watching a movie when Stevie wandered in, walking into the kitchen without even looking over at them. She reached into the freezer and pulled out two popsicles, then opened a cupboard and took out a bowl. She proceeded to unwrap the popsicles and dropped them in the bowl, then put the bowl in the microwave and set it for thirty seconds. Josephine glanced over at her son and saw that he was watching Stevie with a grin. This was obviously normal behavior for her. She reached into the drawer for a spoon and turned around, stopping dead in her tracks as the microwave beeped. She was staring openmouthed at Josephine. It was obvious she hadn't realized she was there.

"Oh… I… oh…" Stevie stammered, grimacing. "I didn't realize anyone was here…" she said, looking at Christian to rescue her.

He grinned. "Mum, this is Stevie. Stevie, this is my mother."

"Hi," she said simply, looking extremely embarrassed.

"Hello," Josephine said.

"Babe?" Christian said.

"Huh?" Stevie said. Christian nodded at the microwave. "Oh!" she said, turning around and taking out the bowl.

"My fiancée doesn't know how to eat popsicles," Christian explained to his mother as Stevie walked over to the couch and sat next to him.

"Actually," Stevie said, grinning ingenuously, "I'm the only one that knows how to eat them right."

She curled her legs up under her. She ate her half-melted popsicles like they were cereal or something. Josephine found herself watching the girl. What she was seeing just didn't jibe with what Christian had told her about the woman. At that moment, Stevie O'Neil seemed so guileless. Josephine wasn't sure what to think.

"How's the shoulder?" Christian asked as Stevie set her bowl on the coffee table in front of her.

"It's better," she said, leaning back against him.

His arms encircled her waist, holding her against him gently. His fingers brushed over a dark bruise on her upper arm.

"What's this?" he asked, raising a black eyebrow at her.

Stevie glanced down at the bruise. "Bad guy, big hands," she said by way of explanation.

"Did ya hurt him?" Christian asked mildly.

"That good old thumb to the palm thing, works every time," she replied, grinning.

"Ouch," he said, grinning too.

"Works every time," she repeated.

"I'm sorry," Josephine said, looking mystified. "What?"

"Oh," Stevie said. "Sorry. This," she said, indicating the bruise on her arm, "was caused by a very big guy who thought he was going to evade being arrested by little old me by grabbing my arm." She took Christian's hand and put it around her arm, showing his mother how the man had grabbed her. Christian did as he was guided, grinning. "So I used a maneuver that I was taught," she said, reaching down and taking Christian's thumb, pulling it up, then turning her wrist so she could press his thumb toward his palm. She stopped when he flinched slightly. "Sorry, babe," she said, taking his hand and putting it to her lips, kissing his thumb. Then she looked at Josephine. "See?"

Josephine nodded, thinking there was definitely more to this young woman than met the eye.

The three of them settled in to watch TV. Christian insisted on ordering Chinese food for dinner.

"I don't want you to have to cook, babe," he said. "You need to rest."

"I'm fine."

"Uh-huh," he said, sounding unconvinced.

She made a face at him. He laughed as he dialed the phone. When the food came, he got up and paid for it. They ate then continued to watch TV. Josephine observed that Christian often leaned forward to kiss Stevie's temple or cuddle her closer to him. Stevie would gently stroke his hands and arms. When his hand would reach up to caress her cheek, she'd turn her head to kiss it softly. Christian would smile warmly at the gesture.

At one point, Stevie turned around to face Christian, and, putting her head against his shoulder, she closed her eyes. Christian looked down at her, smiling slightly. He held her close. Her hand reached up, touching his cheek, tracing his jaw, sliding down his neck, coming to rest on his shoulder. Christian smiled again, then looked back up at the TV.

When Josephine started to yawn, Christian glanced over at her, then down at Stevie, who was fast asleep by that time.

"Time for bed," he said, grinning.

"Definitely," Josephine said, glancing down at Stevie's sleeping form.

Christian shifted Stevie carefully, moving to stand with her in his arms. "The meds always make her sleepy."

Josephine nodded. Christian moved carefully past the coffee table and leaned down, kissing his mother on the cheek.

"Goodnight, Mum."

"Goodnight, Christian," she said, smiling up at her son.

Christian carried Stevie into their room, laying her down on the bed carefully. He went about getting ready to sleep, taking off his clothes and putting sweatpants on. Normally he and Stevie wore nothing to bed, but he felt that with his mother there, he should at least make an effort at modesty. He walked through the house, closing everything up, making sure the doors were locked and things were turned off.

He climbed into bed, turning on his side, sliding an arm under Stevie's neck and putting his hand on her stomach. Sensing him close, she turned over to face him and snuggled against him. He grinned in the darkness. He'd never thought he'd ever enjoy the feel of a woman so much as he did her. When she snuggled close to him, he felt like she was in effect leaning on him, and it made him feel good. She was the one woman he wanted to protect from everything and everyone.

He thought about his mother then, and realized that if Josephine didn't decide to like Stevie, she was going to have a problem with her son. Christian had no intention of ever giving Stevie up again. He'd made that mistake once, and he didn't plan to let it happen again. If his mother made the mistake of expecting him to choose, as far as he was concerned, she could go back to London and stay there. It dragged at him to think that way; his mother had always been the only woman in his life who was a constant. But he knew, beyond a shadow of a doubt, that Stevie was who he was meant to be with, and he was either going to convince his mother or she would have to just deal with it. If that was from afar, then that was how it would be.

The following day, Christian was up first. His mother wandered into the kitchen a half hour after he got out there. Christian knew Stevie was in the shower. They'd had a quick discussion that morning, in which he'd told her that his mother knew about the affair with Joe. He'd known it was something she needed to know, but she'd taken the information better than he'd expected.

She'd shrugged and said, "Well, I knew what I was doing when I ended up with Joe, so I guess now's the time to pay the piper."

He'd stared at her in amazement for a long moment, then shaken his head. He'd kissed her softly, which had quickly turned to heat between the two of them, having been away from each other for an entire week. They made love quickly and as quietly as possible that morning, grinning like kids afterward.

"Mum," he said, "I've got to go into the office for a bit today. Did you just want to stay here, or what?"

"I'd like to see where you work," Josephine said. "I've been here four days and haven't seen your office yet."

"It's boring."

"It's what you do."

"For the moment."

"I know, I know," Josephine said, grimacing.

Christian had told her that he was going to get into narcotics work, and that was the reason for the classes he'd been taking. His mother wasn't altogether pleased with the idea, but she knew better than to try and tell him that she didn't like it. Her son tended to do the exact opposite of what she wanted, especially these days.

Twenty minutes later, Stevie walked into the kitchen. She reached up and took Christian's coffee cup, taking a drink then handing it back to him. He leaned down, kissing her on the lips.

"Good morning to you too," he said with a grin.

Stevie laughed, turning to the high island in the kitchen and smiling at Josephine. "Good morning."

"Good morning," Josephine replied, sipping at her tea.

Stevie stood at the counter, looking at the paper. Christian moved to stand behind her, putting his cup down and bracing his arms either side of her, reading the paper over her shoulder. It was obviously his way of being close to her, even when doing something as trivial as reading the news. Josephine looked on, seeing a very different side of her son since Stevie had returned home. It was very obvious that Christian was very taken with this woman. She hadn't seen his cool, calculating nature in the slightest with this girl.

Josephine hadn't gotten to witness Christian's behavior with too many women. She had seen him with Susan, and even though he had claimed to love her, Josephine could detect his caution and withdrawal from her at times. She had heard about his behavior with other women before, but Susan was at least someone he had loved. Even so, his behavior hadn't been anywhere near as open and loving as it was with Stevie. It did make Josephine question her own thinking.

"My mother's going to drive in with us," Christian told Stevie a little while later.

Stevie glanced back at him, and then at Josephine. "Oh, okay," she said. "We'll have to take the Trans then."

"I figured that," he said, grinning.

"I knew you had," she said, winking up at him.

The three of them left the house an hour later. Christian offered his mother the front passenger seat, but she declined, pointing out that his legs were much longer than hers.

"I'll be just fine," she insisted, climbing into the back of Stevie's car and looking around.

Stevie's car was kept immaculate. She adored it, so took very good care of it. The seats were rich black leather and looked brand new, even though the car was three years old. When Stevie started the engine, the stereo came on, blaring. She grimaced, reaching to turn it down and looking back at Josephine apologetically.

"I'm sorry," she said. "I was kind of distracting myself yesterday."

Josephine nodded.

When they got on the road, Stevie changed CDs on the player. Josephine listened to the music. She had no idea who the artist was, but the words to the song were very strong. She noticed that Stevie sang along, reaching over to take Christian's hand as she did. Josephine had a feeling the song meant something to the two of them. It spoke of being loyal and being the one she'd call. It was sweet, almost heartbreaking.

As the song faded, Stevie stopped at a light. Christian leaned over, kissing her lips softly. "I love you," he said, looking down at her.

"Yeah?" she said, smiling up at him fondly.

"Yeah," he replied with a grin.

"Good thing."

"It is indeed."

She laughed softly.

It was obviously an inside joke with them, but Josephine found it rather endearing. She also noted that Stevie didn't seem to parrot whatever Christian said; she definitely had her own way of doing things.

Once in the office, Josephine got to see her son at work. He was very intense in what he did. He and Erin shot comments back and forth, complaining about this or that. Christian would work on the computer while Erin read things off to him. Then he'd make her sit down and do things on the computer. Christian would stay to the side of her, his arm on the desk beside her; it was obvious the two were quite comfortable working together.

"No, not there," Christian said, grinning. "You put it there and you'll delete all the totals."

"Oh, that would be bad, right?" Erin asked, grinning.

"Yes, that would be bad."

"So I think I'll move it," Erin said, as if it had been her idea.

"Hey, that's an excellent idea."

"Yeah, bite me," Erin said, tapping away at the keys.

"When and where?"

"Oh, sure, and have Stevie after me. Thanks, but no," Erin said, not batting an eyelash at Christian's flirtation. It was obvious they did this all the time as well.

"She's not as good a shot as she used to be," Christian said. "You might get out unscathed."

"Not likely," Erin said, grinning. "Her shoulder still hurting?"

"Yeah, worse now. She jacked it up again."

"I thought Dave was watching out for her," Erin said, raising an eyebrow, having gotten the habit from Christian.

"Yeah, well, there's no keeping tabs on my girl for long."

"She going back to the doctor?" Erin asked, still working away on the computer.

"She needs to."

"But?"

"But she doesn't want to go through another exploratory surgery."

"I can't imagine those feel too good."

"No, she's usually in excruciating pain for a week or so afterward, and it only pisses her off, because they haven't found anything in the last two tries."

"No wonder she doesn't want to try it again," Erin said, rolling her eyes.

"Tell me about it."

At one point Christian stood up to stretch. "I'm going to go get those other schedules," he said. "I'll be back in a few minutes." He glanced at his mother, who was still observing with interest. "You okay over there?" he asked, not sure how she could stand just sitting there watching them.

"Oh yes, I'm fine."

Christian nodded. "I'll be right back."

Josephine nodded, and watched him leave.

Erin glanced over her shoulder at her. "So how has your visit been so far?"

"It's been alright," Josephine said.

"Did you meet Stevie?"

"I met her, yes."

Erin heard the odd inflection in Josephine's voice and turned around. "Is everything okay?"

Josephine looked hesitant, then shrugged. "I want to like the girl, since she's marrying my only son…"

"But?"

"But after what Christian told me about what she did, I just have a very difficult time believing she loves my son enough to have him," Josephine said honestly.

"Oh, she loves him," Erin assured her. "I was sure we'd lose her the day she and Dave found him."

"Found him?"

Erin rolled her eyes. She never could manage to not get herself into trouble, could she? "Stevie and Dave found Christian the day he overdosed."

"Oh," Josephine said. "So what do you mean, almost 'lost' her?"

"She told Midnight, the chief, that if Christian wasn't okay, she was next."

"What did she mean by that?"

"Well, I think she meant that if Christian had managed to kill himself, she'd do the same," Erin said. "She loves your son very much. I just think with a woman like her, who's used to not needing anyone, it's hard for her to accept that she does need him."

Josephine looked back at Erin for a long moment, surprised by the young woman's obvious personal feelings on the issue.

"Why do you seem to care so much about them?" she asked.

Erin grimaced, then shrugged. "I told you, I'm a major romantic. And your son and Stevie are soul mates, I'm convinced of that."

"Soul mates?"

"Yes, there's a theory that everyone has a soul mate—that the other soul completes theirs. And Christian is Stevie's completion, and she's his, even if they're both as independent as they come."

Josephine looked back at the girl for a long moment, surprised by this take on the whole thing.

Later that day, she got an unexpected piece of advice from another source. Midnight Chevalier had come down to talk to Christian. He ended up having to go upstairs to sign some paperwork. Midnight had lingered, talking to Josephine, asking about her visit and so on. Stevie had run into Midnight that morning, and had ended up confiding in the chief the fact that Christian had told his mother about the affair with Joe. Midnight could sense that Stevie wasn't really comfortable with the situation, and Midnight remembered well her confrontation with Rick's family over an affair with Joe as well. So she'd decided to see what she could do to help.

"So everything is going good then?" Midnight asked.

"Well enough," Josephine said.

Midnight nodded, narrowing her eyes slightly. "Josephine, I know that you know about what happened with your son here a month or so ago..."

Josephine looked surprised, but nodded.

"I know it would be really easy to blame Stevie in all this," Midnight said. "But the fact is, your son had just as big a hand in it."

"In her having an affair with his cousin?"

"In her feeling like he didn't want her anymore, and taking a man that did up on his offer," Midnight countered. "It's amazing what having the man you love basically turn his back on you will do," she said, knowing the feeling well. "Stevie is a lot like me, so I know how she felt when things were going wrong. She just wanted to get away so she wouldn't have to examine her failure. But at no time during all of this did she blame anyone but herself for what Christian did. And you know what? She's wrong. It was Christian's fault that he didn't handle things the way he should have. If he loved her that much he should have fought for her in ways other than with his fists.

But that's how men like your son, like Joe, like my husband, handle things. It takes us women to eventually come back and make sense out of everything. And that's what Stevie did in the end. She went to him, knowing how mad he was at her, and after he'd said some pretty nasty things to her and about her, she risked his anger to make sure he was okay. He was never too forthcoming on his own feelings for her—he loved her, sure, but that didn't mean he wanted only her. He'd loved Susan but kept sleeping with other women. In the end, Stevie won him back, and he loves her, so much that losing her made him want to die…" Midnight trailed off as she looked Josephine straight in the eye. "The next move is up to you."

"Up to me?" Josephine asked, surprised to have this turned around on her.

"Yes," Midnight said. "You can either accept Stevie or lose your son."

Josephine looked shocked by that statement. Midnight gave her an apologetic look. "I'm sorry, that sounds pretty harsh, but the fact of the matter is, he loves her. And I think that if you try to separate the two of them, you'll be the one to lose. I'd hate to see that happen— I know you love your son very much. But he's headstrong, and you have to admit, he's always done exactly what he wants to do."

Josephine smiled, nodding. "Yes, he has."

"I'm betting if you ask him, you'll find that he plans to marry Stevie regardless of what anyone thinks. Including you."

Josephine was taken aback by Midnight's directness, but on reflection realized that she was very right. She made a point that day of looking at things differently, doing her very best to set aside Stevie's affair with Joe.

She did find over the next week and a half that she liked Stevie very much. And the girl did have a great deal of spirit, where Christian was concerned. Whenever he tried to bait her on something, she just looked back at him and waited him out.

One evening they were having dinner, talking about the wedding and trying to decide what day they'd actually head to Vegas. Christian glanced at Stevie.

"The guys have been talking about doing that whole bachelor party thing on the strip." His look was pointed, and even Josephine caught the inflection.

Stevie looked back at him calmly and nodded. "Okay, so we'll need to be there… When? A night earlier? Or are we talking major recovery time?"

Christian narrowed his light blue eyes. "You're not going to tell me I can't go?"

"Now why would I do that?"

"Well," Christian said, already sensing he was about to get shut down, "you know the whole bachelor night connotation…"

"Oh, that," Stevie said, nodding.

Christian stared back at her, surprised by how she was reacting—or rather, not reacting.

"So you're saying it's okay?" he asked, pushing it.

"Okay to what?"

He narrowed his eyes again. "To go out and have fun."

Stevie nodded.

His mouth was slightly agape. "You're not saying I can sleep with someone else."

"Are you planning to?" she asked evenly.

"Why?" he asked suspiciously.

She shrugged. "Well, I hear tell there's a bachelorette night too," she said, lowering the boom so calmly.

"You fuck anyone else and I'll kill him," Christian replied just as calmly.

"You fuck anyone else and I'll kill you," she said sweetly.

Josephine was shocked, but then saw that they were both grinning. She shook her head. There was no predicting these two in the slightest.

***

Joe talked to Jordan on the phone on December 22. She was in Paris preparing to do a Christmas Eve show. She called him the minute she got to her hotel room. It was 3:00 in the afternoon. They talked until 8:00 that night. He told her what all was going on with him and the kids. She told him about the tour and the things that had happened here and there on the road.

"So, you're headed home tomorrow morning?" she asked as she glanced at the clock.

She was lying on her bed, staring at the ceiling, picturing him lying in his bed in London. She'd even made him tell her what he was wearing earlier on in the conversation so she could see him clearly in her mind's eye.

"Yeah," he said. "Our flight leaves at nine. We'll get in around eleven a.m. California time."

"And you're going to take the kids back to Randy then?" she asked, having talked with him about this before she'd left on tour.

"Yeah, then go back to have Christmas morning with them."

He was determined to make Christmas nice and somewhat normal for his kids. It was good that he and Randy weren't fighting like cats and dogs. He felt fairly sure that things would go smoothly.

"So what did you get the kids for Christmas?" she asked, realizing they'd never talked about the holiday. She'd bought him something, but wasn't sure if it was even appropriate to give him a gift at this point.

"Well," he said, grinning, "JT's been wanting this race car—it's basically a go-cart, but it's safer. So I found a place that'll do one and make it look like Earnhardt's car. And for Kat, she's been wanting to try painting with 'real paint,' so I got her some lessons, and all the supplies and stuff she could ever use."

Jordan smiled. She knew that Joe loved his kids, but she'd heard of so many men that "loved" their kids but didn't know anything about them. Joe knew his, and it made him even more appealing to her for some reason.

"Did you get Randy anything?" she asked carefully, making a point not to sound jealous in the slightest.

"Yeah," Joe said, sounding a little distant. "I got her a mother's ring. JT's birthday is in August and Kat's is in September, so their stones are that green one—um, peridot—and the other one is a sapphire, so I got a ring that has one band of peridots and one of sapphires that kind of graduate to the London blue topaz, which is Randy's stone."

"Sounds pretty," Jordan said, again amazed that he was so thoughtful.

"Yeah…"

"You okay?"

He was silent for a few moments, then said, "Yeah, I'm okay. I guess I'm just edgy about how this is all going to go. Ya know?"

"Yeah, I can understand that," she said, turning over on her side, tucking the phone under her ear. "Do you think you two will fight?"

"No, I don't think so, but I think things'll be strained."

"That's to be expected, though, Joe."

"Yeah, but expecting it doesn't make it any easier to handle."

"True."

It suddenly hit her that he was going back to America to a woman that was still legally his wife. What if they got things worked out? What if they got back together? She'd never see him again. He was so close right now, but after tomorrow morning he'd be thousands of miles away. Hearing his voice had made her realize how much she really missed him. There were so many nights that she lay in some hotel room wishing she was back at his house, in his arms. She'd come to feel very protected with him, like nothing could hurt her. Suddenly she was back on the road, dealing with Mark all the time; his attitude had gotten worse, though at least he hadn't tried anything. He'd grabbed her a few times, causing bruises on her arms that the makeup people had to struggle to hide for the show. She always made the usual excuses, and she didn't know if they even believed her anymore.

"Joe?" she said, after they'd both been silent for a long time.

"Yeah?" he replied softly.

"I miss you."

On his end, Joe smiled sadly. "I miss you too, babe."

"I hope everything goes okay tomorrow."

"Thanks," he said, sounding a little depressed now.

"The kids are worth the effort, Joe."

"You're right, they are."

Jordan nodded, trying to think of something else to talk about just to keep him on the line. At least she could lie there and hear his voice and imagine he was next to her. Why hadn't she planned on running back to London before this concert? Why was she in a stupid hotel room instead of in his arms? But she knew the answer to that— she'd been too afraid to fight with Mark about changing the original plan. She'd made the arrangements before she'd met Joe, before she'd known there was going to be someone she wanted to see in London before the Paris show. As usual, she'd just let things carry her along, and hadn't stopped to think about what she wanted. Now it was too late. Tomorrow morning he'd fly out of London. Would she see him again? It scared her that she didn't know.

"Jordan?" he said.

"I'm here," she said sadly, her thoughts in turmoil.

"You okay, babe?"

"Yeah." She sighed. "I'm okay. I guess I'm just tired," she said, then grimaced, realizing it sounded like she wanted to get off the phone.

"Maybe you should get some sleep," he said, narrowing his eyes as something occurred to him.

"I'm okay, Joe, really," she said, trying to make her voice sound more normal.

"Jordan, you're going all the time on this tour. You need your rest. Besides, I should get some sleep too. Long day tomorrow."

"Yeah…" she said, trailing off as she fought the urge to beg him not to hang up.

"Can I call you in the morning?" he asked. "Before we leave."

"Will you?" she said, hoping she didn't sound too desperate.

He smiled. "Yeah, I will."

"Great," she said, biting her lip and smiling.

"I'll talk to you in the morning then," he said gently.

"Okay," she said, trying to keep her voice from sounding sad. "Sleep well."

"You too, honey."

They hung up then.

Jordan tossed and turned for another four hours, trying to get to sleep. She was just dozing off when she heard a knock on the door. Her stomach tightened. She worried that it might be Mark; she knew he'd gone out drinking and carousing in Paris that night. If he dared, she thought ominously.

"Who is it?" she called.

"It's the concierge, mademoiselle. I have a delivery for you. I'm very sorry to wake you," replied a French-accented voice.

Jordan sighed, climbing out of bed. She was wearing her brown silk pajamas, and she glanced down at herself to make sure she was covered. She looked through the peephole, and saw that the man standing there did indeed have a hotel uniform on and what looked like flowers in his arms.

She undid the chain and cautiously opened the door.

She was stunned when she saw Joe standing there with a bouquet of Stargazer lilies in his arms.

"Joe!" she said, throwing herself into his arms.

He grabbed her up in a hug as she murmured his name over and over again. He handed the gaping bellboy a tip and then picked Jordan up, carrying her into the room and kicking the door closed.

He looked down at her and saw her staring up at him in wonder.

"You just seemed really down when we hung up," he said by way of explanation.

"I was," she said, hugging him. "I wanted to be there in your arms instead of here."

"Well, now you're here in my arms," he said, walking over to the bed and sitting down with her on his lap.

He kissed her deeply, and she kissed him back with equal fervor. Within minutes they were making love. Afterward they lay in bed, Joe holding Jordan in his arms.

"You're incredible," she said, not for the first time.

Joe glanced down at her with a half-grin. "Why, 'cause I can get on a short flight from London to Paris?"

"No, because you can hear my need for you in my voice, and because of that get on a short flight from London to Paris."

"Who said I only did this for you?" he asked, grinning. He leaned down, kissing her again. "I missed you like hell, Jordan."

She smiled warmly, snuggling against him. Then she glanced over at the lilies, which lay on the end of the bed.

"Shoot!" she said, climbing out of bed.

"Where are you going?" he asked, raising an eyebrow at her but admiring the show of her naked form all the same.

"I need to put my flowers in water," she said, as if he should have known.

"Oh," he said, grinning.

She found a vase to put the flowers in, discarding the roses someone else from the hotel had given her. She made a face as she tossed the roses in the trash. Joe laughed. He'd remembered what she'd told him about hating roses. It had been one of the many things she'd told him in the two and a half weeks they'd been together.

She set the lilies on the dresser next to the bed, climbing back in with him and kissing him on the lips. Pulling back, she looked down at him.

"What was that for?" he asked, smiling up at her.

"For remembering that not only do I hate roses, but that Stargazers are my favorite."

"It wasn't too hard to remember."

"Joe," she said, giving him a patient look, "most men can't remember little things like that."

"They can if they choose to."

She smiled at him, leaning down to kiss him again. She snuggled back into his arms, thinking there wasn't any other place in the world that she wanted to be right then. She fell asleep surrounded by his warmth, waking the next morning to lie and stare up at him as he slept.

He was so handsome. His strong jawline, his perfectly shaped mouth, his dark blond eyebrows that drew together when she said something that perplexed him. And then there was the eyes. So light they glowed against his tanned skin, making her feel their heat almost physically sometimes. He stirred, as if aware that he was being observed, and opened his eyes. He looked down at her and smiled.

"Good morning," she said warmly.

"Good morning," he replied tiredly, leaning down to kiss her lips.

"It's so much better than it would have been," she said sincerely.

"Yeah? How would it have been?"

"Well," she said, settling comfortably in his arms, "I'd have dragged my butt out of bed about 10:30." Joe glanced at the clock—it was only 8:00 a.m. "I would have showered, dressed, and grabbed a cup of coffee. Then I would have spent the day wandering around Paris, wishing I was in London with you…" Her voice trailed off as she realized he would have been leaving London at this point. "Joe, what about your trip?"

Joe had watched her face and had known the minute she'd realized he was supposed to be on a plane to America in an hour.

"What time is your concert tonight?" he asked, ignoring her question for the moment.

"Seven o'clock. Why?"

"What time you looking at being done?"

"I don't know," she said, thinking. "Around eleven or so. Why?" she asked again.

Joe nodded, making a couple of quick calculations. "That'll put us in California about six a.m. or so… That'll work."

"What?" she asked, trying to catch up.

His eyes pinned her. "I want you to come to California with me, and then Vegas for the wedding."

"You do?" she asked, stunned. "But wait, what about the kids?"

"The kids are on their way home, having a great adventure on a plane as 'unaccompanied minors.' They're very excited. I've paid a very discreet nanny a lot of money to leave them alone but keep an eye on them."

"You think of everything."

"Yeah," he said, smiling down at her. "Now, you said you get about a week's break for Christmas, right?"

"Yes," she said, smiling. He remembered that from the conversation over three weeks ago.

"Okay," he said, touching her under the chin. "I want you to spend it with me."

Jordan looked up at him for a long moment, suddenly feeling so happy she could barely stand it. But she had no idea how to tell him that. Instead she kissed him deeply.

"I take it that's a yes?" he asked after a few minutes.

"Oh yes," she said, smiling.

"Good. I need to make a few arrangements."

"Like?"

"Like a flight from here on a fast private jet."

"Oh," she said, grimacing. Then she grinned. "This is going to cost us a fortune, isn't it?"

"Us?"

"Me?"

"No," he said, shaking his head.

"Joe…"

He silenced her with his lips, making her forget the entire conversation a few minutes later as he made love to her. In the end, they got up, took a shower together, making love again, and then went down to have breakfast in a sidewalk café. Jordan got her day in Paris with Joe, and she didn't think she could be happier.

At one point they stopped for a coffee.

"Can I ask for one favor?" Joe asked, watching her over the rim of his glass.

"Of course."

"Tonight, at your show, will you sing 'Damaged' for me?"

Jordan looked back at him for a long moment. "I don't usually do that song."

"Can you do it tonight?"

"Why that song?"

"Because regardless of the background, I like it. It says so much about you." He shrugged. "I don't know…" he said, shaking his head.

Jordan looked at him for a long moment, then nodded. "I'll do anything you want."

His eyes met hers, and he smiled slightly. "Thank you."

"You're welcome."

That night at the concert, Joe stood at the side of the stage watching. Jordan didn't think she'd ever done a better show. She felt his presence the entire time, glancing over at him frequently. She wore a dress of burgundy velvet and black lace that molded to her perfect body. Her stockings were sheer black silk, and her heeled boots laced up to her knees.

The concert was drawing to a close when she walked offstage, picked up a single Stargazer lily, and carried it back on onstage.

"This last song has been requested by someone very special to me," she said, looking over at Joe and smiling. He dropped his head, but smiled all the same, looking back up at her. "This is for the knight that rescued me from loneliness and repaired my damage. I love you, Joe," she said, looking directly at him.

Joe stared back at her as the song began. He was unable to take his eyes off her the entire time, feeling pulled into her as she sang with more emotion than she'd sung anything that night. He had a feeling she was letting herself feel this one for him. It was confirmed when the song ended and he saw tears on her cheeks. Without stopping to think, he took two long strides toward her, wanting to comfort her.

Jordan turned to him, walking straight into his arms, hugging him and looking up at him. Her gold eyes still glistened with tears. He reached out, smoothing his thumb over her cheek, wiping away the tears.

"I love you," she said softly.

Joe stared down at her for a moment, searching her eyes.

"I love you too, Jordan," he said, knowing he had for a while now.

They hugged, and were stunned when the crowd erupted in a huge cheer. It was then that they both realized she still had her headset on, to which was attached her microphone. The entire audience had heard their declarations, and the cameras for the widescreen projection of the concert had also been trained on them. The crowd also heard Joe's mortified "Oh shit," which had everyone roaring with laughter. Joe and Jordan laughed too, unable to deny the humor in the situation.

"Nothing like being famous, huh?" he asked after he'd reached up and pointedly removed her headset.

"Oh yeah," she said, grinning, just before he kissed her.

CHAPTER 7

Donovan lay asleep in the hotel bed the morning after he and Jeanie got to Vegas for the wedding. They'd opted to arrive two days early. Christian and Stevie were getting there that afternoon, as were Midnight and Rick. The rest of the Gang were arriving at various times throughout the day. He and Jeanie had flown over instead of driving the six hours it would have taken. They'd gotten in the night before at seven and checked in at the Monte Carlo. The room was nice, and Donovan had decided to pay for it himself. Even though Christian had offered to pay for everyone, Donovan didn't think he and Stevie should have to do that.

He was just stirring when he felt something touch his forehead. He twitched his nose as whatever it was hit his cheek. Reaching up to rub his face, he opened his eyes. He saw something gold dangling from a ribbon, suspended in front of his face. Blinking to clear his vision, he focused on the item. He glanced at Jeanie, who sat on the bed next to him holding the ribbon.

"Okay, I'm game," he said, peering at her through barely slitted eyes.

Jeanie grinned, untying the ribbon from the gold band it held. She canted her head to the side, looking at him for a long moment.

"Marry me," she said simply.

"Huh?" he asked, looking mystified.

"You know, that whole marriage thing—wife, husband, all that,"

Jeanie said airily.

"You're asking me to marry you?"

"Duh," she said, grinning and holding up the gold band.

"Aren't I supposed to be the one to ask that?" he said, moving to sit up.

"You did that once," she said. "And now I'm asking you."

Donovan looked back at her for a long time. "Why?"

She was silent for a moment. Then her eyes met his. "Because I love you, because I never should have left you, because I never want to lose you again."

Donovan nodded, leaning forward to kiss her lips. "Yes."

"Yes?" she asked uncertainly.

"Yes."

"Now?"

"What?"

"I want to marry you now, Donovan. Right now, today, this morning."

He grinned. "Babe... what's the rush?"

"The rush, Donovan Curtis, is that I want to be your wife. I think our biggest mistake was waiting the first time. It gave me too much time to fuck everything up. And I don't want a chance to do that again. Okay?" she said, giving him a stern look.

"This morning?"

"Yes."

"Your parents will kill you. Randy will kill me."

"So we'll do it again later for them," she said. "The big thing. But I want this now, for us."

He took a deep breath, blowing it out in a rush. "Thought this whole thing out, huh?"

"Yep."

"But I don't have your ring with me…"

She smiled. "Good thing I brought it with me, then, isn't it?"

"You brat," he said, grinning.

"You got it."

"But I don't have a wedding band for you."

"Donovan, don't make me hurt you," she warned. "I don't care about anything but being your wife—I don't care about rings, or anything else, just you. Being yours."

"But then I'll be yours too."

"That's the plan," she said with a brilliant smile.

"I see…"

The phone rang. Donovan reached over and picked it up.

"So what time?" Erin said.

"Huh?"

"She didn't ask you?" Erin said, thinking, *Oh shit!*

"Ohh…" Donovan said, narrowing his eyes at Jeanie. "It was a big plan then, huh?"

Erin laughed. "Yeah, duh!"

Donovan laughed. "I swear, I'm always the last to know."

"No, babe, you were the third to know."

"Same thing," he said, grinning.

"So?" Erin asked.

"So," Donovan said, glancing at the clock. "Meet us downstairs at ten."

Erin squealed in delight. "Awesome, see you two there!" she said, then hung up.

Donovan looked over at Jeanie.

"What?" she asked.

He just shook his head. "Guess I better take a shower, huh?"

"I guess so," she said, having already done so.

"What am I supposed to wear?"

"The suit I packed for you."

"Of course," he said, shaking his head. "How silly of me."

"I swear…" she said, swatting him on the butt as he got out of bed.

"That's considered spousal abuse, Ms. Franco," he said as he walked into the bathroom.

"Not yet, Mr. Curtis."

Donovan climbed into the shower. By the time he emerged from the bathroom, Jeanie was dressed. She wore a silk cream dress that fell to her ankles. It was very simple, but looked fantastic on her. Her hair was up with ringlets falling around her face, and her makeup was perfect.

"You're fast, Franco," he said, raising an eyebrow.

"I'm in a hurry, Curtis."

He nodded, grinning. Within a half hour, he was shaved and dressed. They walked to the elevator hand in hand. Down in the lobby, Donovan told her he had to do something while she looked for Erin. He came back a few minutes later with a dozen red roses.

"You have to have something to walk down the aisle with, besides Elvis."

Jeanie took one rose out of the arrangement, breaking the stem and placing the bud in his button hole, adding a bit of baby's breath to it.

Donovan glanced down. "Acceptable now?"

"Acceptable any time."

Two hours later they had their license and were saying their vows. Erin stood by, doing her best not to cry. She was happy for them, but she was sad for herself. When they were pronounced man and wife, Donovan kissed Jeanie softly. Then they both hugged Erin, and the three laughed like a band of thieves. They went back to the hotel, agreeing to meet in the lobby in an hour.

Up in their room, Donovan promised Jeanie they would have a proper honeymoon eventually.

"I'm not worried about any of that," she said, smiling up at him. "I'm your wife now—that's what I care about."

Donovan nodded, his teal eyes looking down into hers. "I love you."

"I love you too," she said, reaching up to kiss him.

They went back to the lobby wearing normal street clothes, and the three of them spent the day gambling and generally playing.

Joe and Jordan arrived in California at 5:45 a.m. on Christmas morning. Joe took the time to take Jordan by the Hotel Intercontinental, checking her into a room. She told him she thought it was beyond ridiculous that he was paying for a hotel room for the total of about five or so hours she'd be in it. He kissed her softly at the door to the room, then opened it and backed her inside. He set down their bags and grinned at her.

"Sleep, shower, do whatever you want to do to relax, babe. I'll be back by eleven. Our flight is at eleven forty-five."

"Okay," she said, smiling at him.

Joe left the hotel and drove over to his house. He opened the door quietly. Feeling strange, he stepped inside. This wasn't home, all of a sudden. Then he realized that it didn't really bother him.

"Joe?" Randy said from the doorway to the living room.

"Hey," he said, smiling slightly.

"You made it," she said, taking in how tired he looked.

"I wouldn't miss Christmas. Are they up yet?"

"Nope, not yet," Randy said, grinning. "I think they're still a little jet-lagged."

Joe grimaced. "Sorry, didn't really think about that."

"It's okay," she said, gesturing with her head toward the kitchen. "Want some coffee? You look like you could use it."

"Are you saying I look like shit?" he asked, grinning.

"No, I'm saying you look tired," she replied, shaking her head and rolling her eyes. "Come on."

Joe followed her to the kitchen and leaned against the counter as she made his coffee the way he liked it. She handed him the cup, picking up her own and taking a sip.

"So, what time are you leaving for the wedding?" Randy asked.

"I have a flight at eleven forty-five."

Randy nodded.

"You going?" Joe asked, realizing that it could get uncomfortable if Randy was at the wedding with Jordan there.

"Yes, but I'm coming right back afterward. I have too much going on at the center…" Her voice trailed off as she grimaced. "I, uh… I need to thank you."

"For what?" he asked, mystified.

"For the settlement. That was way more than you should have done, Joe," Randy said sincerely.

"No, it wasn't," he said, looking down at her. "You stayed with me for thirteen years—that's a lot of time."

"I was where I wanted to be. I didn't expect to get paid for it."

"Well, I think you deserved at least that much."

Randy was silent for a moment. "I saw that you're seeing someone," she said, her voice not in the least bit accusing.

Joe took a deep breath, nodding. He really hadn't expected Randy to have heard. She didn't really watch TV much, certainly not tabloid-type TV.

Randy nodded. "Kat talked about her a lot. She said that Jordan was very nice to her, and helped her with her artwork."

Joe grinned lopsidedly. "Jordan has a thing for art. Her and Kat seemed to have that in common."

Randy nodded, feeling a twinge of jealousy but knowing that it was just natural to feel that way. She nodded at his left arm then.

"I heard about the tattoo, too. Can I see it?"

She'd been curious what it looked like since she'd heard the report that Jordan had designed it. Joe nodded, pulling up his sleeve. Randy moved closer. She had to admit it did look pretty cool on him. And the Union Jack was so very much Joe.

"Wow, it looks really great," she said, smiling up at him.

"Thanks."

"She's quite an artist," Randy said honestly. "Is she English?"

"No, she's American and Albanian. But she grew up in Europe, and liked England the best," he said, shrugging. "So I guess that's why she has a thing for the Jack. She actually designed this for herself, but decided it was too masculine for her."

Randy nodded. "Yeah, I think it would have been. But it looks really good on you."

"Well, thanks."

Joe was stunned that they were actually having a normal conversation, about Jordan no less.

"And I understand you designed one for her too?" Randy asked, having been curious about that part too.

"Yeah…" he said hesitantly.

"So what did you design?"

"Uh… she has a thing for butterflies, so I kinda cheated. It's kind of flames in a V shape meeting at a butterfly."

Randy nodded. "Sounds interesting."

Joe nodded. "So what's been happening here?"

"Well," Randy said, settling against the counter next to him, "Christian helped Donovan and Jeanie make their case."

"Really now?"

"Yeah, Donny said he did really well too. That he thinks Christian is a natural for undercover work."

"Wow," Joe said, shaking his head. "I suppose he would be. No one would ever expect someone that looks like him to be a cop."

"True. But according to Donovan, Christian has a knack for knowing when to change his tactics too."

"So is he changing jobs, ya think?" Joe asked, raising an eyebrow.

"I hear he already has."

Joe grimaced. He'd missed a lot. "How's the center doing?" he asked, knowing that was the main thing in her life.

"It's doing well," she said. "I think I've got three permanent psychs on staff, and they're all good."

"You're good."

"Well, I need practice. I had a kid go ballistic on me the other day, and Mayers was able to calm him down so quick."

Joe nodded. "Well, it all takes practice, Randy."

"I know, but in the meantime I need people helping me that can do what I can't."

Joe nodded. "Good call. How are the grants coming?"

"I got one, but it's not really that big. I'm still waiting on two more," she said, not looking too hopeful.

"What you're doing is so unique, Randy, it's gonna take a little time before they figure out that you've got the right idea," Joe said. "I mean, Midnight had a hell of a time getting backing for FORS originally too. People figured she was just some broad making noise."

Randy grinned. "Guess she did okay, huh?"

"Yeah," he said, grinning too. "Hey…" he went on, having a sudden thought. "When I was in London, Jordan did a fundraiser for an orphanage there. She made a lot of money for the place. Would you be interested in something like that?"

Randy looked back at him blankly for a moment. "Are you actually asking me if I'd be interested in having some superstar make money for my center?"

"Yeah…" Joe said hesitantly.

"I'm not so proud, Joe, that I won't take help from anywhere, even your newest girlfriend," she said, grinning widely.

Joe winced at the word "newest"—it made it sound like he'd been through a lot of them. He smiled.

"I'll talk to her about it."

"Think she'd want to do me any favors?" Randy asked doubtfully.

"Why not?"

"Um... I am the, uh, ex," she said, testing out the word.

Joe grinned. "You're not the ex yet, and you're still one of the best friends I have," he said, growing very serious on the last.

Randy smiled at that, nodding. "And you're still my best friend," she said, with tears suddenly in her eyes.

Joe took her in his arms, holding her. He was so surprised that they were able to get to this level so quickly. But he realized they'd really been living as friends for a while now. Now that the expectation of a marriage wasn't there, they seemed to be able to talk more easily. It was weird, but he found that it made him feel more comfortable with everything.

The kids came running into the kitchen then, and Joe and Randy separated, grinning at each other. It was a nice morning.

The kids loved their presents, and Randy thanked him warmly for her ring. She'd bought him an Omega Seamaster watch. It was nice, in silver with a deep blue face. It just seemed like him. Randy was right; it looked really good on him. He hadn't had a new watch in years. He hugged her tight, thanking her.

He left the house at 11:00, feeling much better than he had when he'd gotten there. Things were going to work out, he just knew it. He arrived at the hotel at 11:15. He opened the door to Jordan's room and found her sitting on the bed, watching TV.

"Is that your idea of relaxing?" he asked, grinning as he leaned against the doorjamb.

239

She looked up, smiling. "Yes, as a matter of fact."

Joe nodded, pushing off the doorjamb and walking toward her. He sat down on the bed in front of her, picking up the remote and clicking off the TV. Reaching into his jacket, he pulled out a long, flat box wrapped in red-and-gold Christmas paper. He handed it to her.

"Merry Christmas," he said softly, leaning down to kiss her lips.

"Joe…" she said, her voice trailing off as she shook her head. "You didn't have to get me anything. Rescuing me from Paris was enough."

"I didn't rescue you," he said. "I rescued me."

"Uh-huh," she said disbelievingly.

"You gonna open it?" he asked, raising an eyebrow at her.

"Yes!" she said, sighing, but grinning at the same time.

She unwrapped the present, then looked up at him with narrowed eyes as she saw the box was from a prestigious jeweler in London. He grinned back at her, his light blue eyes twinkling. Jordan opened the box, and was literally stunned into forgetting to breathe.

"Oh my God, Joe…"

Nestled in the rich sapphire velvet was a pendant on a beautiful Byzantine chain with intricate, delicate gold links. But what had her breathless was the pendant; it was a perfect, incredible, beautifully detailed butterfly, in the exact colors of the one on her back. The wings were made up of tiny baguette stones of gold topaz at the bottom, graduating to the London blue, perfectly turquoise topaz, and the top parts of the wings were made up of exquisitely rich blue sapphires. There was detailing done in pieces of onyx, to make up the veins of the wings. Jordan was stunned. There was no way he'd bought this out of some case.

She looked up at him and saw that he was thoroughly enjoying her awe.

"You did this, didn't you?" she asked.

He inclined his head. "I had it designed for you, yes."

"Oh, Joe, it's beautiful," she said, realizing she couldn't begin to convey to him the way she felt. It was the most incredible thing she'd seen. "I've never gotten anything this... breathtaking in my life." She felt tears mist her eyes, and looked down.

His finger tilted her face up to his again.

"Thank you, Joe, so much," she said, her voice still showing the effects of her feelings.

"You're welcome. Thank you for saving me from myself."

Jordan grinned, her gold eyes shining. "Well, I got you something, but now..." She shook her head.

"Gimme," he said, grinning.

"It's not near as incredible as this," she said, still holding the box with the necklace in it.

"Bullshit," he said. "If you got it for me, it's incredible."

Jordan looked doubtful, but got off the bed and went over to her luggage all the same. She came back a moment later, handing him a small square box.

"I didn't even have time to wrap it," she said, pouting.

Joe grinned. "Want me to pretend it's wrapped?"

"Brat!" she said, swatting his arm. "I just hope you like it."

He opened the box, and was surprised by what it held. It was a ring. But definitely not a common ring. It was silver in color, in a band style but intricately carved. Set into the band in a channel design were perfect sapphire baguettes. It looked heavy, but delicate at

241

the same time. And it was definitely his style.

"It's platinum," she said, biting her lip. "I just thought it looked like you."

Joe nodded, slowly reaching in and taking the ring out, sliding it on his right middle finger. It fit perfectly. Jordan had taken into account the fact that he was still wearing his wedding band on his left ring finger, and his signet ring was on his right.

"I love it," he said, his light blue eyes shining as he looked at her. "And you."

He leaned forward to kiss her softly, then drew her closer and deepened the kiss. After a few minutes he pulled back, glancing at the clock.

"We'd better get going," he said. "The pilot won't wait all day."

"You chartered a plane?"

"Yeah." He shrugged. "It was easier this way."

She shook her head. "Wait. Put my necklace on me first."

Joe did as she asked, and she went over to the mirror and looked at it on her neck. It shined beautifully, and she glanced up at him in the mirror. He stood behind her, smiling down at her reflection.

"It's incredible, Joe. Thank you so much."

"You're very welcome, babe," he said, glad she liked it. "Let's go."

Joe and Jordan arrived at the hotel at 12:30. Checking in at the front desk, Joe found he already had two messages, one from Midnight and one from Christian. He grinned as he stuffed the pieces of paper into his pocket. Taking Jordan's hand, he led her to the room. Once inside he got on the phone, texting Midnight. As he hit the numbers, he grinned. Jordan watched him, noting that he only punched in five actual numbers, with spaces between. Then he hit send.

"What?" he asked, seeing that she'd been watching him.

"That wasn't the room number—it only has four numbers—and it wasn't a phone number… What did you put in?"

"Oh," he said, nodding. "I put in twenty-two, ten, eight."

"Meaning?"

"I'm twenty-two—Charles twenty-two, to be exact." He could see he needed to explain that further. "Charles is the phonetic for *C* and stands for *captain*, and twenty-two is my radio call number. And then the ten-eight is code for 'on duty.' So basically it said that Captain Sinclair is back on duty."

"Kinda like 'Honey, I'm home'?" she asked, grinning.

"Kinda," he replied, laughing.

They unpacked what little they needed, Jordan taking longer than him because she had to get out her makeup and stuff for her hair. When she finished, she wandered over to the bed, sitting down next to where he lay. He'd been watching her. She grinned at him.

"Like the show, sailor?" she asked.

"Mmhmm," he said, winking at her.

"See anything you want to buy?"

"Oh yeah," he assured her, reaching up to pull her down to him, kissing her lips.

After a while, Jordan laid her head on his chest, sighing deeply.

"What?" he asked, sensing she was troubled all of a sudden.

She shrugged. "I'm just nervous."

"About what?" he asked, his brows furrowing.

"About what?" Jordan echoed, moving to sit up, looking down

243

at him. "About meeting your friends, that's what."

"Why?" he asked, still looking perplexed.

"Um, Joe," Jordan said. "Remember you told me how they acted when you were dating Stevie?"

Joe sighed. "Babe, that was totally different. For one thing, Randy and I weren't even legally separated at that point, and for another, Stevie was with my cousin. I was treading on his territory, and everyone knew it."

Jordan nodded, but didn't look convinced. "What if they hate me?" she asked, sounding very anxious about the possibility.

"They won't hate you, Jordan," Joe said, shaking his head. "How could anyone hate you?"

"Oh, it's real easy," she said, grimacing. "Joe, these people are basically your family. If they hate me, where will that leave us?"

"It'll leave us still in love. Their opinion won't change my feelings."

Jordan looked very skeptical.

Joe moved to sit up, looking her in the eye.

"Babe, I stood against them to be with Stevie, and I didn't love her," he said honestly.

Jordan looked back at him for a long moment, then shook her head as if he wasn't getting it. In truth, he wasn't.

"I don't want you to stand against them for me, Joe," she said. "They're the people you love."

"If they make me make a choice," he said, touching her cheek, searching her eyes, "you'll be my choice, okay?"

She sighed, shaking her head. His lips stopped her. He kissed her softly at first, whispering "I love you" against her lips. Then he pulled her down on the bed with him, deepening the kiss, his hands caressing her.

They were still kissing when there was a knock on the door.

"That's gotta be Midnight," he said, grinning.

Jordan moved to sit up, pushing her hair back, trying to straighten up. Joe thought that even in her casual clothes she looked incredible. She wore a gold silk tank top and faded jeans. She'd had a black leather bomber jacket on earlier and black ankle boots. She wore makeup, but just enough to accent her features. Her hair was in its usual sexy disarray, more so after their making out.

He got up from the bed and walked to the door. When he glanced back at Jordan, he shook his head. She'd picked up a pillow, putting it on her lap. It was a defensive gesture he realized she did whenever she was feeling out of place.

"Quit that," he said.

"What?"

He shook his head, reaching for the door. Midnight and Rick stood outside.

"Hey!" Midnight exclaimed, moving into his arms, throwing hers around his neck and hugging him tight. "I hate it when you're gone so damned long."

"I know, Night, I know."

He nodded to Rick, extending his hand. "Hey, man."

"Hey," Rick said, grinning. "Glad you're back."

"Yeah, so you can stop taking the heat," Joe said, laughing.

"You're so right," Rick said, getting elbowed by Midnight as he did.

Joe stood back to let them in. Then he glanced over at Jordan, who looked distinctly uncomfortable.

"Rick, Night, this is Jordan. Jordan, this is Rick and Midnight Debenshire."

Midnight looked surprised. They hadn't expected Joe to bring her to the wedding. But she recovered quickly, walking over to Jordan and extending her hand.

"It's nice to meet you," Midnight said, her gold-green eyes staring directly into Jordan's.

Jordan took Midnight's hand, smiling slightly. She looked nervous. "It's nice to meet you too," she said, glancing at Joe. "Joe's told me a lot about both of you."

"Oh, shit!" Midnight said, rolling her eyes, then winked at Jordan conspiratorially. "You can like us anyway, you know."

Jordan laughed.

"She was afraid you wouldn't like her," Joe said.

"Joe, shut up!" Jordan said, aghast.

Midnight and Rick glanced at each other, grinning. Then Midnight looked back at Jordan. "Don't worry about it," she said. "As long as you make Joe happy, we like you."

"She makes me very happy," Joe said, gazing at Jordan.

"Then we're cool," Midnight said, sounding pleased. She turned to Joe. "You seen Blue yet?"

"Nope, not yet," Joe said, moving to sit back down on the bed, touching Jordan on the back. She scooted a little closer to him, and he put his arm behind her, his body close to hers.

"What time are you guys doing the rehearsal?" Midnight asked.

Rick went to sit in one of the armchairs near the window. He grabbed Midnight's hand, pulling her down on his lap.

"Rehearsal?" Joe asked, shaking his head. "This is Collins we're talking about. He's gonna wing it."

"Oh Jesus," Midnight said, grinning and shaking her head.

"Tell me about it," Joe said.

"So where's this tattoo you got, old man?" Rick asked, his deep blue eyes sparkling with mischief.

Joe grinned. Leave it to Rick to be blunt. He pulled up his sleeve. Rick stared for a long moment, then put his hands to Midnight's hips, moving her off his lap so he could stand. He walked over to take a better look.

"That's really cool," he said, sounding impressed.

"Yeah," Joe said, grinning. "For an old man."

"Yeah, fuck you."

Midnight had come over to see the tattoo too.

"Joe, that really is cool," she said, and looked at Jordan. "And you designed that?" She sounded impressed too.

Jordan bit her lip. "I was actually designing one for me, but that one just seemed too masculine. But when Joe and I started talking about a tattoo for him, it just seemed like it would be him. Ya know?"

Midnight nodded. "It's definitely him," she said, glancing at her husband, who was still staring at the tattoo, with clear envy on his face now. "Oh shit… now you want one, right?"

Rick grinned engagingly. "Would it be so bad?"

Midnight stared back at him for a long moment, then looked at Jordan again. "You got one too, right?"

"Yes."

"Can I see it?"

"Uh, sure," Jordan said, moving to stand. Then she looked worried. "I kinda have to unbutton my jeans…"

Midnight glanced at Joe and raised an eyebrow. "Where did you have it put, Joseph?"

Joe grinned unrepentantly. "Relax, Chief. It's at the small of her back."

"Ah," Midnight said, reaching up to pointedly cover Rick's eyes. "Go for it, Jordan," she said, grinning as Rick ducked her hand, laughing.

Jordan undid the first two buttons of her jeans, her back to them, then pushed them down just slightly, lifting the back of her shirt.

"Ohh…" Midnight said, her face reflecting her amazement. "That's fantastic."

"It really is great, isn't it?" Jordan said.

"Yeah, it is." Midnight reached down to touch the flames. "I see the *JMS* in here, too," she said, narrowing her eyes as she glanced at Joe. "You'd better have her initials on that tattoo somewhere too, Sinclair."

Jordan laughed. "He does. In fact, he insisted."

Joe pointed out the initials.

"Alright then," Midnight said, still looking at Joe like he'd broken a rule.

"What?" he asked, sounding very English.

Jordan buttoned her jeans, tucking her shirt back in.

"You know what," Midnight said.

"God…" Joe said, rolling his eyes.

"What?" Jordan asked as she moved to sit next to him again.

"Midnight doesn't like any man 'marking his territory' on a woman," Joe said.

"Oh," Jordan said, grimacing. "But he's got my initials too."

Midnight nodded, grinning. "That's the only thing that saved him from a scathing comment."

"Yeah, yeah…" Joe said.

"Watch it, Sinclair. I can still kick your ass."

"Yeah, you and your army."

"Feeling brave today, aren't ya?" Rick said.

Joe laughed. "Oh yeah."

"Okay, look," Midnight said. "We're gonna get out of here and leave you two alone. We'll see you later, okay?"

Joe and Jordan both nodded. Joe got up, walking them out. Midnight reached up and hugged him at the door.

"She's beautiful, Joe," she whispered.

"Yeah, she is."

Joe's eyes connected with Rick's, and Rick nodded approvingly. Joe grinned.

After he'd closed the door, he turned to Jordan. "They like you."

"Yeah?" she asked, still sounding a little worried.

He walked over to the bed, lying down and putting his head in her lap. "Yeah, babe, they like you."

"Whew!"

Later that day, Jordan had gone into the bathroom to freshen up her makeup and brush her hair out. When she walked out, she was stunned to see a man sitting on the bed talking to Joe. He was definitely drop-dead handsome, with jet black hair, tanned skin, and a strong jawline. She realized he was even more so when he looked at her, his light blue eyes alight with interest.

"You'd have to be Christian," she said, smiling.

"That's the name my mum gave me," he said, grinning engagingly. "And you'd be Jordan Tate."

"That's the name someone gave me—not sure which parent though."

Jordan walked over to Joe, who pulled her down to sit between his legs on the bed.

"So," Christian said, his tone changing slightly. "I was watching TV last night…" His voice trailed off pointedly as he looked at Jordan.

She caught it before Joe did, dropping her head and shaking it dismally.

"Huh?" Joe said.

"It was a concert… in Paris," Christian said, grinning at Jordan's reaction.

"Oh…"

"Uh-huh…"

"You just had to see that, right?" Jordan said, putting her hands up to hide her face.

"Oh yeah. It was a very good concert, by the way," Christian said. "With a really interesting, ah, grand finale, shall we say?"

"Oh, shut the hell up," Joe said. "I had no fucking idea her mic was still on."

"That much was obvious from the oh so proper 'oh shit' comment, man."

"You're gonna enjoy this one, aren't ya?"

"Oh yeah," Christian said, smiling. He grew serious then. "Actually, I'm happy for ya. You two make a good-looking couple."

"Easier to say that kind of thing, now, huh?" Joe said.

"Yeah, disgusting what love will do to ya."

"Where is Stevie, by the by?" Joe asked.

"Oh, she's busy being absolutely frantic," Christian said, grinning widely.

"Uh-oh. Why?"

"I guess she forgot some under-thing for her dress. She's calling all over to find one. That's why I decided to take a walk."

"She needs a corset?" Jordan asked.

"Uh…" Christian looked mystified. "Got me, babe. All I know is she doesn't have whatever she needs." He chuckled, as did Joe.

"I might be able to help," Jordan said, moving to stand. "What room is she in?"

"Room 1032," Christian said. "You think you can help?"

"I can give it a shot." Jordan walked over to the closet and pulled out a couple of things. She went back over to Joe, leaning down to kiss him on the lips. "I'll be back."

Joe smiled up at her. "I'll be here."

"Good," she said, grinning.

"Hey, Jordan?" Christian said as she got to the door.

"Yeah?" she said, turning to him.

Christian winked. "Thanks."

"You're welcome, but I haven't helped yet," she said, smiling.

Christian laughed. Jordan opened the door and walked out.

Christian turned to Joe. "Damn, man, she's hot."

"I know," Joe said, grinning.

"So you two are pretty serious, huh?"

Joe shrugged. "Hard to know. I love her, she loves me, but who knows where it'll go. I mean, she's a fuckin' rock star."

Christian nodded. "Fun though, yeah?"

"Oh yeah."

"Then enjoy it while you can."

Joe nodded in agreement.

Meanwhile, Jordan was knocking on Stevie and Christian's door. It took Stevie a few minutes to answer. When she did, she looked at Jordan in absolute amazement. She'd had no idea that Joe was bringing his superstar girlfriend to the wedding, and here she was, standing in front of her.

"Hi," Jordan said. "Stevie, right?"

"Right..."

"Your fiancé said you were having a corset issue." Jordan held up the bag she'd brought.

"Oh my God, are you serious? You have one?" Stevie asked as she opened the door wider, gesturing for Jordan to come in.

"I'm Jordan, by the way."

"I know who you are," Stevie said, grinning. "I don't think there's a human being alive that doesn't know who you are."

"Oh, I'm sure somewhere there's someone that doesn't know

who I am," Jordan replied, laughing.

"Then they don't have MTV, and it's their problem."

"Yeah," Jordan said, making a face. "Anyway, see if either one of those will work. I assumed you'd be wearing white…"

"I am, even if it's a total lie, and I'll probably get hit by lightning for doing it."

Jordan laughed. "I know that feeling."

Stevie went into the bathroom and came out a few minutes later. "You are such a lifesaver!" she said, holding up the corset that worked.

"I don't go anywhere without Lycra."

Stevie looked back at her for a long moment, then shook her head. "I'd kill for a body like yours."

Jordan canted her head to the side. "You don't seem to have any trouble."

"Yeah, well, it's not like yours, trust me."

Jordan shook her head. "Well, I spend a ton of time at the gym. I've sweated for this body."

"See? That's what I need to get back to. I've gotten so lazy. So where are the boys?"

"Back at our room."

"Let's go—they'll get into trouble if they're alone too long," Stevie said, grinning.

Jordan stood up and followed her out of the room. They were back at Joe and Jordan's a few minutes later.

"I see where you go when I need you…" Stevie said, narrowing her eyes at Christian.

"Hey, what the fuck do I know about undergarments?" Christian said, grinning rakishly. "Other than how to remove them, that is…"

Stevie smiled. "Well, you don't get to remove this till later."

"Hey, since we've got both of you here…" Joe said, standing up and winking at Jordan. "We want to give our wedding present to the two of you."

"Man, you didn't have to do anything," Christian said.

"Bullshit," Joe said. "It isn't every day that my cousin gets married."

"Thank God," Christian said, getting slapped on the arm by Stevie for it.

Joe handed him an envelope. Christian looked at Joe, then Stevie. He opened the envelope and took a card out. Jordan moved to Joe, who pulled her in front of him, hugging her close, holding her waist. Stevie knelt on the bed behind Christian, her arms loosely around his neck, looking over his shoulder.

Christian opened the card and read the papers it included. He stared up at Joe, his mouth open in shock.

"You're sending us to Monaco?" Christian asked, awestruck. "For a week? Man…" He shook his head. "This is too much."

"Hey, consider it a combination Christmas present and wedding present. And Jordan helped pay for it too. It's a two-for-one deal," Joe said, grinning.

Stevie was staring at both of them, her mouth open and her eyes wide. Then Christian took out the traveler's check made out in the amount of $5,000. Stevie stared at it like she was going to faint. Joe laughed.

"Better catch her, man," he said, gesturing to Stevie.

Christian chuckled, even as Stevie recovered.

"Joe, this is just too much," she said.

"Hey," Joe said. "It was that or pay off the house for you two. I figured you'd kick my ass if I did that."

"You're right, I would have," Stevie said, getting off the bed and walking over to him. "Thank you," she said, reaching up to hug him.

"You're welcome."

Christian stood, extending his hand to Joe. "Thanks, man, this is fantastic."

Joe clasped his hand, pulling him in to hug him, clapping him on the shoulder.

"So," Christian said, looking thoughtful, "you two wouldn't want to come with us, would ya?"

Joe was surprised by the question. Jordan glanced up at him. Stevie looked thoughtful for a moment, then started to nod.

"Yeah," Stevie said. "You boys could gamble, and me and Jordan can shop!"

"Yeah, but…" Joe said. "Wouldn't you two want to be alone?"

"We wouldn't want to impose," Jordan agreed.

"Bullshit," Christian said. "That's why they put doors on those hotel rooms."

Joe laughed, nodding. "Hadn't thought about that." He looked down at Jordan. "We could upgrade that suite to an apartment…"

"We could," Jordan said, starting to look excited.

"When do you have to be back?" Joe asked her.

"The third of January."

"Cool. That'd even give us an extra day on the other end."

"Cool," Jordan echoed.

"Let me make some calls," Joe said. "You just may have yourselves traveling companions."

"Cool," Christian said.

"You getting dressed over here?" Joe asked him.

"Yes, he is," Stevie said, grinning.

"Do you need any help getting ready?" Jordan asked her.

"I could use some. I have no clue how to get into that dress!"

"Let me get my stuff together and I'll come down in about an hour and half, okay?"

"Great."

It was a bit unreal that she suddenly had a superstar helping her get ready for her wedding, but Stevie found out quickly that Jordan really was just a regular person. They ended up laughing and talking for the whole time that they were getting ready. Stevie found that Jordan had a good sense of humor, making a number of remarks about marriage and weddings that had Stevie laughing, not giving her time to get nervous.

At 6:00 p.m., Christian called the room.

"You ready yet?" he asked Stevie.

"No, I'm not," she said. "Jordan and I have decided to run off together," she added, grinning.

"Oh-ho…" Christian said, laughing. "As long as I get to watch."

"Christian!" Stevie said, laughing all the while. "Besides, you can't see me before the wedding anyway."

"Do you look good?" he asked, his voice dropping an octave.

"Uh-huh…"

"Real good?"

"Uh-huh…"

"Still want to marry me?" he asked quietly.

"Oh yes," she said, her voice full of conviction.

"That's what I need to hear."

"I love you," she said softly.

"Mmm…" he said, closing his eyes. "I love you too. I'll see you at seven."

"I'll be there."

They hung up. Stevie looked at Jordan, who was smiling.

"He's so cute right now, I just want to keep him that way," Stevie said, grinning.

"He's definitely a handful, isn't he?"

"Oh God, yes! Hell, half my problem is keeping other women away from him."

"They can't play if he doesn't," Jordan pointed out. "And I think he's so in love with you he wouldn't."

"Yeah, maybe."

"Maybe? You can't not know how much the guy loves you."

"What do you mean?" Stevie asked, finishing her makeup.

"I mean, after what he did, because he'd lost you…" Jordan said, not wanting to say the words outright.

Stevie glanced at Jordan in the mirror. "Joe told you about that, huh?"

"Yeah. He felt pretty responsible."

"I know he did. So did I."

Jordan shook her head. "Neither of you were responsible for

what Christian did. He made his own mind up as to how he wanted to deal with things. He had other options."

"Like?"

"Like he could have come to you and told you that he couldn't handle losing you, that he loved you, that he wanted you back. Anything like that."

Stevie thought about it. "But that's not the kind of man Christian is."

"Yeah, but what says he can't change the way he does things? Did you think he was the kind of man that would try to kill himself over a woman?"

Stevie shook her head. "Not in a million years."

"So you must mean a lot to him."

"Yeah, but… if I'd lost him. If he'd died…" Stevie shook her head.

"But you didn't lose him, because it wasn't meant to happen that way."

Stevie narrowed her eyes. "You think like my friend Dave."

"I do?"

"Yep, I'll have to introduce you two. He's got the whole 'cosmic forces' thing going on."

"I don't think it's cosmic—I just think it's fate," Jordan said. "Everything happens for a reason, good or bad. There's a grand plan for everything."

"Okay, so you're saying that Christian's attempted suicide was so he and I could get back together?"

"That, and it also sent Joe to England—well, that and the divorce—but in England he met me. So it's impacted my life too. And it was meant to for a reason."

"What reason, do you think?" Stevie asked, curious now.

Jordan was silent for a moment. For the very first time in her life, she wanted to tell someone the whole story. "I think he might be in my life to rescue me."

"From what?" Stevie asked, realizing there was more to the statement than it seemed.

Jordan took a deep breath and then blew it out slowly. It was time. She spent the next twenty minutes telling Stevie the whole story about her and Mark. Including the fact that they were step-brother and sister. She was astounded to note that Stevie didn't look horrified. Or maybe she just hid it well; she was a narc, after all, and from what Joe had said, a good one.

"So," Jordan said at the end of her whole story, describing the last episode with Mark, when he'd raped her after the tattoo incident. "I know it's a sick little thing, but I'm hoping that being with Joe will put Mark farther away."

"Why do you think it's sick?" Stevie asked.

"He's my brother."

"He's not even your own blood. And it's not like you two even grew up together—you were basically grown up before you ever met."

Jordan stared back at Stevie for a long moment, having never looked at it that way before. It was true. Mark had been an adult, and she'd been pretty close.

"I'll tell you, though," Stevie said. "You're really lucky Joe hasn't beaten the shit out of the guy already."

"Why do you say that?"

"Well, I guarantee you that he knows Mark raped you that day, because you told me you hurt when you two had sex two days later. He noticed, and he figured it out—trust me on that. And if he knows that, he basically had to keep himself from going after Mark. That's the kind of man Joseph Michael Sinclair is. So if you asked him not to, that's what kept him from doing it—he was afraid to lose you. But it will happen, Jordan. And I tend to think that if Mark hurts you again, Joe will kill him."

Jordan looked back at Stevie, surprised by what she was saying. She wasn't used to men who felt that strongly about women being protected.

"He's really gallant, isn't he?" she said, smiling softly.

"Oh yeah," Stevie said. "If you're smart, you'll hold on to him with both hands."

"Speaking of holding on to someone…" Jordan said, glancing at her watch. "Let me get my clothes on, and then we'll get you into that dress."

Twenty minutes later, Jordan and Stevie stood looking in the mirror. Jordan was wearing a black crushed-velvet dress that fell to her mid-thighs, flaring from her waist. The velvet had insets of hunter green satin and jewels that buttoned up the front that looked like emeralds. Under it she wore a black lace corset. The reception was taking place in a bar located in the hotel. It was Christian and Stevie's intention to simply party after the wedding, throwing all tradition out the window.

Stevie wore a halter-style sheath dress. The bodice was ivory satin covered with seed pearls and insets of lace. The style left her arms and shoulders uncovered, her year-round tan making her skin seem to glow. The skirt was satin as well, with the pearl and inset detailing on the bottom section. Her hair was arranged around a V-shaped beaded headpiece, the veil at the back. The rest of her hair fell down her back in silken auburn waves. Her makeup was light, but well done; Jordan had an artistic flair for that as well. She'd used colors to enhance Stevie's emerald green eyes, showing her a few things she'd learned over the years. Stevie couldn't believe the difference it made; the green of her eyes seemed to emanate from her face. Her cheekbones were highlighted with rich blusher, and on her lips she wore a rich brown with just a touch of burgundy to it, making them look sexy and pouty. Stevie was fairly sure Christian was going to have a heart attack.

"Hell, I look so good, I want to do myself," she said, laughing.

Jordan winked at her. "That's the idea."

"You look really good too. You have the most incredible wardrobe," she said, having seen pictures of Jordan in a number of outfits.

"I spend most of my money on clothes," Jordan said. "What are you planning to wear for the reception?"

Stevie grimaced. "I don't know. I wasn't sure about leaving this on—it'll probably get ruined—but it seems like a huge waste to take it off right after the wedding…"

"Well, since it's a two-piece, you could leave the top half on and change to a skirt…" Jordan said, narrowing her eyes. "I've got this really good emerald green skirt, if you want to borrow it—it would look great on you."

Stevie thought about it. It was the skirt she was worried about, since it fell all the way to the floor. If she could change that, then at least she'd get some wear out of the bodice, which was the most detailed part anyway. She smiled.

"I think you and I are gonna get along just great," she said.

Jordan laughed. "As long as I don't run out of clothes, right?"

she asked, grinning.

Stevie nodded. "Yeah."

"I'm going to head down," Jordan said, glancing at Stevie, who suddenly looked extremely nervous. "You okay?"

Stevie took a deep breath and blew it out slowly, nodding.

"God, this is huge," she said, biting her lip, her green eyes glittering as she stared at herself in the mirror.

"You love him."

"More than life."

"Then get yourself together and go down and marry him," Jordan said, looking around the room. She spotted a bottle of tequila and went over to pick it up. She poured Stevie a shot.

Stevie grinned, taking the shot and downing it.

"Oh yeah…" she said as she felt the alcohol go through her. She moved her head around, closing her eyes, centering herself. "I'll be down in ten minutes."

Jordan nodded. She left the room.

Down in the lobby, Jordan located Joe with a group of guys. She was taken aback by how good he looked. He wore a tuxedo, the same as Christian, only without a vest. The coat was different, high collared, very chic, not in the least bit traditional. The men were all drinking shots, including the groom.

Christian looked fantastic too, wearing a modern black tuxedo with a deep blue vest. It fit what seemed to be his style perfectly.

Jordan walked over to them and heard their toasts.

"To love and marriage," said an Asian man.

"To avoiding it as long as humanly possible," the sandy-brown-haired guy with blue eyes said, grinning.

"Oh yeah, like you did," Rick said, laughing.

"Yeah, only to have her have him so wrapped he'd mortgage his ass to buy her a Mercedes," the Asian man said.

"You bought her a Mercedes?" Joe asked.

"Yeah—where were you?" Rick asked.

"London," Joe replied, grinning.

Rick laughed. "Oh yeah, falling for a rock star."

"Jealous?" Joe countered.

"No, I got a chief, thanks."

"Can I fuckin' drink yet?" Christian asked, grinning.

"Drink!" the other men all said.

"Um…" Jordan said, touching Joe on the back.

"Hey." He turned and put his arm around her, his eyes moving over her appreciatively. "Guys, this is Jordan. Jordan, that's Spider, Dave, Kyle, Donovan, and Tiny. You met Rick and Christian."

"Nice to meet all of you," Jordan said, smiling.

All five men looked back at her with varying degrees of appreciation.

"Joe," Jordan said, turning back to him. "Stevie's gonna be down in ten minutes. I think you guys should get in there."

Joe nodded. "Thanks." He turned to Christian. "Time to go."

Christian nodded, taking another quick shot.

"I gave your fiancée one upstairs too," Jordan said, grinning.

"She needed one, huh?" Christian asked, raising an eyebrow.

"Oh yes," Jordan said. "But she also said she loves you more than life, so I think you're safe."

Christian smiled brilliantly. Jordan could see how women's

hearts would be breaking everywhere now that this one was off the market. He was definitely a dangerously handsome man.

CHAPTER 8

The guests were all seated, and the men went to join their respective spouses. Josephine Collins sat in front, watching her son. She was surprised to note that Christian didn't look the least bit nervous. Christian's eyes trailed over to his mother and connected with hers. He smiled warmly, winking at her. Josephine laughed softly. It was very obvious to her that he did indeed know what he was doing marrying Stevie O'Neil. She'd never actually imagined this day would come, despairing that her son would never settle down from his wild ways. It had alarmed her to know how desperately Christian was in love with this woman, and to think that she was simply toying with him. It had eased her mind to see that Stevie O'Neil did seem to love Christian as much as he did her. Perhaps she could make him happy forever, the way she obviously did now.

A mother could only hope for the best.

Jordan found herself looking around curiously. It was interesting to see these people together. Joe had told her a little bit about them, and she felt like she was staring a lot at all of them.

She saw Susan, who was Joe's kids' nanny. She didn't look like a nanny; she was a beautiful blonde with perfect skin, perfect hair, and fantastic bones. This was the woman Dave had mortgaged his "ass" to buy a Mercedes for. Jordan could see why.

Tiny's wife was also a beauty. Did these guys marry ugly women at all? She had red hair and creamy skin. She was very small next to her very large husband, but Jordan could see how gently he touched her, even holding her hand. She smiled up at the big guy like a ray of sunshine, so it was obvious she was in love with him.

There was also Kana, the tough-looking Samoan woman, with a diminutive but gorgeous woman sitting next to her. Jordan thought the woman looked familiar, but couldn't figure out where she'd seen her before.

Then there was Spider and his wife. Tammy Nguyen looked very pretty; she was not as outrageously beautiful as the other women, but pretty in a very quiet way. No one had obviously ever gotten her to play up her looks, but she looked happy the way she was.

Lastly there was Joe's brother-in-law, Donovan, who sat with three women. There was a pretty blonde who looked very young. There was a very pretty woman with long chestnut hair and big brown eyes—that had to be Jeanie, Donovan's girlfriend. And the other woman must be Randy Sinclair.

Jordan did her best not to stare, but there was no denying how beautiful Randy was. She had long, rich blond hair down to her waist, and beautiful teal blue eyes set in a very pretty face. She also didn't look like a woman who'd borne two children. She was trim and lovely. Jordan felt plain all of a sudden. She glanced up at Joe, at the front of the room, and saw him looking at her. His eyes were narrowed slightly, as if he was trying to read her mind. Then he winked. Jordan looked down and grinned to herself. Boy, this was weird!

The wedding went off without a hitch. Kyle Masterson walked Stevie down the aisle, giving her to Christian. Rhiannon was Stevie's matron of honor, wearing a deep blue dress. More beautiful people. Jordan knew that Rhiannon was Stevie's older sister. While they looked alike in some ways, it was obvious who the wild child was.

Stevie's looks were just more sexy. Rhiannon was incredibly beautiful, but in a very reserved way.

The vows were quick and simple. The ring exchange was interesting, since apparently neither had seen the ring the other was giving them. Stevie's was a Celtic infinity knot band, with a second band containing marquise-cut diamonds and emeralds set on the sides.

"Christian…" Stevie breathed, looking up at him.

"I know you're close to your heritage," Christian said. "And that infinity knot represents the love and desire I have for you."

Stevie reached up, touching his cheek. He closed his eyes in response as everyone looked on.

The ring Stevie gave Christian was an engraved platinum band in a rope design. It was very masculine-looking and fit him perfectly.

"Wow…" he said, his eyes shining at her.

Stevie shrugged. "It just seemed like you."

"It is."

The justice of the peace pronounced them husband and wife. Christian touched Stevie's cheek, his fingers sliding along her jawline, his eyes connected with hers. His hand slid to her neck, and he pulled her to him, kissing her deeply. The catcalls started immediately, followed by whistling and applause. Christian and Stevie kissed undaunted, until Joe finally elbowed Christian pointedly, causing the couple to start laughing.

While people were still milling about, Jordan found herself suddenly face to face with Randy Sinclair. She wasn't sure what to say. She had no idea if Randy even knew who she was and that she was with Joe. Randy solved that dilemma immediately.

"You're Jordan Tate," she said, smiling and extending her hand.

"I'm Randy Sinclair."

Jordan took the proffered hand and nodded. "It's nice to meet you," she said, not sure at all what to say in this situation.

"I'm surprised you could make it to the wedding," Randy said, nodding toward Christian and Stevie, who were talking to everyone who was crowded around them. "I understand you're in the middle of a tour."

Jordan was surprised. She hadn't expected Randy to know anything about her. "I, well, yes, I am… but I was coming up on a break, and I was kind of miserable. I, uh…" Jordan stammered, not sure what she should say.

Randy nodded. "I know, Joe came and rescued you," she said. "He does that kind of thing a lot," she added, without a trace of anger or resentment in her voice. "He's definitely got the knight in shining armor thing down. He's always where he needs to be when you need him. You'll find that a lot with him."

Jordan was stunned. Randy didn't seem to mind that her soon-to-be ex-husband was already rescuing other women. Nor did she seem bitter or even angry with him. Before Jordan could form a reply, Joe was at her elbow. Jordan also noticed Midnight coming up behind Randy, an intent look on her face. Were they rescuing Randy or Jordan?

Joe and Midnight had seen the two women talking at that same time, and they'd both gone into motion. Neither of them were even sure there was a problem, but they both wanted to make sure nothing happened.

Randy glanced up at Joe, then canted her head to the side slightly as her teal blue eyes narrowed.

"Joseph Michael Sinclair," she said. "You don't trust me?"

Jordan glanced up at Joe; he was grinning. "I trust you," he said simply.

"Uh-huh," Randy said, nodding as she glanced over at Midnight, who now stood with them as well. "You too?"

"Hey, I'm just a spectator," Midnight said, holding up her hands and grinning.

"Jordan, it was nice to meet you," Randy said.

"You too, Randy," Jordan said, smiling.

"Sorry the troops thought it necessary to break it up," Randy said, nodding as she turned to walk back over to her seat.

"I'll be right back," Joe whispered to Jordan, then went after Randy.

Jordan watched as they talked for a few minutes. Randy looked up at Joe, shaking her head as she spoke. Joe reached out, touching her shoulder, staring down into her eyes. It was very easy to see that they knew each other very well. When she dropped her eyes from his, Joe's hand touched her under the chin, bringing her face back up. Jordan could see by his expression that he was speaking very softly to his wife. She felt a twinge of jealousy, knowing that the two of them were very close and that she may never get that close to Joe. Randy had shared thirteen years of marriage and a lot of experiences with him. Jordan felt a tug at her heart, even as she felt someone tap her on the shoulder.

She turned, meeting Midnight's eyes.

"Joe needs to make sure everything in his life is settled," Midnight said by way of explanation as she gestured at Joe and Randy. "He can't feel like he's out of control too much."

Jordan nodded, trying to understand.

"Jordan," Midnight said, stooping slightly to get under Jordan's downcast eyes. "It doesn't mean he doesn't care for you. He just has to feel like he's got everything in his life settled."

Jordan nodded. "Randy is the mother of his children, and he loves her."

"Yeah," Midnight said, nodding. "But he must feel an awful lot for you, if he brought you here."

Jordan didn't reply.

"We're like his family, Jordan," Midnight said. "And by bringing you here, he's wanting us to know that you're important to him."

"Yes, she is," Joe said, having come up behind Jordan. He reached out, touching her shoulder and pulling her back against him.

Jordan leaned back against him gratefully. His arm snaked around her waist, holding her close.

Midnight nodded, smiling. The three of them talked for a few more minutes, and then Midnight was called away.

"You okay?" Joe asked, leaning down to whisper in Jordan's ear.

She turned to him, glancing around for Randy.

"She left," Joe said.

"Because of me?"

"No, because she had to get back to town. She's okay with this."

Jordan nodded. They talked about other things then. Jordan refused to discuss her insecurities about Randy. At this point, she had no reason to believe she was a permanent part of Joe's life, so she didn't feel like she had much place to talk about her concerns. She left it alone.

Christian stood staring out the window at the Vegas strip. He heard the door open and glanced back. His mother stood watching him.

"So? What did you think?" he asked.

Josephine walked forward, reaching up to hug him. "I think I want you to be happy in whatever you do, Christian."

Christian pulled back. "I love her, Mum," he said sincerely.

"I know you do."

"She loves me too."

"I believe that now."

"Are you happy for me?" Christian asked, his tone boy-like.

Josephine touched his cheek fondly, then reached up to stroke his hair, like she had when he was a boy. "I'm happy for you, love," she said softly.

Christian hugged her again, relieved that his mother seemed to have put to rest her reservations about Stevie. He really hadn't wanted to have to choose, but he had known that Stevie was a permanent part of his life now. He loved his mother, but he needed Stevie more than he could ever explain to anyone.

When he glanced up, he saw that Stevie had come into the room. She was watching him and his mother with a soft smile on her face. He stared at her, still holding his mother. *God, she's beautiful,* was all he could think.

He straightened and put his hand out to Stevie. She walked over to him, taking his hand and looking at Josephine.

"You two ready to go do this reception thing?" Stevie asked.

"I'll be along soon," Josephine said. "I want to freshen up a bit."

"Do you want us to wait?" Stevie asked, not wanting to leave her all alone.

"Oh, no, I'll be fine, dear," Josephine said, sounding very English. "You two kids run along and have a good time."

"You sure?" Christian asked, suspecting his mother wouldn't show up at all.

"Yes, love, I'm sure," Josephine said, smiling up at him. She reached out and took his hand, taking Stevie's in her other hand and looking at them both, then straight at Christian. "Christian Joseph Collins, you have made me very proud today. You have married a lovely girl, and I know that the two of you will be very happy together. I couldn't be more proud of the man that I raised, the man that you've become. I love you."

Christian smiled fondly, then reached down to hug his mother again. He knew she was telling him that she really did approve of what he'd done. And he was grateful to her for being able to change her mind.

"Are you sure you won't come down with us?" he asked.

"I'm sure, dear. You go have a good time," Josephine said, winking at them.

Stevie and Christian laughed, then nodded and left a few minutes later. As expected, Josephine never did come down. She spent the evening in her room relaxing and reflecting on the difference in Christian from when he'd lived in England, happy that he'd changed so much.

The reception was held in the Monte Carlo Pub and Brewery. Christian and Stevie rented it out for four hours, wanting everyone to be able to drink and have a good time before other people came into the bar. It was a nightclub, so they had live music and a DJ. The band didn't start till later on, so the DJ was on first.

The toast was done with shot glasses rather than champagne.

Stevie and Christian had doubles. The boys drank, the women danced. Jordan had retrieved the skirt for Stevie so she could change, and Stevie did so after the toast. It did look really good with the bodice of the dress. Stevie was thrilled, and Christian was floored. The skirt was short, not obscenely so but enough to show off his new wife's beautiful legs. Their first song was played, Darren Hayes' "Insatiable." It was the first song they'd liked together, and it described them perfectly. It spoke of both love and lust, stating that their love was insatiable. Christian and Stevie danced, and eventually others joined them on the floor.

Later, the party proceeded with Midnight leading the way to the bar for the women, while the men moved to tables to take up positions next to the dance floor across the room. Raising her shot glass to Stevie, Midnight said it was about time someone caught Mr. Collins. Jordan was included in everything, and she found that the women in this group were indeed fun.

There were a few long moments of silence, and even the music quieted a bit at one point when a large Samoan woman walked in. Standing next to her and holding her hand was the woman that Kana had been sitting with at the ceremony. She had long, dark hair and very definite Hawaiian native qualities, not the least of which was the flower in her hair. She was a very pretty girl, standing next to the very buff-looking woman. Jordan knew that this was Kana, but didn't think anything of the fact that she was holding another woman's hand. But then she glanced at the faces of everyone in the group, and it was obvious they were all surprised.

The bigger woman looked back at everyone as if challenging them all to say something. Jordan looked at Midnight, who was staring at the big woman almost askance. Then Midnight ordered three shots, and picked them up before walking toward the Samoan.

Kana met her halfway. Midnight knew everyone would follow her lead. They stopped a foot from each other.

Kana's eyes were wary, but she inclined her head to the young woman next to her.

"Palani, this is Midnight Chevalier. She's the Chief of Police, my boss. Midnight, this is Palani, my girlfriend." There was no mistaking the challenge in Kana's voice.

Midnight looked at the young woman and smiled warmly.

"Nice to meet you, Palani," she said, handing her a shot and giving another to Kana. Lifting her glass, she said, "To finding happiness within oneself."

Kana looked taken aback for a moment, but then drank the shot. Jordan watched as the big woman's eyes met Joe's across the room. Joe raised his glass, inclining his head. Kana grinned, nodding. Apparently this was new territory for her, Jordan surmised, and she was asking acceptance from her family.

"Go hang out with the boys, Kana," Midnight said, grinning. "We girls are over there drinking our asses off. I'll take care of Palani for you."

Kana laughed. "You want to go hang out with the girls?" she asked Palani.

It was obvious to Midnight that the young woman was just plain nervous about being there and not sure if she would be accepted. Midnight put her hand out to her.

"Come on, we don't bite—much," she said, grinning.

Palani laughed softly and nodded, reaching up to kiss Kana quickly on the lips. Kana stood staring after Midnight and Palani for a long moment, then walked toward the guys who were hanging out near the stools and bench seats at the other side of the bar. She snagged a waitress on the way and ordered another shot, a double, and a beer. As she walked up, she caught Tiny's look. She narrowed her eyes at him, and he grinned, nodding in approval.

Back at the girls' bar, Midnight made introductions all around. Palani was stunned to meet Jordan Tate. "The Jordan Tate."

"Oh my God, I have both your albums. You are fantastic!" she said, smiling broadly.

"Well, thanks," Jordan said, smiling too.

They drank a few more drinks, and then they all went back out to the dance floor, taking Palani with them. The women danced, while the men and Kana watched and drank. At one point a slow song came on. Christian nudged Joe as he walked out to join Stevie on the dance floor, pulling her close and kissing her. Joe nudged Rick, then walked out and took Jordan in his arms. Rick nudged Dave, and so it went until all of them were dancing with their respective spouse or loved one. Even Kana joined Palani on the floor. It was the first time they'd danced together.

Jordan grinned up at Joe. "You've got a pretty cool group here."

Joe glanced around, nodding. "They're family."

"Then you have a pretty cool family."

Joe looked down at her for a long moment, then leaned down to kiss her softly.

During the course of the evening, it was discovered that Donovan and Jeanie had actually done "the deed" as well. Joe gave his brother-in-law a pointed look.

"Randy's gonna kill ya," he said matter-of-factly.

Donovan grinned, holding up a hand. "I know, I know, but we're gonna do it again for everyone."

"I just wanted this made more permanent," Jeanie put in, standing next to Donovan and smiling up at him.

"Yeah, before she can chicken out on me again."

Donovan was promptly jabbed in the ribs for that comment. He laughed and hugged Jeanie to him. There were a number of toasts and rounds at the bar in honor of their upgraded marital status. Everyone got happily drunk.

Later in the evening, the bar was opened to other patrons. Many of the men saw the women all dancing together. A few were foolhardy enough to attempt to zero in on one or another of them.

Joe caught them at it first and nudged Rick, who glanced in the direction Joe was looking.

"Oh really now?" Rick said, loud enough for most of the other guys to hear.

Joe and Rick strolled pointedly toward the dance floor. They were followed shortly by the rest of the guys. The women, of course, saw them coming, and grinned. Midnight, Jordan, and Stevie were the current objects of attention by the foolhardy men. Joe, Rick, and Christian made a point of standing at the edge of the dance floor nearest to their respective ladies. Stevie glanced over her shoulder at Christian and grinned. Turning to him, she beckoned with a finger. Christian walked over obligingly.

"Hey," the guy who was attempting to dance with her said, before he caught the rather dangerous-looking group standing near the dance floor looking intently at him.

Christian's eyes narrowed at the man. Then, as he made a point of taking his wife's left hand, he lifted it to make sure it was apparent that she wore a wedding ring. The man swallowed a few times and glanced over at the ominous group, many of whom were grinning with very definite malicious intent. He disappeared shortly thereafter.

Joe's eyes were on the man attempting to get Jordan to notice him. She glanced at him helplessly. He nodded and walked over to her, taking her by the waist and pulling her to him. The guy made a move like he intended to do something about it, and actually was fool enough to step toward Jordan and reach for her. He was snatched up off his feet by a six foot, two inch Englishman.

"You want something?" Joe asked dangerously.

The man looked back at him, his eyes already wide. "Uh, no… no, man."

"The lady is with me," Joe said. "Got it?"

"Yeah, man, I got it."

"Good," Joe said, and set the man back down on his feet. He made a quick retreat.

The last man made an almost fatal mistake. He actually put his hands on Midnight's waist. Just as she was about to react, Rick was there.

"Let me make this easy for you," Rick said, his deep blue eyes narrowed dangerously. "You take your hands off my wife, or I'll take your head off right here."

The foolhardy man made the mistake of taking a swing at Rick. Rick ducked the punch, grabbing the man's arm as it passed him, twisting it up behind his back and taking him to the floor in the same motion. Rick then put his knee in the man's back, leaning down to his ear.

"Now, see, that was not the wisest thing you could have done," he said.

"Let me up!" the man yelled, embarrassed and mad.

Rick hauled him to his feet, used to handling criminals the same way. He let go of the man's arm, which had the guy turning around to try and start something. He took one look at Rick, and then the group standing behind him, waiting for him to be stupid, and decided against it. Rick grinned. Midnight moved to lean against her husband, staring up at the man who had made the mistake of trying to accost her.

"Sorry," she said, her look passive. "But my husband has issues with other men." She shrugged. "Go figure."

The man looked at her for a long moment, then held his hands up in defeat and walked away. Midnight glanced back at her husband.

"We really need to work on your people skills," she said.

"I know, I'm really bad with PR," he replied, not sounding the least bit sorry.

The rest of the evening passed uneventfully. Most of the club's patrons figured out rather quickly who not to touch.

Later, in their hotel room, Christian lay in their bed, waiting. He smoked a cigarette, the smoke curling toward the open window. They were on the top floor.

"Are you comin' out ever?" he asked.

"Yeah, eventually," Stevie answered from the doorway to the bathroom.

Christian looked up and found himself speechless. She was wearing a silk-and-lace vision of a nightgown.

"Oh Jesus…" he breathed, his eyes shining as he stared at her openmouthed.

Stevie grinned and walked over to the bed, looking down at her husband. He was bare-chested, which was enough to get her going every time.

Christian sat up, reaching out and pulling her to him, kissing her deeply. Their lips met over and over again, and within minutes the nightgown lay on the floor and their bodies were entwined. A couple of hours later, Stevie still lay over him, trying to catch her breath. He never ceased to astound her with the myriad ways he could make her body react to him.

His hands were in her hair, stroking it, touching her back, holding her to him.

"I love you," she said, kissing his chest again.

"I love you," he replied softly.

They lay together for another half hour or so.

"Oh, I almost forgot," Christian said, and reached beside him into the bedside table drawer.

He withdrew an envelope and handed it to her. She looked at him, then at the envelope. She narrowed her green eyes.

"What is that?" she asked suspiciously.

"Just a little something," he said, grinning as he shrugged.

Stevie moved to sit up, straddling his waist. She opened the envelope, taking out the paperwork contained inside. She read it over, her eyes widening as her mouth dropped open.

"Christian… this…" she said, shocked. "This says you paid twenty thousand on the house."

"Yes," he said, reaching up to touch her cheek. "On our house."

Her eyes met his. "Twenty thousand?"

He grinned lopsidedly, then shrugged. "My bonus from the Seattle job."

"Kind of ironic, don't you think?" she asked, grinning now too.

"Rather."

She leaned down, kissing him deeply, then moved back to look into his eyes.

"Thank you," she said softly.

"You're very welcome."

"Now…" she said, leaning over and pulling a box out from under the bed.

"What did you do?" he said, raising a jet black eyebrow at her.

"Well, nothing as grand as you," she said, shrugging. "But I think you'll like it."

"You weren't supposed to do anything," he said, narrowing light blue eyes at her.

"Just open it, Collins, or I'll kick your ass."

Christian chuckled. His new wife certainly was a romantic, wasn't she? Still grinning, he sat up as she moved to his side. He opened the box and stared at what lay inside, nestled in tissue paper.

"Oh my God…" he said, awed. "Steve…" He was shaking his head in wonder. "You got me the Vaio," he said, reaching in and lifting the ultra-thin laptop out of the box.

"You said it was better," she said, grimacing, hoping she'd made the right choice.

"Babe, it's fantastic," he said, his eyes taking in the laptop's streamlined shape.

"Well, it's got all the bells and whistles. I even upgraded the memory and RAM. The CD is writable, and it's the top speed for those," she said, trying to remember everything about the laptop.

"Ohh…" he said, grinning. "I love it when you talk dirty to me."

Stevie laughed. "You perv!" she exclaimed, leaning over to kiss him. "You like it?"

"I love it, babe—I love it," he said. "Here, look." He took her hands and turned them palms up, then put the laptop on them. "Feel how little this weighs?"

"Yeah," she said, nodding. "Your other one weighs a ton."

"Yeah. And it kills my shoulder to carry it all the time."

She bit her lip. His shoulder hurt him all the time anyway. It was the shoulder that had been hit by AK47 fire when he had saved her life. It still made her feel guilty fairly often.

"Stop it," he said, leaning forward to kiss her deeply, knowing her well enough to realize exactly what she was thinking about. "I love you," he said, pulling back to look down at her. "You are worth every twinge."

"Let's see if you're saying that in twenty years," she said, grinning.

"I will be," he said, drawing her to him and kissing her deeply as he set the laptop aside. They made love again then.

Like everything in life, there were never any guarantees. It was all just a roll of the dice.

You can find more information about the author and series here:

www.sherrylhancock.com

www.facebook.com/SherrylDHancock

www.vulpine-press.com/midknight-blue-series

Also by Sherryl D. Hancock:

The *WeHo* series follows a group of women from Los Angeles as they navigate the ups and downs of love, life, work, and everything in between.

www.vulpine-press.com/we-ho

The *Wild Irish Silence* series. Escape into the world of BJ Sparks and discover how he went from the small-town boy to the world-famous rock star.

www.vulpine-press.com/wild-irish-silence-series